Escape from Castro

Escape from Castro

Mario Lamar

BRANDYLANE PUBLISHERS, INC.
White Stone, Virginia

❀ Brandylane Publishers, Inc.

P.O. Box 261, White Stone, Virginia 22578

(804) 435-6900 or 1 800 553-6922; e-mail: brandy@crosslink.net

Copyright 1999, by Mario Lamar
All rights reserved
Printed in the United States of America

Library of Congress Cataloging-in-Publication Data

Lamar, Mario, 1931–
    Escape from Castro/Mario Lamar.
         p.   cm.
  ISBN 1-883911-20-6
    1. Castro, Fidel, 1927–   —Assassination attempts—Fiction.
  2. Cuba—History—1959– —Fiction. I. Title.
PS 3562.A42165E83 1998
813'.54—dc21   98-54097
                                                             CIP

To my talented wife, Karol, for it was her idea that I write this book. Without her invaluable help and encouragement *Escape from Castro* would never have been written.

In rare instances it has been necessary to make slight changes in the description of the topography in order to accommodate the plot.

Acknowledgments

Robert Pruett, for his help in making *Escape from Castro* a better book.

Armando Valladares, whose book *Against All Hope* was an inspiration from the very beginning.

Richard Green, from Seal Teams 1, 2, and 6, who was always willing to help with his technical knowledge.

Ed Moore, my friend behind the computer.

At 0400 hours on January 12, 1959, in the San Juan Valley of Oriente Province, Raul Castro watched as seventy-one men, mostly students, were lined up in front of a freshly opened ditch forty meters long. Castro gave the officer in charge of the firing squad a nod, and those who were about to die heard one last word, "Fire!"

Of the seventy-one, only five had been formally charged or had gone to trial.

The reign of terror that would seem to have no end had begun on the island of Cuba, ninety miles from our shores.

Two Years Later

Chapter One

On a small key six miles off the southern coast of Havana Province stood the ruins of what once had been a luxurious vacation retreat. The grounds sloped gently to the shore where a well built pier had endured two years of neglect. At the highest point of the island a handsome two story stucco house and its adjacent guesthouse commanded a dramatic view of the coastline. Security fences and surveillance equipment surrounded the property.

An old militiaman by the name of Ortiz had been placed in charge of the key to prevent further looting by fishermen and revolutionary thugs. It was close to midnight when Ortiz finished loading his nineteen foot boat with provisions, started the engine, and set course for the supposedly deserted key. After half an hour of rough riding on a choppy sea, he directed the narrow beam of his spotlight toward the boat house and sent his pre-arranged signal: one dot, one dash. Feeling uneasy after a few unsuccessful attempts to contact his party, he started to head back to the mainland. Just as his magnetic compass was settling at a new course of 031°, he saw a flashing light off the port quarter. Through his binoculars he confirmed the reply: one dash, two dots. Finally his signals had been acknowledged; he wouldn't have to come back tomorrow. He pulled the throttle back and with the help of a dim light at each end of the pier, he was able to bring his small boat alongside—although not without first bumping a couple of times against the tires that served as fenders.

The old fellow swore under his breath as he threw a line to the dark figure standing on the pier. "Lousy weather to be at sea tonight," he said looking up at a starless sky—ominous darkness occasionally laced by lightning—the background rumbling of thunder leaving no doubt about an impending tropical storm. "Not that I mind at all coming out here, Boss," he added. "I'm more than happy to be of some help."

"I understand, Ortiz, and we really appreciate your efforts," came the young voice from the pier. "Now let's go ahead and start passing the supplies while the weather holds. That way you'll be able to head back before the seas get any rougher."

"I don't mind the weather, Señor Nicky. I can help you take the boxes into the guesthouse. Oh yeah, I mustn't forget," he said pulling an envelope from the inside pocket of his poncho. "I have a letter for you fellows. It's marked urgent."

"Thanks, Ortiz," Nicky said as he took the letter. "Start off-loading, and I'll give you a hand as soon as I get back from the house."

Inside the main house Nicky sat at the breakfast table and waited for the older man beside him to finish reading the coded message.

After a few long minutes Raul put the message down on the table and, looking straight at his young friend, said, "Nicky, wake up Julio and get the weapons into the boat. We are going to the safe house in Havana as soon as Ortiz leaves."

"Does this mean that the waiting is finally over?" Nicky asked gravely.

"Yes, it looks like this is it." Raul glanced at his watch and muttered almost to himself, "In fifty minutes we'll be on forty-eight hour alert."

THE FOLLOWING DAY
AT THE CUBAN NAVAL ACADEMY, MARIEL

The messenger of the watch at the Bachelor Officers Quarters (BOQ) knocked at my door. "Come in," I said.

Escape from Castro

The messenger opened the door but didn't come in. Instead, after clicking his heels and coming to attention, he responded, "Lieutenant, the comandante wishes to see you."

"Very well," I replied, looking up from the tests I was grading. "I'll be there right away."

"I'm sorry, Sir, but my orders are for you to accompany me without delay." His voice was polite but firm. He had been briefed.

Silently, I reached for my garrison cap and prepared to follow the messenger when I noticed that he was carrying an AK Kalashnivok assault rifle not usually issued to duty personnel. I could only hope that my face did not betray the sudden chill which had rushed over me. Could they have found out about my activities, or counter-revolutionary betrayals, as they would undoubtedly be called? But no, I had harbored the same fears for over a year and a half, and they had always proved unfounded.

It was now almost 7:00 P.M., somewhat late for Comandante Mario Pinto, the superintendent of the academy, to still be in his office. The sun was setting behind the green hills of Mariel, making the Moorish architecture of the main building look ominously beautiful. As we walked up the stairs, my hopes of this being just another false alarm faded rapidly; I had just spotted three brown sedans of the type used by G-2, the most feared of the repressive organizations in the Cuban military, parked on the left side of the building. By now, my heart was pounding so loudly that I was half afraid that someone would hear it.

Damn, I'd better pull myself together or I'll wind up like Midshipman Martin, I thought.

How long had it been since poor Martin was whisked away at two in the morning in one of those G-2 sedans? Not long enough to forget, but who could ever forget? His agonized screams woke most of us as the car drove with deliberate slowness past the midshipman's pavilion. A loud shot followed, echoing forever—or so it seemed. They say he was dead before the car reached the main gate—dead at seventeen!

As we approached the quarter-deck, the pounding of my heart kept pace with the bitter memories. Should I make a run for it? I asked myself without much conviction. I knew only too well that I didn't have a chance to make it out of the academy's grounds alive. Well, I'd soon see how much the bastards really knew.

We entered the building through the rear entrance, passed the officer of the day's spaces, and started up the stairs toward the comandante's office. As we walked into the waiting room, I saw my friend, Lieutenant Junior Grade (LtJG) Miguel Nodal, standing on the balcony which overlooked a Roman-style atrium encircled by classrooms. He was talking to two men in civilian clothes. Both were obviously armed as the bulge of the side weapons beneath their jackets attested, and both were obviously jackals from the G-2. The instant Nodal saw me, he dismissed the messenger of the watch with a slight movement of his head and approached me smiling and stretching his hand out to shake mine. He was making a noticeable effort to make the whole affair look like a casual meeting.

Miguelito, as most of his friends called him affectionately, had been first in his class at the academy. He was also a graduate of the prestigious Underwater Demolition Team (UDT) School of the United States Navy at Little Creek, Virginia. Now twenty-nine, Nodal was an athletic man of medium height and sharp military bearing. Relegated to obscure engineering ships' billets during the last few years of the Batista regime, Miguel was rapidly becoming a rising star in Fidel's navy. His success was due not to any revolutionary prowess since he was strictly a career officer without any political affiliations, but rather to the fact that he had been a classmate of our new chief of staff, Capitan de Fragata (Commander) Castiñeiras. Nodal also owed some of his success to the lack of qualified officers which had resulted from the purge of senior officers following the triumph of La Revolucion.

"Carlos, old buddy, where the hell have you been hiding yourself?" Miguel inquired, his cheerful voice interrupting my gloomy thoughts. "I looked all over for you last weekend. Don't you know we're on a twelve hour alert?"

"What's so special about being on twelve hour alert? We're always on some kind of asinine alert."

Before Nodal had a chance to answer, the comandante's door opened and his assistant and political advisor, Lieutenant Calderon, stuck his head out and signaled for Nodal to come in. Although we had known each other for years, his eyes somehow skipped over me. As the door closed behind Calderon and Nodal,

I felt someone approaching behind me. I looked apprehensively over my shoulder and saw the gentle old face of Chief Miranda, the academy's chief steward. He was carrying the customary silver tray on which were neatly arranged cups of cafe espresso and glasses of water. He had just ignored the two G-2 gorillas, I noticed.

"Buenas noches, Lieutenant," he said, while gesturing for me to take a cup. I could see by his expression that he had realized that I was in a tight situation. As he handed me a glass of water, I smiled, trying to look reassuring. Good old Chief Miranda, I thought. He had been a second class when I entered the academy seven years ago, and he had never stopped seeing me as the carefree midshipman I had been in those happy, uncomplicated days.

"Attention on deck!" shouted the guard stationed at the superintendent's door. Everyone came immediately to attention. I could hear the six sailors of the honor guard running down the main deck toward the entrance where the comandante's car was already waiting, its back door open and its driver standing by. It was customary for the honor guard to render honors whenever the superintendent arrived at or left the academy grounds. The honor guard was normally given a warning of at least ten or fifteen minutes, but this time there had been no warning at all, an indication that Comandante Pinto had an abrupt change of plans, probably a phone call from the Estado Mayor (headquarters).

As Comandante Pinto hurried down the marble stairs with their polished brass handrails, he turned around and looked at me briefly, a glance totally devoid of expression. Nodal followed the comandante, but he was back in a matter of minutes.

"Carlos, let's go eat," he said. "Mario apologizes for keeping you waiting so long and then not having time to see you, but Castiñeiras (at least he uses the CNO's *last* name, I noted with amusement) summoned him to headquarters."

Was this an honest invitation, I wondered, or was Nodal supposed to be keeping track of me? "No thanks," I replied with a gesture of regret. I had better go home since I'm driving my father's car, and he might need it. That is, if it's all right with you if I leave the academy." Well, at least now I'll know where I stand, I figured, holding my breath as I waited for the answer.

Nodal hesitated for a moment that seemed to last an eternity. Finally he smiled and said, "Of course it's all right. As you wish." Then as he turned and began walking briskly down the stairs, I stood transfixed with relief, almost afraid to believe my good luck.

Within three minutes I was driving down the hill where the academy stood overlooking the Port of Mariel. I checked my watch—9:15 P.M. The lights of the small town and those of the merchant ships in the harbor glowed warmly in the distance. The night was cool, and the clean, crisp air tasted faintly of freedom, but I still had to pass the guard at the main gate. I took my .45 from its holster, placed a round in the chamber, and laid it underneath a sweater on the passenger's seat. I was determined to leave, and one guard was not going to stop me. If things were that bad, I was better off making a run for it.

The guard, I saw, was not Navy—only a militiaman. That would surely make it easier to pull the trigger if I had to, I thought with some relief. The militia was composed mainly of losers, frustrated hooligans trying to make up for their lack of action during the Revolution by fanaticism and abuse. This particular militiaman was a short man in his forties with long hair and a hard unshaven face. He was dressed carelessly in an old army jacket and dirty navy blue pants. As I approached the gate, he walked slowly and importantly to the center of the road, signaling me to stop while holding his AK-47 conspicuously in his right hand. He flashed a light on my face and then made a sweep through the inside of the car with his powerful flashlight. Finally, he produced a crude imitation of a military salute.

"Lieutenant," he said in a swaggering voice, "I need to see that book written in American that you got in the back seat." He was referring to the copy of *Navy Proceedings*, a U.S. Navy sanctioned professional publication to which the academy subscribed.

"No problem," I replied, "but just let me add a note for Lieutenant Carraso (executive officer of the academy and a good friend)."

"A note?" the guard questioned. "I suppose it's all right." Now, he was overwhelmed with his importance. Here he was harassing an officer who had been a member of the useless upper class of the past, a man who had no place in today's Cuba. Even better, he had caught this officer with an imperialist magazine.

On the inside cover of *Proceedings* I wrote in English: "Antonio, from what gutter did you pick up this cretin? Carlos." I returned the magazine to the guard and drove away, leaving the cretin happily contemplating the praise and recognition he was bound to receive from his bosses. At least, so he thought.

I drove west along the coastline toward Havana, relishing my relief and enjoying the humming of the finely tuned engine of my father's Mercedes. The drive had already begun to lift my spirits; if there was one place in all of Cuba where I felt a special pride in my country, it was this twenty-five mile stretch between Mariel and Havana. The road wound along about fifty feet above the sea, always closely hugging the coastline as if afraid to be separated from some of the most beautiful waters in the world. To every change in light, the ocean responded with a change in color: pure blue or turquoise in the bright sunlight, then deep blue-violet as the evening shadows approached. One thing never changed though—the clearness of waters so pure that you could trace the outlines of the coral growing along the bottom. The countryside along the road was just as beautiful—all lush green, gently sloping hills which were mercifully free of the billboards that were such an eyesore in other countries I had visited.

As I drew nearer to the city, I turned on the radio. The station was playing the music of Los Chavales de España. Ironically, the beautiful songs depressed me instead of making me happy as they had done so many times before. How could everything have changed so fast, I wondered? Whatever had happened to those incredibly happy years when no one had known or cared who Fidel Castro was? How did that poem go?

Treinta años
Quien Diria que al cabo de ellos
No tendria yo
Sino blancos mis cabellos
y mi alma apagada y fria

Thirty years ... who was to say
That by the end of my last candle count

I would have but my hair grey
And my soul defrauded of warmth never found

Well, at least I was not thirty, but only twenty-four, and my hair was black instead of grey. Still, living on close terms with fear and repression had certainly taken away much of the warmth and light from my life.

A glance through the rear view mirror before changing lanes suddenly jolted me back into reality. Following closely behind me was a squat brown sedan obviously tailing me. I had little doubt that I could lose the sedan in the now heavy traffic of the city outskirts, but I decided this would be a mistake. Let them follow me. I drove slowly through the tree lined streets of El Vedado to my parents' house. As I pulled the car into the garage, I watched the familiar brown sedan of the G-2 park blatantly almost in front of my home. I wondered if Nodal was getting reports of my whereabouts. I was allowed to leave the academy; the leash had been lengthened, but I could still feel the heavy hand of mistrust at the other end.

I left the garage and walked with deliberate slowness into the house. Only the dog was awake to greet me. I went upstairs to my room and quickly changed from my dress blues into civilian clothes—blue slacks and a white linen guayabera. I opened a window which overlooked the backyard, and with the help of a trellis and the ivy which covered the back of the house, I eased my way down the wall and into the garden. By cutting through the neighboring yards, I was able to come out onto a street and, within moments, I had picked up a taxi and left my neighborhood behind.

I had the taxi drop me off at the intersection of Calle 6 and Fifth Avenue in Miramar. Here, I paid my fare and pretended to enter a house I had never seen before. Only when I was certain that the taxi had left, did I begin to backtrack, walking those long Miramar blocks to Tony Capó's apartment. As I hurried along, the idea that had slowly been breeding within my mind became stronger and stronger—all these unusual events were happening because we had been successful—and Fidel was dead!

As I walked along Fifth Avenue, I felt increasingly conspicuous, for this was the main artery of a wealthy residential area and not a place where people normally walked alone for long distances. I consciously slowed my speed and did my best to resemble a resident out for a late night stroll. At least, the slower pace gave me a chance to observe things I never would have noticed while driving. Flowers and shrubs still grew in the median strip which divided the four lanes into two sections, but the flowers were losing a battle with the weeds, and the untrimmed shrubbery looked scraggly and unhealthy. On both sides of the street the imposing residences were also beginning to show neglect. One house stood guarded by an iron gate which sagged on broken hinges; another wore a coat of peeling paint; a third was surrounded by uncut grass and weed-smothered gardens. Well, I speculated bitterly, the high officials of Fidel's government and their Soviet friends were obviously too busy to keep up these confiscated homes for the legitimate owners who had fled Cuba. My contempt for these hypocrites who preached equality while living in stolen luxury knew no limits.

After walking for about twenty minutes, I finally reached the apartment building where my old friend Tony and his wife lived. Tony, now thirty-one years old, had been a captain of the University of Havana football team during his college years. He was still a solid man of strong will and firm convictions (one of the firmest being that Communists had no business taking over his country.) Set in a quiet neighborhood of wide, tree-lined streets and beautiful lawns and gardens, the rather ordinary building with its stone balconies and underground garages gave an illusion of peace and security. Not a bad illusion for someone engaged in Tony's activities, I found myself reflecting.

As I was climbing the stairs to Tony's second floor apartment, the lights came on abruptly. Tony appeared at his door, wearing a heavy black cardigan and a forced smile. "Come right in," he said. "I heard you coming." He closed and locked the door before inviting me to make myself comfortable.

"Sit down and relax Carlos. I'll bring you a drink—which you're going to need when you listen to what I have to tell you."

"Great! Just what I needed at this time of night—a cheerful greeting."

Tony disappeared into the kitchen and I settled myself on the comfortable sofa. While waiting, my eyes wandered appreciatively over the apartment which was tastefully decorated and furnished with second hand mahogany furniture that glowed with rich, dark-red highlights. I knew that Cathy had meticulously searched out each piece with the zeal of a big game hunter. Her greatest prize was the grand piano which occupied most of the living room and which was still open and covered with sheets of music. Cathy must have been giving lessons that afternoon.

Within minutes Tony came back with a tray containing glasses of ice, a plate of anchovies, and a bottle of Buchanan scotch. He laid the tray on the coffee table, sank back into his favorite chair, and took a good look at me. "You're going to need this for more reasons than one," he said as he poured me a stiff drink. "Who ever told you that white guayaberas are something to be worn in January?" (By Cuban standards temperatures in the fifties and sixties called for wool and fur, not linen).

"Well, let's skip over my guayabera and get to the point," I replied, beginning to feel exasperated by all the preambles. "We're not here to discuss the local dress code."

Tony's face turned somber, and he abruptly dropped all preliminaries. "We expect Fidel to make the trip any time within the next twenty-four hours. You know how unpredictable he is, but there is little doubt this time."

"So we haven't moved yet," I exclaimed, torn between feelings of relief and disappointment. I thought for a moment before speaking again. "Have you called Oviedes?" I asked.

"Yes, I have. He'll drop the station wagon as agreed in the event that we can't get out through La Via Blanca. Now, I think it would be a good idea for you to stay here tonight, in case this thing goes sour."

"Of course, I'll stay. And you're right; it could very well go sour if it doesn't take off soon. I don't know exactly what is going on, but listen to what happened today at the academy and tell me what you think." I went through a rapid narration of the day's events. By the time I had finished, it was almost one o'clock.

Tony sat thinking for a moment before commenting on my story. Finally he responded, "Carlos, they may have some vague suspicions, and there is no doubt that they are trying to hassle you. But frankly, if they had any idea that we were stalking the Maximum Leader, do you think you'd be here now—drinking expensive scotch? No, I don't think they know anything. Anyway, we'd better try to get some sleep. God only knows what lies ahead."

Still awake, staring at the ceiling of Tony's guest room, I listened to the clock chime one bell. I never heard the two bells; my exhausted body must have finally overwhelmed my mind.

Chapter Two

Not far from Tony's apartment in the U.S. Embassy office building by the waterfront, Fidel Castro was the main topic of a different type of conversation.

In the embassy's briefing room, Michael Armstrong, the senior officer of the Central Intelligence Agency (CIA) in Cuba, handed the message to the attractive young woman sitting in front of him:

> Fm: Station Chief—Cuba
> To: CIA Deputy Director for Operations (DDO)
>
> Top secret. For green eyes only.
> Immediate. 050510Z Jan.
> There are strong indications that young naval officers are about to attempt to overthrow Castro. Specifics unknown at this time due to extreme secrecy in their camp. UNODIR (unless otherwise directed) will provide support if requested.
>
>   Condor

After reading the words carefully, she nodded and handed the message back to Armstrong. "I don't think we'll have to wait long," she said quietly.

Armstrong looked at his watch. It was past midnight. He

had arrived at the embassy at 0700, and the long hours were beginning to show in the dark circles under his eyes.

"I'll have this message coded and sent immediately. By the way, how are things at Pan-Am? Are they being cooperative?" Armstrong asked as he gathered his papers into a leather attaché case and prepared to leave.

"Very—I have complete flexibility with my flight schedule. No questions asked."

"Excellent, I must let the ambassador know. He will be pleased. Have a restful night. And Lourdes," he paused on his way out of the door, "be very careful."

At 0400 the same morning Ensign Antonio Quesada was standing his watch at Navy headquarters in downtown Havana. Quesada was a dedicated naval officer, but also a fanatic anti-communist, fanatic almost to the point of reckless insanity. At about 0450 Quesada was called to the Communications Center where a priority immediate message had just been received from Fidel's Mobile Command Post. The message was a request for naval support for Fidel's projected trip to Tarara, a resort beach twenty miles east of Havana. The estimated time of departure was to be 0700.

Traditionally, whenever Castro stayed overnight at a resort area, the navy provided a small craft for the pleasure of the Comandante and for close support from the sea. Standing out about four or five miles, there would also be a larger vessel, usually one of the three Cuban frigates if one was available. All units would be in constant communication. These requests never came with more than two or three hours of advance warning. The not-so-obvious purpose of this apparent lack of planning and organization was to avoid an attempt on Fidel's life.

After receiving the message, Ensign Quesada returned immediately to the OOD stateroom. There, (a chance he knew he had to take) Quesada called Tony Capó and relayed the message.

Tony had been sleeping by the phone and grabbed it even before the first ring had stopped echoing in the silent apartment. His face reflected no emotion as he listened to Quesada's rapid explanation. After hanging up, Tony paused only a second before calling his close friend, Raul Ramirez. Raul, a lawyer and former classmate of both Tony and Fidel, was a short, wiry man with a sharp, bony face and thin lips. He gave the impression of being an intense, no-nonsense individual—which he was. The conversation between the two friends was also intense and no-nonsense, totally devoid of the usual pleasantries.

"Raul, our friend will be leaving at 0700 for the beach. Why don't we join him?"

"Excellent! But it's now almost 5 A.M. There is not time for you to come along; you could never make it . I'm truly sorry. I know you would have enjoyed this outing."

"Mierda! This is my party too! I'm on my way!" Tony slammed down the receiver without waiting for an answer and hurried into the guest room.

"Carlos! Wake up! I've received confirmation from Quesada. This is it!"

I sat bolt upright in the bed. The news had awakened all my senses simultaneously. "Finally!" I exclaimed. "I'll stop at the club and make sure that The *Sirius* is gassed up." The *Sirius* was a powerful twenty-four foot cabin cruiser that my cousin Alonso Carnot and I had bought with the idea of eventually using it to get out of Cuba. As a member of the military, I would never have been allowed to leave the country. Now, if all went well, the boat would soon be used for a better cause.

Tony picked up his FAL automatic rifle and placed his .45 in the shoulder holster. "Wait at the academy for our call," he instructed as he walked toward the door. Then he added softly, "Think of a good reason to give Cathy. I just couldn't talk to her now. Don't let her worry too much, Carlos."

I nodded.

At 0640 I arrived at the academy, having already checked on the boat, and stopped along the road for cafe con leche. I parked my Opel Capitan in the staff parking lot and went straight to my classroom, deciding to skip my usual breakfast in the Wardroom in order to avoid the unavoidable stares which would await me there. In a small school like our academy nothing went unnoticed—and certainly not the dramatic events of the previous evening. The early morning air was clear and calm, and the academy lay peacefully stretched out across the handsome grounds. As I walked into the rear entrance of the main building, I had to shake myself mentally to believe that this was truly the scene of last night's traumatic close call.

But somehow as I began walking through the superintendent's foyer, the events of the night were once again a cruel reality. I glanced into Comandante Pinto's office as I walked past and found myself remembering only too well the agony I had lived through while my future was being decided behind these closed doors. Now, other agonizing thoughts were occupying my mind; only a few miles to the east, young Cuban men were about to risk their lives for our cause.

"Lieutenant Dumas!" I heard the familiar voice of Cdte. Andreas, math wizard and much respected professor at the academy, calling me.

"Si, mi comandante. Como esta usted?" I responded.

"I'm fine, but I didn't see you at breakfast, and your friend Nodal (did I detect a slight irony in that remark) was wondering why you weren't sharing empanadas with us, as usual."

"He was, was he? Well, he won't have to wonder much longer. Here comes the devil now."

Nodal soon joined us, and after we exchanged the usual greetings, said to me, "I think that we'll have an interesting mission coming soon. I'll tell you about it at lunch. You are joining us for lunch, Carlos?" The seemingly casual question contained an element of command.

"Of course," I replied. "It's about time we got underway. We haven't been near the water in over a week now." Of all my numerous duties in the Navy, the most interesting by far was my position as executive officer of the Underwater Demolition Team (UDT) which was commanded by Nodal and manned by two officers, Nodal and myself, one warrant officer, and seven enlisted men.

The conversation obviously over, Nodal and I saluted Andreas and left for our respective classrooms.

At exactly 0700 the senior man of my first class of the day was standing outside my classroom door. As soon as I opened the door, he said, "Permission to come in, Sir. All midshipmen present or accounted for."

"Permission granted!" I replied.

The midshipmen filed quietly into the classroom and took their places. This class was studying intermediate English, and all of the students had achieved some proficiency in the language. I usually enjoyed teaching this particular group of midshipmen, but today I knew my mind would be elsewhere. A rapid glance at my planning book reminded me where we had left off the preceding day. "Today, we will continue yesterday's vocabulary drills," I announced. These drills consisted of having one student write a word on the blackboard in Spanish while another student attempted to rapidly translate the word into English. After twenty words had been completed, the students would reverse their roles of teacher and translator.

I looked at my watch: 0710. Mother of God, please help them, I prayed silently. Then, leaning forward on my desk, I called Midshipmen Delgado and Diaz front and center. Delgado was a nervous young man with a bad case of acne who was not doing well in any of his classes except for political indoctrination. Diaz, blond and cocky, had the well-earned reputation of disliking Delgado and all his type—those who used their allegiance to the Revolution to cover their personal and academic inadequacies.

"Midshipman Delgado, You will be the first to write the words in Spanish," I said.

Looking in my direction, but avoiding eye contact, Delgado took the chalk in his hand and wrote his first word on the board: CONSPIRADOR. The classroom filled with icy silence, and tension mounted steadily as the drill went on.

When Diaz's turn came to write the words in Spanish, he chose a red piece of chalk with great deliberateness. Then, while looking Delgado directly in the eyes, he wrote his first word: BASTARDO.

Chapter Three

At 0630 a black Oldsmobile sedan with Raul Ramirez at the wheel was crossing the Havana Bay Tunnel. Next to Raul sat twenty-two year old Nicasio (Nicky) Berrocal, a dark, athletic young man almost six feet tall. Nicky had resigned his commission just after graduating from the Naval Academy. Even though he had not served the required four years after graduation, Nicky's resignation had been accepted on the grounds that he was "politically immature," a euphemism used to describe those who could not unconditionally support the Revolution. His mother's American nationality had not been overlooked. Nicky was now busy going through the check-off list—for the second time. He was grateful to the list for keeping his mind off the overwhelming responsibility with which he had been entrusted.

In the back seat, Julio Acosta was carefully examining the weapons one final time. Julio, a serious young man of twenty-five, was of medium height and a light build. He wore glasses and always seemed absorbed in his thoughts. Julio taught math at the University of Villanova in Havana, when not engaged in the dangerous business of counter-revolution.

As a former member of the rifle/pistol team at the academy and by far the best shot on the team, Nicky would be the one to handle the FAL (fusil automatico ligero) with the telescopic sight—his mission: to fire at Fidel, and at no one else, when given the signal by Raul. He would also be the first man to open fire.

Nicky's attack would be followed by Julio's firing his Browning automatic rifle loaded with incendiary rounds at Fidel's car. Raul's first function would be to use his binoculars to make positive identification of Fidel. This mission fulfilled, Raul would drop his binoculars and engage the most threatening of the targets or whoever was returning the fire most effectively.

About 200 meters from the tunnel's exit, Raul pulled the car off the road and hid it behind a line of pine trees which ran parallel to the road. Within five minutes, the three men had assumed their familiar, often practiced positions on a small elevation in the terrain which, although covered with relatively heavy brush, still offered an unobstructed view of the tunnel.

Fidel's party, leaving the tunnel and travelling east in the early hours of the morning, would be facing the rising sun, which Raul's men would have at their backs.

It was 0655. In another five minutes Fidel would probably be leaving Celia Sanchez's apartment. Then, twenty minutes of driving would bring Fidel's entourage to the tunnel. A total of twenty-five minutes! An eternity, thought Julio as he opened a soda and reached for an empanada de guayaba. He would need the energy he would get from a high sugar meal. But then he remembered that if he were to be shot in the abdomen, his chances of survival would be poor if he had been eating. Julio decided to remind Nicky not to eat but turned aside in sorrow when he realized that his young friend was deep in prayer. Nicky was standing off to the side looking out to sea, his scapulary medallion in his hands. Julio knew that during the two long weeks of isolation while waiting and training for the mission Nicky had experienced great difficulties reconciling his deep religious convictions with his present activities. Now, Julio said under his breath, "Dios mio, what kind of system is this communism that forces decent kids like Nick into killing?"

Within a minute, Nicky turned to his friend and asked, "Julio, were you calling me?"

"No, I was just talking about you, Nicky."

"You were, were you? Don't you worry about me or about anything else, Julio. Tonight we'll be together sipping daiquiris in Coral Gables." Nick's parents and his younger sister, whom

Julio much admired, had gone to live with their American relatives in Coral Gables, Florida.

Julio looked intently at his friend. "I only know that tonight we'll be together. I promise you that. But it will be God's will as to where."

Both men leapt to alertness as the sound of brush crackling not far away but relaxed when they saw Raul making his way back up the trail. Raul had finished placing the anti-personnel mines on the only trail that branched off the main road. "All taken care of," he said and then went through a detailed explanation of how Nick and Julio could avoid the mines on their way down, especially if he were in no condition to lead them. All was ready; there was nothing left to do now but to wait and to mentally rehearse every move.

The tunnel exited onto La Via Blanca (The White Way) with the Atlantic Ocean only a kilometer away on the north side of the road. The strip of flat land between the highway and the ocean was covered with brush and pine trees and was very sparsely populated. The land to the south of the highway was equally unpopulated, but rose up gently to form elevations which did not quite qualify as hills. The road now lay almost deserted under the early morning sun. Because it was January, a month in which no self-respecting Cuban would dream of swimming in the ocean, no significant traffic to the resort area was likely. This fortunate factor practically canceled the possibility of innocent victims being caught in the cross-fire, a situation which was presently offering much consolation to the men.

At 0715 within five minutes of Fidel's estimated time of arrival, the three men exchanged handshakes and took their positions. Raul, the only one standing, had his eyes glued to his binoculars. Nick and Julio, both lying on their stomachs, aimed their weapons toward the tunnel.

At this precise moment three sedans, two black Mercedes following a silver-gray Buick, were rapidly approaching the western entrance of the tunnel. From its right fender the first Mercedes was flying a red and black flag with a star in the center. The automobiles crossed the blue and white tiled tunnel at great speed—as if in search of what now could not be avoided. As they shot out of the eastern exit of the tunnel, they were instantly spotted by Raul who spoke in a chillingly calm voice, "Here they come. Nick, you first."

The three cars were traveling much faster than the men had calculated. Through his binoculars Raul spotted Fidel's flag flying from the first Mercedes. He saw a big man next to the driver just lowering the visor to shield his eyes against the blinding rays of the rising sun. The visor now obscured his view of the bearded passenger, but Raul had to make his decision instantly; he knew the speeding cars would be out of range in less than fifteen seconds. To Nicky, he called out, "Nick—the car in the center—next to the driver. Fire!"

Almost before Raul could finish speaking, the bearded man sitting next to the driver was in the center of the crossed lines of the FAL's telescopic sight. With the same sequence of deliberate movements ingrained in him by years of competitive shooting, Nick held his breath and gently squeezed the trigger. The first bullet smashed through the windshield, striking its target in the middle of the face. Flesh, blood, bone, and teeth splattered across the interior of the car, momentarily blinding the driver. Nick fired again and again although he could no longer see his target. The car was now swerving all over the road—the driver desperately trying to regain control of his speeding vehicle but hindered by the splattered blood which covered his face and by the dead weight of the body which had slumped against him—the body of Comandante Miguel Rivera.

Miguel Rivera's resemblance to Fidel Castro was uncanny; both men had the same build and coloring and both wore similar beards. Whether Rivera was in Fidel's car as a deliberate decoy could never be known. What was certain was that his allegiance to his look-alike leader had cost him his life.

According to plan, Julio now fired his Browning automatic-rifle at the Mercedes' gasoline tank. The third shot hit its mark, and the car was instantly engulfed in flames. Within seconds a thunderous explosion shook the air, and blood and metal rained down onto La Via Blanca.

In the distance the driver of the lead Buick was reacting to the attack. He had shifted down, reducing his speed enough to safely apply his brakes, and the desperate sound of squealing tires now filled the air as the Buick swung 180 degrees and reversed its course—back toward the tunnel. As soon as the car neared the elevation where the attackers were hidden, the man in the back seat thrust half his body out the window and began firing his M-14 rifle.

His primary mission now completed, Nicky shifted his attention to the Buick. With his usual accuracy he silenced the M-14 and shot the right front tire, causing the Buick to spin out of control and crash into one of the pine trees which lined the road—not more than twenty feet from where Raul's Oldsmobile was hidden.

Two armed bodyguards stumbled out of the bullet-ridden car, leaving their dying companion sprawled across the back seat. Realizing that the Oldsmobile was the intended getaway car, the men quickly shot the tires and after a moment of rapid consultation began climbing toward their enemies.

Chapter Four

The minute the first shot had been fired, the last car in the caravan had increased its already breakneck speed and had quickly left the Dantesque scene behind. The well trained driver had without the slightest hesitation followed the cardinal rule which had undoubtedly been ingrained into him time and time again: Get the hell out of any trouble spot, no matter what the cost! At the first sign of trouble all the passengers in the rear of the car had disappeared from sight, obviously seeking the relative safety of the floor of the luxurious sedan. As the car sped out of sight, Raul noticed one disheartening detail: not one of the rounds fired at the second Mercedes had penetrated the windshield or windows. Now, oddly detached from the terrible scene it left behind, the black car disappeared into the east, toward the sun and Tarara.

By now the east exit of the tunnel had been closed to normal traffic, and G-2 sedans were beginning to join the regular blue police cars which had arrived moments earlier. There was little doubt that the fleeing Mercedes had alerted the pack! Realizing that the escape through La Via Blanca was impossible, Raul ordered Nicky and Julio to start heading toward the back road that led to the small town of Casablanca. Raul himself was to stay behind to make sure that they were not going to be followed.

After ridding himself of all nonessential equipment, Nicky slung his ammo belt over his shoulder and started to run down

Escape from Castro

the trail; Julio, now sweating profusely, followed close behind. The men were following their alternate plan which called for escape in an inconspicuous old Ford station wagon which was to have been hidden on the north side toward the end of the trail. As they ran, Nick and Julio could only hope that Lt. Oviedes had been able to place the car according to plan.

The two body guards from the Buick were soon in view of the high point from which the attack had taken place. The younger man, eager to be the first to engage the enemy, pushed past his companion and burst into the clearing at the top of the elevation. "Wait, Juan! Don't move!" the older man shouted. Instincts sharpened by two years of fighting in the hills with Fidel had warned him that there was something unusual about their surroundings. But the warning came a second too late! Juan, the younger and more impetuous, had taken his next and final step.

From his hiding place 100 feet away, Raul heard first the explosion, then terrifying screams, and finally muffled groans which soon faded into silence. Having no desire to witness the destructive power of a mine upon human flesh, Raul turned away quickly and began descending the trail toward his friends. His regret for human suffering was mixed with some satisfaction; at least, he found himself thinking, no immediate danger would threaten them from the head of the trail.

Nick and Julio had reached the end of the path and had decided to wait for Raul before making their run across the dirt road to the area where the station wagon was supposed to be hidden. As Raul rushed down the trail, he spotted his friends. "Thank God, they're safe!" he murmured, pausing for a second to catch his breath and to wave his rifle over his head to make sure that Nick and Julio had seen him coming. No sooner was Raul's rifle in the air than a shot rang out loudly. Raul's rifle fell to the ground. He stumbled, lost balance, and rolled slowly a few feet before coming to rest at the end of the trail's final slope.

Nick and Julio stood frozen, appalled by what they had just witnessed. But shock and disbelief quickly yielded to fury, and Julio, following his emotions, rushed toward Raul, stopping once to fire aimlessly at the wooded area from which the shot had come. "Julio, come back!" Nick shouted, while taking cover and using his keen eyes to desperately search the wooded area for the enemy. His trained mind told him that their lives depended on his ability to kill the sniper before he had a chance to fire again. Too late! Another shot rang out, and Julio fell to his knees, but this time Nick had spotted the flash of his enemy's weapon. He opened fire and was almost immediately rewarded by a sharp cry coming from the wooded area. A moment later, a man's body dressed in military uniform came crashing down from one of the trees which overlooked the dirt road. Struggling to keep his thoughts clear, Nick waited a few seconds to see if other shots would be fired. He knew that the exchange of fire would have alerted the enemy that must be rapidly enclosing them. Hopefully, the man in the trees had been scouting ahead of the rest of his unit, but Nicky was far from satisfied that he had been alone. Now, there was no time to lose, no time to wait for the enemy to make the next move. Raul's body lay motionless in a contorted, unnatural position, and Nick had no hope that his comrade had survived the attack. But Julio had moved slightly from the spot where he had fallen! Without another thought, Nicky rushed to Julio's side, hoisted his wounded friend onto his back, and staggered off toward the thickest part of the forest.

Chapter Five

As he ran, bowed almost double beneath the burden he carried on his back, Nick fought down his rising anguish. So much had been lost! Raul was dead, and Julio had been bleeding profusely from a chest wound when Nicky had rescued him. Now, after only a few minutes of running, Nick could already feel the back of his shirt dripping wet with his friend's blood. Julio was stirring slightly, as if struggling to regain consciousness. Nick laid his friend gently down under a tall tree and began to administer emergency first aid. He knew that they only dared to rest for a moment, and he hoped that he could stop the bleeding before they continued their desperate flight.

Julio's eyes opened abruptly and for a second he stared wildly at Nicky—without recognition or comprehension. Then, sorrow seeped over his features as he began to remember. "Nick, where's Raul?" he asked, making an obvious effort to articulate the words. The effort visibly drained him, and his pale face broke out into tiny beads of sweat.

"Raul is dead, Julio," Nick answered in a low voice while avoiding his friend's eyes. "We must go, viejo. If we can make it into the deep forest, we'll be safe. Try to hold on. I'm going to have to move fast."

"Nicky!"

"Yes, Julio?" Nick's voice was choked with sorrow.

"I can't breathe."

"Yes, you can. And you will." As Nicky gently placed his friend on his back, he felt closer to Julio than he had ever felt to another human being. Between them lay the bond of Raul's death. "Now hold on. We'll be safe soon." He spoke softly, reassuringly.

As he ran, Nick could hear Julio's labored breathing, but he did not dare pause. With the last of his strength he ran deeper and deeper into the pine forest. The increasingly thick brush and the small saplings offered a natural cover, but they also increased Nick's labor. Twice the toe of his boot caught in roots beneath the pine needles, and each time Nick came within an inch of pitching forward to the forest floor. Sweat poured into his eyes, but he could not let go of Julio long enough to brush it away.

Once he stumbled upon a small brook and forced himself to wade along it for several hundred feet although the slippery stones made it almost impossible to keep his footing. At least, when he continued on dry land, the enemy would have more difficulty following his trail. In the distance he could still hear the wailing sound of sirens from the police cars and ambulances. He knew that he had to get farther away before the enemy closed in upon them.

"Nicky, please put me down," Julio implored. "I hurt too much. Can't keep up this pace. Your chances would be better alone."

"No, I won't," Nicky replied and he continued walking—now with great difficulty. Once again, he was aware of his friend's blood wet against his back. Nick was struggling desperately to keep the sun on their left and to keep from walking in circles. But as the forest grew thicker, it became increasingly difficult to maintain a sense of direction. The ground was now cluttered with dead trees and matted undergrowth, and everywhere lay a thick cushion of pine needles. At last, the thickness of the deep forest was beginning to filter out the sound of sirens.

Julio's arms had gone limp; he was no longer making any efforts to hold on. His head now rested on Nicky's shoulder. Utterly exhausted and fearful that he too might pass out, Nicky realized that he would have to rest. He stopped and stood still for a second—listening. Finally, satisfied that only silence surrounded them, Nick very slowly lowered his unconscious friend to the ground, placing him within the protection of two fallen trees.

"There, Julio, isn't that better?" he asked gently. But there was no answer, no movement at all. Then, more to himself than to his friend, Nick said, "Now, let me check that wound." With great care, Nicky tried to open Julio's shirt, but dried blood had sealed the garment firmly to the skin. Nicky carefully eased the shirt away from the wound. Even in the safety of unconsciousness, Julio shook violently and made a gasping sound.

The bullet had made a hole below and to the right of the right nipple. Nicky changed the compress that he had fashioned earlier, this time using a handkerchief which he pulled from his own pocket. Satisfied that his friend was resting quietly, Nicky began to gather dead branches to camouflage their position.

With branches heaped about them, Nick almost felt an illusion of safety. He settled himself next to his friend and closed his eyes for a moment's respite. Then he felt Julio shudder and quickly knelt beside him, looking down into his face.

"Nicky, Nicky," Julio whispered.

"Yes Julio. I'm here. What is it?" Nicky had to place his ear closer to Julio's mouth to be able to hear him.

"Don't . . . leave . . . me."

"How can you even say that? I would never leave you."

The effort to speak utterly exhausted Julio, and he was overcome by a coughing spasm. With great sorrow, Nick saw that he had begun to cough blood.

"Nicky, I'm cold," Julio whispered. His face was now gray, his eyes closed.

"Oh God, dear God, help us!" Nick pleaded as he covered his friend with his field jacket. He took off his scapulary medal, and praying fervently, placed it around Julio's neck. Once again, Julio sank into merciful unconsciousness.

Time went by slowly as Nick watched over his friend. Restless as the ocean which pounded away relentlessly in the distance, the wind sighed through the top branches of the pines. To Nick, the sounds seemed to merge and blend into a low, sorrowful dirge. At last, the welcome darkness slowly engulfed the forest, bringing an end to the longest day Nicky had ever endured. One by one, the stars emerged, shining with frightening brilliance in a sky untouched by human misery.

Julio opened his eyes slowly and whispered, "Nicky, hold

my hand." Nick had been holding his friend's clammy hand for over an hour, but now he increased the pressure and answered, "Sure Julio. Don't worry. I'm right here."

"Nicky, me han matado (they have killed me)," Julio whispered.

Rage, mixed with terror, washed over Nicky. "No! No! You promised me! You promised! You said we would be together tonight." He leapt to his feet, fists clenched, face contorted, now shouting—emotions finally out of control after the horrors of the day. "I hate you! Bastard! You can't leave me alone! I didn't carry you all this way so that you could die on me!" Then, overwhelmed with exhaustion and weakness, yet somehow relieved by his outburst, Nick sank to his knees and buried his face in his hands. He knew that Julio would not have heard his words, and that even if he had, he would have understood. He held his face next to Julio's and wept. Julio opened his eyes and said in an almost clear voice, no longer a whisper, "No, Nicky . . . No . . . Don't watch me die."

Chapter Six

I didn't see Nodal at lunch as we had agreed. Instead of joining the rest of the staff in the wardroom, I retreated to my stateroom. Staterooms at the academy were functional cubicles furnished with two bunks, two desks, and a phone, but seldom occupied by more than one officer, so privacy was not a problem.

In order to keep my mind on an even keel, I decided to work on a small project I had been assigned. I was to make a short presentation to a couple of Soviet naval officers concerning the Cuban Navy's modest contributions to the Allies' battle against the U-Boats during World War II. "On 15 May, 1943," I jotted down, "the Cuban subchaser SC-13 commanded by Ensign Mario Ramirez sank U-176 in the Straits of Florida at 23° 21' north latitude, 80° 17' west longitude, thus avenging the sinking of a Cuban freighter two days earlier."

The hell with it! I slammed my book shut. Enough research, I said to myself. I just couldn't continue writing about something that had occurred almost two decades ago when actual events that could shape the future of Cuba were hanging in the balance at this very moment. Fuck the Soviets! I lay on my bunk and did the only thing I could do—wait and hope.

The radio and television stations had been transmitting their regular programs with no indication that anything unusual had happened. To most of the listeners, the brief radio announcement that the Havana tunnel had been temporarily closed due to an accident meant nothing. To a few of us it meant a great deal. There could no longer be any doubt that the "atentado" had been carried out, but had it been successful? It wouldn't be long before we knew; it was just going to seem long.

Tony had called at about 10:00 to tell me that (as Raul had indicated) the other members of the team had not been able to wait for him. After missing the rendezvous, Tony had tried to cross the tunnel but had been turned back by the police. Luckily, his car had not been searched. He was feeling depressed and was determined to find out what had happened, one way or another. He had promised to call me back.

When the phone rang, I grabbed it eagerly, sure that it would be Tony with more news. Instead, the unmistakable, over—confident voice of Midshipman Diaz greeted me. "Yes, Diaz, may I help you?" I responded none too cordially.

"Sir, aren't you coming down to the boathouse? The Snipe is ready and so are we. Remember, we have practice this afternoon." Diaz took his duties as part of the academy sailing team more seriously than some of his academic subjects, I thought.

"I'm sorry Diaz, but I'm buried in paperwork right now. You go out with Quintana and try to lay a course like the one we used in the last regatta. Just make sure not to bull your way around the buoys. If you wreck a Snipe, I'll have your ass."

"Aye, aye, Sir. I think that I'd better stop by your stateroom later and let you know how we did. With your permission, that is."

"Very well, I'll see you later," I answered. That's strange, I reflected after hanging up the receiver. We don't have a practice scheduled for today. I know I wouldn't have forgotten making any such arrangements. What does Diaz really want? Well, no problem. Knowing Diaz, if he wants something, he'll make sure that I don't wonder what it is for long.

More pressing and less pleasant matters pushed this casual conversation from my thoughts. I picked up the phone again and dialed a number at the Naval Base across the bay.

"Lieutenant Alberti speaking." The voice on the other end of the wire was self-assured and authoritative. Alberto Alberti, a career officer in his early thirties, was the best air navigator in the Navy and a highly qualified instructor at the Air Academy.

His pleasant features and easy smile helped to mask a determined nature and a fierce hatred of communism. He had been conspiring against Fidel from day one.

"Alberto, how are you doing?"

"Carlos, good to hear from you. But I'm the one who should inquire about your health. I heard that you had not been feeling well (a reference to my recent close call)."

"That was a couple of days ago," I responded, somewhat amused at the speed with which news traveled within our "huge" navy of 7,000 men and 400 officers. "I feel fine now. Although you never know; there could always be a relapse."

"Oh... well, let's hope not. Listen, I need help with some translations. If you're not in a hurry, I'll stop over to show you what I have and to share a beer or two before you take off. By the way, you never mentioned why you called."

"Nothing important... just to offer you a ride home. I was planning on leaving soon and remembering how cheap you are, I thought you might want to save some gas."

"Cheap, huh?"

"I'll tell you what. Come on over. I translate and you buy."

"Talk about cheap! I'll be there in fifteen minutes."

As promised, after fifteen minutes of low flying his old Ford through the narrow, winding back road that led to the academy, Alberto miraculously arrived in one piece. I was waiting for him in the parking lot. Grinning with pride at his record driving time, Alberti climbed out of his battered Ford. After he had returned the salutes of two midshipmen, he put his arm around my shoulders and said with amusement in his voice, "I heard about the other night with your friends from G-2 wanting to take you for a nice little ride."

"Yeah, I can't say I'm sorry to have made them go home alone. But I'm sure they'll try again. That's why I called you. I need to know if you could introduce me to your contact from the American Embassy. I'd like to have a back-up to get out of the country if I have to. You know... in case I can't get to the boat."

"Too bad you didn't call me earlier. I was with him this morning. Anyhow, my contact knows very well who you are. If you need him for anything, call the embassy and ask for Michael Armstrong." Alberti's expression suddenly changed. Looking over my shoulder, he had seen a car coming up the road. It was now hidden from view by the high walls covered with red-violet bougainvillea which guarded the road at the entrance to the academy.

"What's the matter?" I asked. "You look as if you just spotted your worst enemy."

"Carlos, let's get out of here. Nodal will be with us in a minute." Lately, Alberti's reputation as one not to be trusted had been growing. Naturally, Nodal, always in touch with the times, did not care much for him.

"O.K., let's take a walk toward the pool," I said. The academy was the ideal place for taking a stroll. Immaculate grounds with manicured lawns and lush tropical plants and flowers combined with a breathtaking hilltop view of the bay, the town, and the coastline far below—enough to impress even the most jaded beholder.

As we walked, Alberti spoke with the excitement of one who knew more than he could reveal. "Carlos, the Americans are preparing something big. In Miami they are beginning to recruit Cubans, especially those with military backgrounds. As I was about to tell you before our friend made his appearance, my contact just this morning told me it's now unquestionably official; President Kennedy has given the green light to a plan to form a Cuban Brigade, to train it, and then land it in Cuba with full military support."

"It's about time," I exclaimed excitedly. Oh God, let it be, I thought. What a pleasure it would be to put all those Vende Patria (sellers of the Fatherland) where they belong.

"Listen, Carlos, here comes Nodal," Alberti said, interrupting my outburst. "I'll talk with you tomorrow. I wouldn't want him to see me alone with you. You've had enough trouble as it is."

Ignoring the warning, I answered, "What do you mean by that?"

"You'll know soon enough. Be sure to bad-mouth me. Just don't overdo it," he called as he walked quickly away, turning only once briefly. He was gone before I could ask another question. It would be a long time before I would see Alberti again, not so long in a matter of months or years, but in a matter of lives changed and lost.

I walked briskly and purposefully, hoping to avoid Nodal. The day was finally drawing to a close; the temperature had already dropped and a soft, blue-gray dusk was settling slowly over the academy. I was halfway across the Parade Grounds when Colors was sounded, and I stood at attention and saluted the flag as it was lowered by the honor guard. Glancing at my watch, I noted that the sun had set at 1830 at Mariel's latitude.

When I entered my room a few minutes later, I found Nodal with his feet on my desk reading my latest copy of *Carteles*. "I hope you've made yourself comfortable," I remarked.

"I decided that I'd better stop and see you here. You looked as if you were on your way to the Quinta Avenida, and there I would not have felt comfortable."

Quinta Avenida? Was Nodal referring to the home of my girl friend, Thais Encheverria, on that street? But what would have led him to believe I intended to visit Thais? Then, I understood. There was little doubt that Nodal was referring to a certain green house on Quinta Avenida, better known as the G-2 house of horrors. Ignoring the bait, I answered casually, "No, I wasn't planning on seeing Thais tonight. In fact, her whole family is vacationing in Costa Rica right now."

"Good for them," Nodal replied caustically. "Anyway, I just wanted to give you a heads-up; we have a job to do tomorrow in the bay of Havana."

"Another Russian ship?" I asked.

"Yes, the *Komsomolets*, and it's a big one. It's going to be tied up on the east pier."

"What time are we leaving?"

"Early. I'll pick you up at 0600. Where will you be?" he asked as he got up to leave.

"As I mentioned earlier, I'll be at my parents. I'll meet you there."

"Il ya vas uvizhu zavtra," he said in heavily accented Russian.

"Yes, I'll see you tomorrow," I replied in my best English.

One of the main tasks of the Cuban Underwater Demolition Team was to stand guard under Russian munitions ships while they were being off-loaded. This mandatory guard duty had been established after the French ship *La Coubre* had been blown up while off-loading weapons in Havana. Since the *La Coubre* incident, most of the ships carrying munitions were off-loaded at other Cuban ports and, whenever possible, while at anchor. Nevertheless, once in a while there would be a need to bring such a ship into Havana Bay.

At least, I was relieved to see that I was still in fairly good standing or I would not have been called for such a sensitive mission. I was also relieved to learn that this underwater watch was going to be during the day since most of the ammo off-loading was carried out at night.

The long day of constraint and pretense was over at last, and I was finally free to find out what had happened to my friends. I hurried out of the Bachelor Officers Quarters toward the staff parking lot. As I approached my Opel, I saw the shadow of a man in uniform sitting next to the driver's seat. I quickly opened the car door with my left hand while holding my 7.65 Beretta in my right. The car light came on, illuminating the friendly face of Midshipman Diaz.

"Diaz, what the devil are you doing in here listening to my car radio?" I barked.

"I told you I wanted to talk with you, didn't I, Sir?" answered Diaz, somewhat disconcerted by the sight of my drawn weapon.

"Yes, you did," I admitted. "But why here?"

"Why here? Because Lieutenant Nodal was in your stateroom, and he would not have approved of my conversation."

"O.K., go on," I said, lowering myself into the driver's seat and closing the door behind me. "But make it short; I'm in a hurry."

"Well, last night I was in the library at about 2230. You know how we're not supposed to be in there after 2200 . . ."

"I can't hear a thing you are saying, but go on anyway," I replied, pretending not to want to know that he had broken yet another academy rule.

"I heard Lieutenant Calderon and Lieutenant Nodal come into the library. I hid in the head. I didn't want any more demerits if I could help it. Lieutenant Nodal was making the rounds since he was the officer of the day. Anyhow, I heard Lieutenant Calderon telling Lieutenant Nodal that an order had come straight from Comandante Castiñeiras' office to take you out of Havana for awhile. Nodal seemed delighted and he said, 'If we're going to save his neck, we've got to get him out of here before it's too late.' It sounded to me like in their own weird way they wanted to help you."

"Yeah? Maybe," I replied. "But it isn't as altruistic as you think. Because during the Revolution I opposed Batista and because of my connections with Fidel and some of his people, it would be a victory of the G-2 over the Navy to get me down. They would argue that if I had proven to be disloyal to the Revolution, then how could they trust any other naval officer? The G-2 ambition of having the right to interfere in the internal affairs of the Navy would seem justified. And wouldn't G-2 love to destroy the last vestiges of tradition and pride of our military! That is partially why Lieutenant Nodal and Lieutenant Calderon are trying to help me."

"And partially because of what else?" asked Diaz, delighted with the confidence and trust I had placed in him.

"And partially because they, like most Cubans, are not truly communists, and friendship still means more to them than the party line."

The music on the radio suddenly stopped and the somewhat doleful voice of the announcer began to speak as martial music played in the background. "We interrupt our regular broadcast to announce that, as a result of burns suffered this morning in an automobile accident outside the tunnel, one of the greatest heroes of the Revolution, Comandante Miguel Rivera, has just died. Five members of his staff also perished in the accident; their names are being withheld pending notification of their next of kin. Our Maximum Leader, Fidel Castro, was in Oriente province at the time of the accident, but he is expected to arrive very soon at Jose Marti International Airport . . ."

Without waiting to hear the rest of the report, I started the engine and turned to Diaz, who seemed to be trying to figure out the truth behind the announcement. "Diaz, I'll speak to you again soon, but now I must leave immediately. Just don't forget that you are only five months from graduation; don't take many chances."

As he climbed out of the car, Diaz answered, "I won't, Sir, unless they seem worth taking."

As I drove away, I looked back and saw Diaz walking past

Midshipman Delgado who was standing by the door of the hall. Apparently, he had been watching us as we conferred. Oh, well, Diaz can take care of himself, I thought, trying to reassure myself. But as I drove toward my parents' house, my thoughts were with other courageous young Cubans who had taken a risk that they believed was worth dying for.

Chapter Seven

Julio had kept his promise to be together with Nicky that night; he had not died until the first hour of the new morning. Nicky had lain awake next to his friend most of the night until, toward dawn, his exhaustion had forced him to sleep. The sunlight filtering thorough the branches of his make-shift shelter finally awakened him. He reached for his pistol and stood silently, feeling that he had heard noises. Or had he been dreaming? But a crackling sound in the brush answered his question; there was no doubt, he had been discovered. He pushed the branches aside and almost shot the intruder. A young woman wearing riding breeches and holding a horse by the reins was standing there, staring down at them.

His sudden movements had startled the high-strung thoroughbred which was now rearing and whinnying as the young woman desperately tried to settle it down. Nicky, who had been around horses all his life, grabbed the reins from her and controlled the animal. When he turned his attention back to the girl, he was startled by the absolute terror which was reflected in her face. He put away his pistol and said, "I'm sorry if I frightened you."

"Oh, no, it was my fault. Please, I didn't mean any harm. I was just riding home when I heard screams, so I came to see if someone needed help. When I saw you and your friend sleeping under those branches, I realized that one of you must have been crying out in a nightmare."

Nicky watched intently as she spoke, trying to make a rapid assessment of the new situation. She had the air and manners of one to whom life had denied very little. Although not new, her riding clothes were of excellent quality, and her horse was obviously a fine animal. Even the plain but expensive saddle reflected a restrained elegance. I think I'm on safe ground, Nicky thought. "What is your name? And who is with you?" he finally asked.

"My name is Elena . . . Elena Marten, and I'm alone. Please, let me go," she implored, her voice shaking with fear.

What do I expect? Nick reflected. After twenty-four hours of hell . . . dirty and unshaven . . . my clothes torn and covered with blood . . . What must I look like to a young girl like her?

"I'm not holding you. You are free to do whatever you want," he said with a sad smile, regretting having to lie. He knew he couldn't allow her to leave.

For the first time she really looked at him. Now, only a few feet away, she realized how young he was. His straight black hair fell over his forehead, almost covering his eyes. From time to time he would push it aside with a disarmingly boyish gesture. His speech was educated and warm. She found it hard to believe that an evil, violent soul could be trapped inside those striking good looks and gentle manners. Who he was, she did not know. Nevertheless, it was obvious to her that he must have been involved in the shooting she had heard the day before. For a few moments, not a word was spoken as Elena struggled to deal with the rush of thoughts flashing through her mind. They had spent the night in the most secluded part of the forest—armed—blood all over their clothes. Their pursuers had to be closing in on them. Time was running out and they needed her help desperately.

But who had helped Marco? She asked herself. The vision of her brother seemed to replace the reality of the moment. She could still see him being dropped unconscious at the front gate after one night in the hands of the G-2—his young face swollen under a mat of clotted blood, his open mouth gasping for air. And Marco's fate would be pale compared to what would await this man. It was a guilt she could not bear. There was only one thing to do—she would help.

She broke the silence. "I must warn you that the G-2 has

searched my home twice since yesterday. The last time they assured us that we were not going to be bothered again. Still, who would trust them? Now, you must tell me the truth."

"The truth is obvious. I can tell you nothing except that I need your help. I haven't had anything to eat for twenty-four hours and very little to drink. I'm so thirsty."

Tears of pity came to her eyes. He looked like a hunted animal making its last stand—with dignity but without much hope. "Don't worry. My father and I don't live far from here, and we will try to help you both."

"Just me. I'll take care of my friend."

"But why only you? Is he all right?"

"He is dead," Nicky said as he handed her the reins and walked toward where Julio lay.

For several seconds Elena did not move as she fought to absorb yet another shock. Too much was happening too fast. But when she saw Nicky coming out of the shelter with his dead friend in his arms, she realized that all she wanted to do was to help this young man whose name she did not even know.

Chapter Eight

At about 8:00 P.M. I arrived at my home on Twenty-First Street. I started to pull into the driveway but realized the impossibility when I saw that it was already filled with the cars of relatives and friends. I shook my head and smiled; the time-honored Cuban custom of dropping in unannounced on friends and relatives and visiting for hours on end never failed to amuse me. As I walked up the stairs that led to the main floor, I recognized the car of Luisita Olivella, the wife of a well-known physician and a dear friend of my mother. Her chauffeur was sitting behind the wheel, looking very contented and eating a plateful of croquetas. He waved at me and tried to mutter a greeting through the huge bite he had just taken. I sure hope Jacinta made enough croquetas tonight, I thought ruefully.

I slipped into the house unnoticed since everyone was engaged in animated conversation out on the main terrace. I went directly to my room and quickly changed into civilian clothes. On my dresser I found a note from my mother: *Tony wants you to call as soon as possible*.

Using the phone in my parents' room, I dialed Tony's number. When he answered, I said, "Tony, what's up?"

"Nothing good. The party was a disaster."

"I was afraid of that," I replied as my whole body shivered involuntarily.

"Where are you now?"

"At home."

I'll be there in a few minutes. Don't go anywhere."

"No, the house is full of people. Let's meet at El Carmelo."

"Okay, El Carmelo then," Tony replied.

I put down the receiver and stood motionless for a moment, staring at the large painting of the Sacred Heart which hung on the wall over my parents' bed.

The door opened and my mother entered the room. "Oh, I didn't know you were home, Carlitos," she said.

I turned around, kissed her and said, "I just got in. I hope you don't mind my using your phone."

"Oh sure, I mind." Affectionately, she cupped her hands around my face and said, "How come you are so handsome?"

"Oh, I was just careful to find a set of parents with the right genes—especially the mother," I replied.

Then, looking me straight in the eyes, she said, "Don't believe that you fool me for one minute with that charming smile and those clever jokes. Tell me what's worrying you."

"Mamy, don't be silly. It's nothing—at least nothing I can't take care of. I'll tell you more soon."

"Are you leaving now without even eating?"

"I'm afraid so. It's urgent."

"Jacinta is going to be very disappointed. She made the croquetas that you asked for. Besides, Luisita stopped by on her way to the theater to see an operetta. She has an extra ticket and was hoping that you would join her and her house guest."

"I'm really sorry, Mamy, I just can't. Let's go downstairs. And please make my excuses to Dad and to everyone else."

It took less than ten minutes to drive to El Carmelo Cafe on Calzada Street. As usual, the place was crowded with familiar faces. If there was any safe place to meet, this was it, for El Carmelo patrons tended to be well-dressed and cultured; G-2 men and Fidelistas would have a hard time blending with the crowd. Always an exception to any rule, Fidel, accompanied by his usual crowd of lackeys, often visited this elegant gathering place. It occurred to me that considering the present circumstances and the radio announcement that he was in Oriente, tonight we didn't have to worry about him.

I wondered how long it would be before this way of life would disappear. I had little doubt that Fidel was going to make good his promise to wipe out the different classes in Cuba. Soon everybody was going to be the same—poor and miserable.

Tony was sitting at a table next to the large glass windows which faced the street. He waved as he saw me approaching, and we shook hands warmly.

"It was bad, huh," I said as we settled ourselves at the table. It was more a statement than a question.

"Yes, really bad," he replied. Then, he narrated the day's events exactly as they had taken place. "All my information comes from our contact in G-2 who was at the scene no more than ten minutes after the fact," Tony stated grimly. "Anyway, Raul is in the Hospital Militar in coma. The G-2 is still looking for Julio and Nicky."

The waiter approached the table and took our order: hot chocolate and toast. After he had left, Tony leaned forward and spoke in a low tone which was drowned out by the background music, lively conversation, and laughter which surrounded us. "Carlos, they have to be alive or the bodies would have been found. The G-2 is combing the whole area; not a stone has been left unturned."

"Do they know who they're looking for?" I asked anxiously.

"They have some idea, I'm afraid. We have to find Nick and Julio before they do or . . ." Tony cut his remarks short as the waiter approached and placed the rich chocolate and thick, buttery slices of toast before us. We ate, but without appetite or enjoyment.

After a few moments, Tony repeated with greater urgency, "Carlos, we must find them."

"No," I answered, "we could never find them. The only thing we would accomplish by trying would be to get caught wandering around the area. And without a good, solid explanation, we would be in a heap of trouble."

"Yeah? And what do you suggest we do?"

"I'll tell you, Tony. We won't have to look for them because they are going to find us. You can be sure that the minute they can, they'll call my house, as planned."

Tony finished his hot chocolate and put the cup down slowly. Finally, after weighing my observations, he said, "You know, Carlos, you're right. Just make sure that everyone at Twenty-First Street thinks that you are interested in selling your Opel."

"They do. I've told everyone at home to make sure that I'm notified right away if any calls come in about my car. If anyone calls and asks about the Opel, it has to be Nick, or Julio using the code. And they will give us instructions about how to get in touch."

"And if they don't call soon?" Tony asked.

"Then we had better get ready for the worst," I replied.

Tony nodded glumly. "Well," he finally said, "I'd better go now. I've hardly seen Cathy these last days; she must be a bag of worries by now. As he rose, he glanced out the window at the Auditorium, Havana's famous performing arts theater. "That's quite a crowd across the street," he remarked off-handedly. "I wonder what's going on at the Auditorium."

"Oh, it's the Cuban National Ballet Company's first home performance after their European tour. It looks like half of Havana is there to welcome them home."

Tony nodded. "One of these days Fidel is going to claim that before him, there was no ballet in Cuba—just the way he claims to have instituted free education and free medical services."

"Well, we know he's the greatest demagogue of the century," I said as I laid down my napkin and rose to leave.

Tony sat back again and motioned me to stay. He looked around our table and, satisfied once more that there was no way that anyone could hear our conversation, said, "At this stage of the game perhaps it's better to stay ignorant of some of Fidel's atrocities, but anyhow listen to what I just found out."

I sank back into my chair and leaned forward so that he would not have to raise his voice.

"My Aunt Margot lives next door to the Sori-Marins. Well, as you know, Humberto Sori-Marin fought next to Fidel in the mountains."

"He sure did, and later he became part of Fidel's inner circle," I added.

"Exactly. They were really buddy-buddy—so much so that Fidel became an almost daily guest at Sori's home. He loved Humberto's mother's cooking."

"Yes, I've seen plenty of pictures in the newspapers of Humberto and Fidel practically eating out of the same plate."

"Anyway, Humberto's mother told Aunt Margot that when she found out that her son had been arrested on charges of conspiracy, she went to see Fidel. Castro listened intently and was apparently moved by the old lady's suffering. He even stroked her hair and reassured her that her son was going to be all right— he promised. Within twenty-four hours, if you can believe this, following Castro's direct orders, the infamous firing squad spilled the blood of one more of Fidel's closest friends."

"Unbelievable! What a monster!" I was shocked. "A poisonous snake could take lessons from our Maximum Leader. If he did that to Sori, you can imagine what he would do to us, but especially to you, Tony."

"As if I didn't know it! But Carlos, before you go, I must ask a favor," Tony said in a low voice.

"Sure, anything. What is it?" I answered.

If you find out that they've got me, don't try to help. It would be useless. Just get in your boat and get out."

"I'll see about that, but I make no promises," I replied as we walked out of the cafe into the cool evening air. "In the meantime, try not to get caught."

I got into my car but didn't start the engine. Tony's request had shaken me more than I wanted to admit, and I needed time to collect my thoughts. I sat behind the wheel of my Opel Kapitan watching him as he stood outside El Carmelo, surrounded by friends and looking casual and confident. Who could have guessed just a few years ago when he, Fidel, and Raul Ramirez were all law students at the University of Havana that their lives would turn out the way they had.

Back in 1946 Tony had been a freshman; Fidel a sophomore. Tony played football; Fidel politics. Castro's ambitious goal of becoming President of the University of Havana Student Association, a highly visible position much sought after by student leaders with political aspirations, seemed to be eluding him. In spite of his high academic standing and considerable personal magnetism, Fidel could not rally enough support to get elected. His biggest drawback was his growing reputation as a student gangster. Through intimidation and fascist tactics he and his less intelligent friends were trying to lead students who did not want to be led, at least not by him.

One cool morning in October of 1946, Fidel was having a violent public argument with Raul at the Plaza Cadenas, the main square of the University of Havana. The Plaza was surrounded by academic buildings whose impressive columns and elegant marble steps reflected the obvious influence of classical Greek architecture. Somehow the civilized Greek influence didn't seem to have much of an effect on Fidel Castro that day. Playing to the crowd and looking pointedly at Tony who was standing next to Raul, Fidel said to Raul, "Why don't you get one of your friends who is more my size to step forward?"

Tony immediately stepped forward and said in a low, defiant voice, "I am his friend. I am also your size. What now?"

Surrounded by a large crowd of students, Tony and Fidel began walking toward the stadium to vent their anger with their fists. As they walked, Fidel remarked boastfully, "I have money to bet on this 'little fight'."

In the football field, now encircled by several hundred students, Tony Capó and Fidel Castro faced each other. The exchange of hard blows between the two solidly-built men, each over six feet tall, soon brought blood to the face of an astonished Fidel Castro. Unrattled by warnings that the police were on their way, the determined young men continued fighting without either man showing any sign of dwindling courage. But it wasn't long before Fidel began to tire, and the outcome of the fight started to unfold. Tony, accustomed to the rigorous and aggressive training of a football player, was able to knock Fidel down three consecutive times. Determined not to lose face, Castro launched a desperate right. Tony moved fast; the right failed and Fidel's unguarded face was met by the fury of Tony's left fist. Fidel for the rest of his life would show a black tooth as the result of the "little fight."

Castro's friends, annoyed that Fidel's forecast of an easy fight was taking an unexpected turn, took out their pistols and began firing into the air. A football player named Besada hurried to Tony's aid. As a result of his assistance, one of Castro's gangsters had to be rushed to the hospital. Ultimately Fidel's goons put their weapons away and the bout ended with the intervention of the University Police.

The bright headlights of a car parking next to mine brought me back to the present. I looked at my watch: 2230. I started the engine and headed home, reassured that I had a solid partner in Tony Capó.

Chapter Nine

Nicky lay Julio's body next to the spot he had chosen. He broke off a pine branch and with its sharp end and his own bare hands began to dig his friend's grave. Wishing he could have been alone, he turned to Elena and said, "I'll be ready to leave as soon as I finish what I have to do."

"I'll help you," she offered.

"No, I can take care of it," he replied, abhorring the idea of a complete stranger touching Julio's body. Nick's lips felt dry and his forehead was cold and clammy with perspiration. For a second he thought he was going to pass out, but he continued to dig. When he was finally finished, he covered Julio's face with his jacket and then recovered his friend's pistol and all of his personal belongings except for the glasses, which he placed in Julio's shirt pocket. He wrapped the rifle and buried it under a fallen tree. Then, he knelt, and Elena, looking away, heard him praying in a low voice, "Hail Mary, Mother of God . . ."

Time passed, and still kneeling next to his friend, Nick seemed oblivious to his surroundings. Elena walked away a few feet, but Nicky still did not move. Finally, after about twenty minutes, Elena began to fear that someone might come. She walked back to the grave and leaning down, she touched Nick lightly on the shoulder and said, "I'm afraid it's time. We mustn't stay here any longer."

Without saying a word Nicky touched Julio's hand, stepped

out of the pit, and turning his face away began to fill the grave. Over the freshly moved dirt he threw small branches and handfuls of pine needles. Then he used a pine branch to erase his footprints. As he surveyed the area, he thought with relief that even he would have difficulty finding it again.

Elena and Nicky began to walk slowly toward her home. Elena led her horse by the bridle, and Nick followed about twenty-five feet behind her, forcing himself not to look back. About 400 feet from the forest's edge stood her family home, a large, handsome two story stucco house with a red tiled roof and a small stable in the back. Nick was amazed to find the house so close; he had believed that he and Julio were alone at the ends of the earth. As for Elena . . . he would soon know if her sympathy and offers of assistance were only motivated by fear.

Almost as if she had read his thoughts, Elena said, "You must trust me. I really want to help you. Wait here until I make sure that everything is clear. And don't worry about intruders; the nearest house is more than a kilometer from here."

"But what about your family?" Nick asked.

Everyone except for my father and myself is in Miami, and my father won't be home until late this evening. Only our maid of twenty years is here now. I'll get you something to eat and drink, and then we can decide what to do next. "O.K.?"

"Yes, fine. But are you sure you want to go along with all this?"

"I have never been more sure of anything. Still, I'll have to call my father and explain the situation. I'm sure you can understand that."

"But what if he . . ."

"You don't have to worry about my father," she interrupted. Without waiting for his reaction, she began to walk toward the stable to put up her horse.

Nick watched the stable until he saw Elena go into the house through the back porch. Then, after satisfying himself that he was alone, he walked toward the house, hoping to be able to watch Elena through the windows. It had occurred to him that she was now free to summon help if she had not been telling him the truth. The ferocious barking of a large dog inside the house made him change his mind and head for the stable instead. Once inside the stable he moved gently so as not to frighten the horses, but he soon realized that although there were six stalls, only one was occupied—by Elena's thoroughbred.

Nick noticed a sink by the stable door, and now he gave it his full attention. He turned the faucet on and reveled in the sight— clear, cool water gushing out, pouring over his cupped hands. He drank and drank until his terrible thirst was almost quenched. At last, he forced himself to stop, fearing stomach cramps. He peeled off his filthy shirt and washed away the stench of sweat, blood, and death. Dripping wet, but beginning to feel alive, he walked into a tack room across from the stalls. Next to the tack room was a small sitting room furnished with an old couch, a few chairs, and a small refrigerator. In it he found two bottles of Hatuey beer, a half-full bottle of coke, and a few stale slices of ham. He sat down on the couch, ate the leathery ham, and drank a bottle of beer in slow, appreciative gulps. Then he lay back on the dusty old couch and rested.

The wall in front of him was decorated with dozens of ribbons and with photographs of Elena and a young man participating in horse shows. When the ribbons and photographs began blending together, Nick realized that he was falling asleep. He forced himself to stand up, knowing it was dangerous to let his guard down for even a few minutes. He decided to check the rest of the stable. Outside the back door under a pile of soaked, dirty wood shavings, discarded bedding from the stalls, he hid his blood stained jacket. Back inside the stable Nick climbed to the loft over the stalls. There he lay down on a pile of alfalfa next to a small window which commanded a view of the back of the house. There had been no movements at all around the house, and the dirt road, which was about 300 feet from the front of the house, seemed deserted. Half reassured that there was no immediate danger and half not caring anymore, Nicky closed his eyes and fell into a deep sleep.

Chapter Ten

By the time I got home it was nearly midnight. When I stepped out of my car to unlock the gate, I heard our dog, Dago, barking and growling in a dark corner of the yard. Suddenly, a bearded man emerged from the heavy shrubbery which bordered the house. As I watched, he climbed the wrought iron fence and began running across the street toward a car which was parked with its engine running. I started toward the car, shouting, "Stop right there!" but the driver had opened a back door to let the bearded man in, and the car was already heading down the street. I drew my pistol and fired a shot into the air as they drove away.

Hoping that they had gotten the message, I returned to the house. Once inside the gate, I noticed that Dago was sniffing a large piece of meat which was lying on the driveway. I picked it up and hurried into the house to have a better look at it. My first intention was to take the meat to a laboratory to have it analyzed, but second thoughts brought the realization that any such action would make me very conspicuous. I tossed the meat into the garbage. Anyway, I had very little doubt that those characters marauding around the house were not trying to supplement Dago's diet. They could have saved their cyanide or whatever they had put into that meat, since Dago was trained to accept food only from family members.

The kitchen door opened, and our maid Lucila, a tall, handsome black woman, appeared in her house robe.

"Carlos," she questioned in an agitated voice, "did you hear that noise? It sounded like a shot."

"Yes, I did. I was the one who fired—to scare away a couple of hoodlums who were hanging around the house." I didn't want to alarm her unnecessarily, but I did want her to be alert in case they tried it again. "Keep your ears open," I said calmly, "but don't tell los viejos. I'd like them to get a good night's sleep."

"Don't you worry. They went to the theater with la Señora Olivella. It's the best thing they could have done since they got pretty upset listening to the evening news. You must have heard about the officers who were killed outside the tunnel."

"Yes, I did hear about the accident," I replied.

"Well, people are saying that it was no accident—that those men were gunned down. Do you believe it was really just an accident?"

"Yes, Lucila, of course I do. The officials have no reason to lie." I couldn't risk having her quote me the wrong way on this subject.

"Well maybe . . . if you say so," she finally answered, doubt still heavy in her voice. "Would you like me to fix you something to eat?" she asked, putting aside her curiosity in response to my seeming lack of interest.

"No thanks, what I need is to go to bed right away. I'll be leaving about 6:00 A.M."

"I'll have cafe con leche ready for you when you get up."

"No, Lucila. It would be much too early. Please don't bother; I'll get something along the road."

"Sure you will. You come to the pantry; it'll be ready at quarter till six, and don't you let it get cold. Buenas noches," she concluded in her usual bossy but affectionate tone.

"Buenas noches, y gracias, Lucila," I said as she left the kitchen.

I went to my room and took off my clothes. On the way to the shower I glanced at the mirror, noting with disapproval that I looked both tired and underweight. Determined to get a few hours of sleep for a change, I went back into my room and poured myself a generous glass of Cointreau. Back in the bathroom I filled the tub with hot water and sank gratefully into the nearly overflowing bath. Before the water had even had a chance to cool off, I had finished the Cointreau. Somehow, though, my mind was still wide awake. Deciding that I might as well enjoy the night air and the view from the balcony, I put on my comfortable old terry cloth robe and walked out onto the terrace.

The cool air smelled slightly of evergreen, and the ocean was clearly visible thanks to a sky brightened by the lights from Morro Castle. I settled myself in a lounge chair and tried to let the peaceful scene sink into my tired brain. It didn't work though; the thoughts that crowded into my mind were uniformly unpleasant. Why the attempted poisoning of Dago? I hoped it was just the work of common burglars and not of the local milicianos. Anyway, this new incident was minor compared to my real worries: Raul in a coma and under round-the-clock G-2 surveillance, Nicky and Julio—God only knew where. The worst part—even worse than the uncertainty—was knowing that there was absolutely nothing I could do to solve any of the problems. Once somebody wrote, "Long is the night that does not rush toward dawn." Whoever he was, I thought, he really knew about nights like this. I shivered violently; the chill of the night had finally reached me. With a sigh, I got up and went inside to my room. I sank into bed, refusing to even glance at the clock.

A few hours later I was on our front porch waiting for Nodal who had insisted on picking me up at home. He arrived promptly at 0600, pulling up in front of the house in his beaten-up Oldsmobile. "What about some breakfast?" I asked him as I opened the gate.

"It depends on what's on the menu." he replied as he climbed out of his car.

"You'll have to ask Lucila about the menu, I'm afraid."

"If Lucila's doing the cooking, I'll take my chances," he answered with a smile.

Feeling revitalized after a quick but tasty continental breakfast that included plenty of coffee, we headed toward Nodal's car. We drove along the Malecon, passed the American Embassy and the monument to the USS *Maine,* and then made our way through downtown Havana, pleasantly devoid of its usual horrendous traffic at this early hour. It was a few minutes before 0700 when we pulled alongside the pier. Our conversation had been impersonal and strictly related to our immediate task. Better that way, I pondered, although I surely would have enjoyed knowing exactly what Nodal had on his mind.

The ship was almost 700 feet long, had a beam of about 80 feet, and appeared to be of fairly new construction. We had to wait a few minutes while the Russians finished tying up with the assistance of two powerful tugs. As soon as the accommodation ladder touched the pier, we went up. We showed our identification papers and were turned over to a rough looking, middle-aged sailor who escorted us to a compartment where we could change our clothes. The compartment contained only a couple of unpainted, splinter-laden benches and a few dilapidated metal lockers. "Not exactly the Queen Mary," I remarked to Nodal.

"Don't worry about it," he answered brusquely. "We're just here to do a job."

"Yes, you're right," I replied, a little amused by his defensive attitude, "but before we start that job, let's make sure that Ivan understands that the propeller has to be engaged before we go down."

The sailor who awaited us outside the compartment could not understand a word of Spanish or English, giving Miguel an opportunity to show off the Russian he was so avidly studying. With some difficulty, he finally let the sailor know that we needed to speak to the OOD. We were led back to the quarter-deck, where the officer of the day informed us in quite serviceable English that all the necessary safety precautions had been taken. He asked us not to worry, claiming that he personally would be responsible for our safety. It was more than a turning propeller and the expectation of finding deadly explosives attached to the ship that worried me. Once in the dark waters of the bay, I could be disposed of easily, and no one would question what would appear as a readily explainable accident, considering our mission.

We went into the water by the stern since the first places to check would be the propeller and the rudder. Fortunately, this ship was a merchant vessel and had only one propeller and one rudder; naval vessels usually had two of each—to ensure better handling and greater maneuverability. The water was unusually cool and just as polluted as always. Havana Bay's narrow entrance was a great advantage in that it offered protection against both weather and intruders; unfortunately, this bottleneck opening also prevented the tides from cleansing the oil spillage and discharged debris which afflict all large harbors.

Nodal and I went down together to check the stern, mainly by feel since our visibility was nearly zero. Our two underwater lights were both malfunctioning, and the fact that we had just placed an order for top-notch Italian underwater equipment offered us little consolation as we groped our way through the murky water.

It's amazing how overwhelming a ship can look from underneath, especially when the visibility is poor and you don't quite trust your partner. I made sure that my knife was within easy reach on my right calf, as Nodal and I split up to pursue our separate tasks. I slowly felt my way underneath the keel from starboard side to the port side. Luckily, nothing unusual showed up. I surfaced and looked for Miguel. When I didn't see him, I figured he must have moved toward the bow. I was now sandwiched between the pier and the ship, to the dismay of half a dozen onlookers who were gesturing wildly and shouting, "Don't do it. Don't try to go through." They were obviously aware that if for any reason the ship shifted its huge bulk half a foot toward the pier, I would be crushed like a fly. I went down anyway since I knew that a 40,000 ton ship wasn't about to move half a foot sideways without the help of tugs or gale winds. I maneuvered slowly down the hull, always within touching distance of the pier, worked my way under the ship and finally surfaced once again on the starboard side. I continued making similar passes under the ship, always feeling for any unusual bulge, grateful that my sense of touch had become a kind of second vision.

The lack of visibility and the polluted waters always had their worst effect on me the first time under. After that, I became accustomed to the darkness and the oil in the water and didn't mind them so much. By now, I had already been in the water for a couple of hours and was totally adjusted to the conditions. My next pass was from port to starboard. Since the ship was berthed on her port side, once I crossed the keel, I swam up, searching for the balance keel (a wing-like projection on the side of the hull which was designed to increase stability, especially during heavy seas). The balance keel was unfortunately also a convenient location to place an explosive device.

Halfway up, I was startled by the sudden warmness of the hull and by the vibration caused by the power plants and pumps within the vessel. Some atavistic danger response within me brought a spurt of adrenaline and irregular breathing, and before I knew it, I had managed to get some of the filthy water inside my mask. I lay back and forcefully blew air out of my nose to evacuate the mask, but a small amount of water refused to budge. I had been over that balance keel once, and once would have to do. I started up, and in my eagerness to reach the surface, brushed my left leg against the razor-like barnacles that infested the ship's hull. The result was a long slice up the side of my thigh which looked exactly as if it had been made by a surgeon's scalpel.

Damn! I thought. Serves me right for not wearing the bottom half of my wet suit. On the surface Nodal was waiting for me.

"What took you so long?" he demanded. Then he noticed the red stain in the water around my leg. "What happened? What's all that blood?" he asked with sincere concern.

"Oh, just a cut on the leg. The barnacles got me on my last pass," I answered, sounding nonchalant although I was beginning to worry a little about sharks.

"We'd better get out of the water before we get some uninvited company attracted by all that blue blood," Miguel suggested after he had quickly checked the wound.

"That sounds fine to me," I said, thinking that he sounded more like the old Miguel, an encouraging sign that my leg didn't look all that bad.

We climbed to the pier by means of a slippery Jacob's ladder—no easy chore with the weight of the double tanks on our backs. The accommodation ladder was almost as steep, and it was a relief to finally set foot on the quarterdeck. We noticed with satisfaction that the off-loading was nearly finished and so would be the need for our services. The sailors, unaccustomed to our type of activity, were staring at us as much as they dared. Among them, I noticed several women working as deck hands, and I couldn't help feeling sorry for those poor women as I thought what their duty must be like during heavy seas in the Russian latitudes.

When we got to the head, we found an old sailor with a large first-aid box under his arm waiting for us. Without wasting time, he signalled for me to lie down on a bench and went to work immediately. With dirty hands and even dirtier fingernails he proceeded to expertly clean and suture the cut on my thigh. No longer did I have to worry about an open wound, I reflected; now all I had to worry about was an infection—a Russian infection.

As I was getting off the bench, my bandage securely in place, the OOD, followed by a sailor, burst into the head. Looking agitated and embarrassed, he took off his cap and rubbing a nervous hand along his receding hairline, said, "Comrade lieutenants, you must excuse us. We were not informed of your rank." With a snap of his fingers he indicated to the sailor standing by him to pick up the clothes. "Please follow me," he motioned. "I'll show you to the wardroom."

Nodal glanced at me, shrugged his shoulders, and gestured for me to go ahead. We did follow the officer of the day, but no longer through cold, bare decks and unpainted bulkheads. We now walked through a carpeted passageway which exited into a small but tastefully decorated wardroom. It had a large, round table in the center and comfortable, upholstered chairs. Built-in shelves filled with books covered two of the bulkheads. Adjacent to the wardroom was a large head with real showers, huge, fluffy white towels, and two types of soap. Miguel, looking embarrassed at the obvious differences which existed in this supposedly classless society, said very little. Not the best time to rub it in, I thought, deciding to let him off the hook and to just enjoy the facilities.

Chapter Eleven

The afternoon sun pouring in through the small window was rapidly turning the loft into an oven. Lying on top of the clothes that he had spread over the alfalfa, Nicky was drenched with perspiration, and discomfort was gradually displacing sleep. As his mind and body struggled to throw off the heat-induced stupor, Nick became aware that what was really waking him up was the feeling that someone was staring at him. Before he had a chance to react, he heard a soft voice calling his name and he opened his eyes to the sight of a young girl looking down at him with gentle concern. "Nick, how do you feel?" she asked.

Embarrassed that he was wearing only his shorts, Nick sat up and quickly wrapped his shirt around his waist. "Fine, just fine," he replied. "I must have been sleeping for quite awhile."

"Just around the clock," Elena answered, not knowing where to look and trying very hard to sound casual. "I checked on you a couple of times and you were really out. The house is empty now, and I thought that this would be a good time for you to shower and to have something to eat."

"That's very kind of you, uh, uh . . ." Feeling ashamed, Nicky struggled desperately to remember the name of this girl who had risked so much to help him.

"Elena. Remember me?" she asked, slightly disappointed that he couldn't remember her name right away.

"Yes, of course. Elena, my guardian angel," Nick replied,

trying to make up for his lapse of memory. Now fully alert, he felt as if he had just awakened from a nightmare only to find that the nightmare was a reality. The terrible memories filled his mind, and he struggled to force them down.

". . . and I have some of my brother's clothes that should fit you," Elena continued. Nick realized that he had missed part of what she was saying. "He's about your build and height. I'll go now; come when you are ready."

"I'll only be a minute. But, please, before you go, tell me if there is any unusual news on the radio."

"Not any more. Two days ago they announced that there had been a terrible accident outside the tunnel and that several high-ranking officers had been killed. That was the official report, anyway."

"What do you mean, official?" Nicky asked abruptly.

"Just that the accident occurred at a time when we heard a lot of shooting. But you wouldn't know about that, would you?"

"Who was killed?" Nicky answered her question with his own.

"Comandante Rivera and four others. Fidel was said to have been in Oriente at the time of the accident, but he returned the next day in time for the funeral."

"So Fidel was not with Rivera, eh?"

"No, not according to the radio report."

"Oh, well, what difference does it make?" Nicky finally said, making an effort not to reveal too much.

Elena looked at him intently, but said nothing. "Well," she spoke at last, "I'll meet you at the house. . . . Do you see that window to the right of the porch?" she added as they peered together out the tiny loft window.

"The one with the venetian blind?"

"Yes. If you see that the blind has been lowered, don't leave the stable. Otherwise, come a few minutes after I leave." With these words, Elena turned and began to climb down from the loft. Through the window, Nick watched her cross the yard and enter the house. After several minutes, the blind remained up.

Nicky quickly threw on his clothes and left the stable through a side door. He walked rapidly toward the house, his right hand on his pistol which was concealed under his shirt. He waited a moment outside the house and then decided to take a look inside through a large window which faced the driveway. As he reached through the protective wrought iron bars to open the window, a huge dog literally launched itself at the window and just missed tearing off his hand. Nicky jumped back, but not in time to prevent the animal from scraping his wrist. Immediately, Nicky heard Elena calling the dog. "Stay, Suki, stay." she commanded in a controlled voice. Still growling, the dog obeyed reluctantly by retreating to a corner of the room.

"Now I understand why your father doesn't mind leaving you alone," Nicky said from behind the window.

"Nick, come in—that is if you're now satisfied that I am alone."

"I will, as long as you keep your friend under control."

"I'll introduce him to you, and you'll see how nice he can be to people who come into the house through the door instead of the window," Elena said as she patted her dog.

Nicky went in, but refused to let Elena examine his wounded hand. "It's just a scratch," he insisted.

She had prepared a large (and beautiful, Nicky thought) Cuban sandwich with different kinds of meat and cheese folded into a crusty roll. "Do you mind if I eat it after I take a shower?" Nicky asked. "I can't stand how filthy I am."

"Of course not. In fact, if you prefer, you could take a long, hot bath while I exercise the horse."

Again, Nick felt embarrassed as he realized that Elena's sense of decorum would make it necessary for her to leave the house while he bathed. At every turn, he seemed to be making this girl's life difficult.

"That sounds wonderful," he answered, "but . . ."

"Don't worry," Elena said, misinterpreting the cause of Nicky's concern. "I'm not expecting anyone to drop in. Most of our friends and neighbors are already out of Cuba—like my brother Marco Antonio. You'll find a change of clothing in the bathroom—Marco's, by the way. If the phone rings, I'll answer from the extension in the stable. You are welcome to listen, if you like."

"Thank you, Elena," Nick answered. "You are more than kind."

"Try to relax," she said as she left for the stable. Suki, left

Escape from Castro

behind to alert Nicky if anyone approached the house, was now half wagging his tail as if in the mood for reconciliation. I always heard that you have to watch out for Dobermans, Nick thought, eying the dog warily as he walked slowly toward the bathroom. It was an oversized room with elegant Cuban tile stretching all the way up to the ceiling and a large sunken tub. Lying in a tub of hot water, Nick thought almost cheerfully of the sandwiches and beer which awaited him. With his mind temporarily at ease and his body recuperating rapidly, he was beginning to think that he might pull himself out of this crisis after all. Then, without warning, the mental image of G-2 men bursting into the bathroom exploded onto his still traumatized brain. He could see them lift their automatic weapons to fire the deafening barrage at point blank range. He seemed to watch his mutilated body sink into the water rapidly turning red with his blood.

Desperately, he looked for his pistol, but he remembered that in his illusion of safety he had left it on a table out of reach. He lunged out of the bathtub and retrieved his weapon. "They won't catch me in the water," he said between clenched teeth as he grabbed a towel and rushed out of the bathroom.

Once he left the confinement of the steamy room, Nicky immediately felt better. Still, he took the time to search the area before going back into the bathroom to look for the clothes that Elena had set out for him. He dressed in the hall, determined not to tempt the return of his nightmarish vision. Marco's clothes were a perfect fit, and Nicky felt less vulnerable the minute he had finished dressing. Civilized again, he thought, but not so civilized as to leave behind the pistol that he concealed underneath the tweed jacket.

He checked the house again—this time with Suki at his side; his former foe was now his best guarantee against someone sneaking up on him. Recovering his sandwich and beer from the refrigerator, Nick walked to the kitchen door. As he looked out across the back porch, he could see Elena on her horse practicing dressage exercises. She was remarkable, he found himself thinking as he really looked at her for the first time—a beautiful girl who was apparently not aware of her loveliness. But it was her kindness and courage that first impressed me, Nicky reminded himself, and not her beauty.

When Elena had finished exercising her horse, she started back toward the house, nervously tapping her right boot with her crop as she walked. Her sun-bleached, light brown hair fell softly and naturally over her shoulders, and her face was flushed from the vigorous exercise. Admiringly, Nick watched her from inside the house, grateful that she could not see him staring. He shook his head slightly as he went to open the door for her; he could not help but wish that they could have met in another place, at another time.

"Is that really you Nick?" she exclaimed, amazed by the transformation.

"You didn't expect to still find me dirty and in rags, did you?" Nick replied, a little embarrassed.

"No, but I didn't expect my brother's clothes to work such a miracle. You look so relaxed and natural in them."

"The clothes are great, but what really worked the miracle was the wonderful ham on that sandwich you made for me. You don't think there could be any more where that came from, do you?"

Elena laughed. "Ham and anything else you would like to eat. Let's see what we can fix. I'm starving too." As they began to walk into the kitchen, Suki suddenly rose to his feet and started to growl. Nicky and Elena stood motionless as the front doorbell rang. She looked at him fearfully.

"Don't worry," he whispered as he positioned himself against the kitchen door where he could not be seen. "Open the door and see who it is. Sound natural, but try to speak loudly enough that I can hear you."

"Be careful," she said, placing her right hand on his before she left to open the door. The bell rang repeatedly, with an obnoxious insistence. "Coming, coming," she shouted.

Nicky took out his pistol and released the safety catch. He could both hear and feel the violent beating of his heart. He waited, straining to hear Elena's voice.

Elena stood in front of the heavily carved wooden door, controlling Suki and trying to control her own nervousness. Slowly, she opened the massive door and pushed open the wrought iron gate.

"Buenas, Elena. Como estas?" said a short, stocky boy of

about fourteen. He had broad, rustic features and a pushy manner which bordered on insolence.

"Buenas, Gilberto. What can I do for you?"

"Nothing. I came to bring the weekly eggs and vegetables, as usual. Where is Mercedes? How come she didn't answer the door?" The youngster was craning his neck in an effort to look inside the house over Elena's shoulder.

"Mercedes is visiting her sick daughter, and that's why she didn't answer the door. How much do we owe you?" Elena replied dryly.

"Oh, nothing. My father will collect for the whole month later on," Gilberto answered while continuing his efforts to snoop and giving no indication of leaving. Then, the sound of a car pulling into the gravel driveway attracted the boy's attention. He turned his head and saw Elena's father's Cadillac pulling up in front of the house.

"Well, that's all I came for. Adiós," he said abruptly as he turned to leave. Going down the marble steps of the front entrance, he turned toward Elena's father and said in a tone very different from the one he used to address Elena, "Buenas, Doctor. Como esta usted?"

"Fine thank you, Gilberto," Dr. Marten answered as he stepped out of his car. Gilberto made some kind of bow and left.

"Daddy! I'm so glad to see you," Elena exclaimed as she threw her arms around her father.

"Well, the pleasure is certainly mutual, mi hijita. Now, where is our guest? Has he awakened yet?"

"He surely has, and I can't wait for you to meet him. I know that you'll like him." As Elena spoke, Nicky approached them, his head high and his manner confident.

Elena's father stretched out his hand and said, "I am Marcelo Marten. I'm very happy to meet you and to welcome you to our home, or what's left of it." Crates and boxes stacked in every corner of the house made it clear that the Martens were planning to leave for good—soon.

As they walked together down the long corridor, Nicky spoke in a low voice, "Doctor, I want you to know that there are no words to express my gratitude to your daughter and to you. I must explain, though, in more detail the huge risks you are taking for me."

"Nick, before you agonize any more, let me tell you about my only son, Marco Antonio. He was severely beaten by the G-2 and only thanks to the fact that I had been a strong financial supporter of our great leader (the sarcasm was unmistakable) was I able to pull him out on the condition that he would leave the country and never return. Do you know what terrible crime Marco Antonio committed against the revolution to deserve such treatment? He refused to join a communist student group at the University. Marco's situation is just an opening. I could go on forever about how I feel about the usurpers who now govern our country."

"I understand, sir," Nick answered, "but you must hear me just the same."

"All right, but first let's sit down and enjoy a daiquiri. Although Elena does not drink them herself, no one can prepare a daiquiri better than she does."

"I'll also fix some snacks," Elena said. "I'll be back in a few minutes."

Listening to Dr. Marten, Nicky felt elation and relief. He had liked Elena's father from the moment the doctor had stretched out his hand to welcome Nick to his home. The firm handshake, the way Marten had looked him straight in the eye and accepted him without reservation had assured Nicky that this man in whose hands his immediate future lay was a man of character, accustomed to success. He almost gives me hope, Nicky thought.

By the time Elena returned pushing a cart laden with hors d'oeuvres and drinks, the essentials of the conversation had been ironed out and Dr. Marten was saying, "I'll make sure that Marco lets your parents know that you are O.K. and that hopefully you will be joining them very soon."

"Thank you, sir. Thank you."

"Nick, you make me feel old. Marcelo will suffice. And now, a toast." He handed Nicky a glass of daiquiri, gave a glass of white wine to Elena, and raising his own drink, said, "To courage."

Chapter Twelve

Two weeks after the ill-fated attempt on Fidel's life, I was at the yacht club with my cousin going over the boat to make sure that it would be ready when needed. The boat, a twenty-four-foot Prowler with two 135 hp Chrysler inboard engines, was able to do thirty-eight knots. It had a nice cabin, and more importantly, a large fuel tank. We had chosen it carefully for the task of getting us out of Cuba, and I had no doubt that it would do just fine when the time came.

The last two days had been very frustrating because of the lack of news. Through Tony's brother Rene, a physician at the military hospital, we had learned that Raul was out of coma but still in the intensive care unit. According to Rene, the rope of security which surrounded Raul was the tightest he had ever seen. The G-2 had made several attempts to question Raul, but his only answer had been, "My name is Raul Ramirez, and I have nothing to say until I am represented by an attorney." Probably because of his delicate condition, and because of the presence of the medical staff, the G-2 had not pressed Raul too hard. But they were waiting like vultures, knowing that it wouldn't be long before they could get Raul out of the hospital—delicate condition or not.

Before leaving the club, I decided to call home to let the family know that I would be there for dinner. After six rings, Lucila answered, sounding out of breath and more than a little irritable.

"Well, I'm sure that the Señores will be glad to hear that they're having company for dinner," she said.

"Come on, Lucila, it isn't as if they haven't seen me for years; I was there just three days ago."

"Well, that's true," she replied, relenting a little. "By the way, you got your first call from someone interested in buying your Opel."

"What! They called about my car?" I exclaimed. I shouldn't sound so excited, I thought, and in a calmer tone, I asked, "Any messages? Tell me exactly what they said."

"Goodness, I didn't think it was a matter of life and death," Lucila grumbled. "Wait, Carlos, I wrote the information down. I'll go get it."

She returned to the phone in a matter of seconds and read me the short message: "They are very interested in the car, and they want you to call them tonight around 6:00. The number is 62956."

I looked at my watch—6:15. "Thank you, Lucila," I said. "I'd better call them now; it's already getting late. Tell the family that I'll be home soon."

"No, wait just a second," she insisted.

"Lucila, I'm in a hurry. What now?"

"I thought that you would like to know about those vandals that tried to poison Dago the other night, the ones that you fired a shot at, remember?"

"Yes, yes, I do, although I fired into the air, not at anyone. But, what about them?"

"Well, they were caught last night trying to break into the Alvarez's residence and . . ."

"Great, Lucila," I interrupted. "Great news, but I really have to go now. Adiós." I hung up without waiting for more details. I was relieved that the intruders had turned out to be nothing but run of the mill burglars, but somehow the whole episode didn't seem to matter at this time. I left the club's bar and walked back to the boathouse where I used a public phone to dial 62956. The phone rang repeatedly, but there was no answer. I hung up and with shaking hands dialed the number again. This time the unmistakable voice of Nicolas Berrocal answered, "Yes, may I help you?"

"You already have," I replied. After two weeks of silence, I felt almost as if Nicky had come back from the dead. I could not control the excitement in my voice even though I waited a moment before trying to speak again. "Thank God! Are you all right? Can you talk?" I stammered.

"It's good to hear your voice too," Nicky answered, his voice resonant with emotion. "I'm fine, and I can talk. What about your end?"

"A public phone. Go ahead." I answered.

"I didn't get a scratch, but Julio and Raul didn't make it." Nicky said, speaking in his fluent, unaccented English.

"Raul did." I answered also in English just in case somebody might be listening. "You had good reason to think he was dead; he was in coma for several days. But he's recovering now at the military hospital."

There was silence on the line. "Are you still there?" I questioned anxiously.

"I'm sorry. Yes, of course I'm still here. It's just that I left Raul and instead I carried Julio with me, only to lose him that same night. He died in my arms."

"Listen, Nicky, the important thing now is to take care of you. Tell me where you are, and I'll be there right away."

"I'm close to Tarara," he said and gave me directions to the phone booth he was using. It was located outside a small roadside bar which appeared to be closed, and Nicky thought he would be safe enough waiting for me inside the station wagon which he had driven to the phone booth.

The drive from Miramar to Tarara in the evening traffic usually takes about an hour; it took me an endless forty minutes. I felt guilty to be so glad that Nicky had been the one to make it, but the fact was I had known Nick all his life. We had traveled together through Europe in the days when my father was stationed in Rome and Nicky was studying in Switzerland. Together, we had skied the slopes of St. Moritz and of St. Johann-Alpendorf in Austria, our favorite.

Even in adolescence, Nick had been deeply religious. When he had decided to take this assignment, I had felt it was a great mistake—even if he escaped the bullets the guilt would get the best of him. But it had done me no good to try to talk him out of the mission; he was committed and his sense of duty and hatred of communism were greater than any other consideration. If Nicky didn't make it now, it would be a great waste. He was one of the most gifted people I had ever known.

As I drove down the steep street which led to the rendezvous point, I thought I saw a station wagon like the one Nick described, but in the dark I could not be sure. I decided to drive past slowly enough to check out the car and driver and to circle back if all appeared to be in order. My plans changed abruptly when I drew in close enough to see that a militiaman was standing next to the car talking to the driver—Nicolas Berrocal. With a quick wrench of the steering wheel, I swerved onto the deserted side street and parked behind the station wagon. I was out of my car in seconds, propelled by the obviously violent and antagonistic manner of the militiaman and by my fears of the reaction of Nicky's already overstrained nerves.

The militiaman took me in with a glance, his manner changing as soon as he saw the uniform. I understood his exaggerated attitude of respect when he addressed me as "Comandante." Evidently, the star on my shoulder boards which signified an officer of the line had confused the young man who had interpreted it as my rank.

"What seems to be the problem here?" I questioned brusquely, determined not to lose the advantage of his mistake. I need not have worried—the militiaman was obviously too drunk to either see or think very clearly. He was a young punk of about twenty-one—full of alcoholic courage and just itching to exercise his recently acquired authority.

"Buenas, Comandante. The problem is this individual who has been sitting here for almost an hour and who doesn't have any identification. He'll have to come with me to G-2," he added in a belligerent tone, glaring at Nick.

"Stand aside; I'll be with you in a moment," I said to the militiaman. Then, leaning into the car and placing a hand on Nicky's shoulder, I whispered, "Don't make a move. I'll take care of this." Nicky's face was flushed with anger which he was obviously trying to contain, and his right hand was ominously concealed under his jacket.

Now turning my attention back to the militiaman, I questioned, "May I ask what prompted you to demand that this man identify himself?"

Something in my voice seeped through the alcoholic fog just enough to trigger the young man's defensive responses. He fingered the rusty .38 which was jammed into his belt and muttered, "He's been parked here a long time with no good reason. Besides," he added, jerking his head toward Nick, "he doesn't look like one of us."

"What is your name? And what is your militia unit?" I demanded.

"Emeregildo Valdes from Troop 2 of the Neighborhood Vigilantes for the Revolution-Casablanca," he answered, beginning to realize with astonishment that I was not going to commend him for his diligence.

"What did you forget to use when addressing an officer? Or haven't they taught you even the basics of military courtesy?"

"Oh, yeah. Sir," he replied reluctantly.

"Well, listen to me now Valdes. This individual happens to be my cousin, and he has been waiting for me. As for you, you're dirty, drunk, and a disgrace to the uniform you are wearing. You'll get the hell out of here right now, or you are the one who is going to be arrested. Do you understand me?" I spoke in a loud, intimidating voice, hoping that this misfit would not persist in his demands. In a final effort to defuse the situation, I turned my back on the young punk and said to Nick, "Start your engine and follow me."

I got into my car and pulled ahead of the station wagon. The militiaman, now confused and demoralized, turned away and walked erratically toward the roadside bar. I drove onto the main road and noted with great relief that the station wagon was right behind me. Within a minute Nicky had passed me, and all I had to do was follow him to our destination.

In less than fifteen minutes we were pulling into the Marten's driveway. We got out of our cars, walked toward each other, and after a moment of silent appraisal, we fell into a heartfelt fraternal abrazo. Then, still with an arm around my shoulder, Nick directed me toward the house.

Dr. Marten and Elena had already retired to their rooms, obviously to let us meet in privacy, and only a large Doberman pinscher welcomed us when we opened the door. Nick stopped to pat the dog, and then led the way through the house to the back porch where we sat down on comfortable rattan chairs under huge ceiling fans now idle for the cool winter months.

"Would scotch be all right?" Nicky asked, acting as host and obviously feeling quite at home.

"You bring the glasses, Junior, and I'll do the pouring," I said, changing the serious mood which had ruled us until now.

"Si, mi comandante," he replied, mimicking the militiaman.

After a couple of hours and half a bottle of Black Label, we had reached no agreement about our next move. Nicky seemed more interested in Elena than in his own safety, a big change from his usual cool, detached attitude toward the opposite sex.

At about 0100 Nicky put down his drink and said, "Carlos, you'd better stay here for the night. It wouldn't be wise to leave at this hour; you'd be too conspicuous." Then he rose from his chair and added, "Come on, there's an extra bed in my room."

"O.K., Nicky," I agreed, "but I must be on my way at 0600."

"And when will you be back?"

"I'll be back for you tomorrow evening; be ready about 9 P.M."

"Is that an order?" he asked, the underlying plea obvious beneath his joking tone.

"It is," I said, trying to sound matter of fact.

♦ ♦ ♦

My alarm clock never had a chance to go off; instead I was awakened at 0530 by Nick's terrifying screams. Realizing that he was in the grip of a nightmare, I rushed to his bed and, gently holding him by the shoulders, tried to wake him up. With a final blood-chilling scream he jolted to a sitting position and stared at me with unseeing eyes filled with fear. Then, slowly the awareness returned to his eyes, and the trembling of his body subsided. Last night, well dressed and looking sophisticated, busy playing the host, Nicky had given no indication of what was going on inside him. Now, as he pushed his too-long, dark hair out of his face and struggled to regain control, the mask had slipped. But only for a moment. Nick was already looking at me with embarrassment, explaining away his anguish with an off-hand remark about how a doctor friend had once told him that all nightmares had their source in physical discomfort. "That scotch left me with a headache, Carlos. You'd think I would have had the sense to have taken an aspirin or two before hitting my rack," he said, getting up and opening the French doors which led to a small terrace overlooking the forest.

Fresh, cool air swept into the room, bringing with it the sound of the wind moaning through the pine trees. Nick stood silently by the door, looking out into the forest.

"Are you all right, Nicky?" I finally asked.

Without turning to face me, he replied, "Oh sure, I'm fine," and then added, "Are you leaving now?"

"I'm afraid I have to. Why?"

"Oh, nothing. Just wondering. . . . Well, maybe there is something."

"Fine, let's hear it," I said as I began to get dressed.

He came toward me and sat on the edge of the bed. "Don't pass any judgements until I'm finished. O.K.?"

"O.K., I won't. Go ahead," I answered, striving for the right tone of encouragement and acceptance.

"After our fiasco . . . with Julio lying dead only a few hundred meters from here, I didn't care if I lived or not. I didn't even dream I'd be able to get out of Tarara alive. But then Elena came, and taking great risks and ignoring my hostility and suspicion, she saved my life. She is a courageous and beautiful person."

"I agree," I said. "I noticed some of her pictures downstairs."

He continued, "It's not how beautiful she is. . . . It's that she's so real—like no one I've ever known—and she is in love with me."

"And what about you?" I asked.

"I think I'm in love with her, too."

"Nicky, why are you telling me this?" I asked gently.

He got up, closed the doors, and returned to his bed. "Because I think I'm a marked man after killing Rivera and attempting to kill Castro himself."

"And?" I questioned.

"And I don't see much point in leaving this house. I just want to be with her, at least until they leave Cuba. Then I'll do whatever you want me to, although I don't believe there's a way out for me."

"Are you finished?"

"Yes."

"Well, you're wrong about a few things. In the first place, if you really care about Elena, you must get out of this house before you compromise her and her father. Then, you overestimate the Fidelistas. They don't know what you did. They suspect everyone, but they are still disorganized and undisciplined. Ten years from now, if they are still in power, it will be different, especially with the Soviet help. But now ... now they are nothing but a band of fanatic, inefficient monkeys. I could have you in Miami tomorrow, if I wanted to."

"Are you serious? Then why don't you?" he asked incredulously.

"Because there is no immediate danger and because I could not leave my family behind if I defected. They must leave first."

"When could we leave?"

"Very soon. We are working on it. But we must get you to the other side of the bay. In any emergency, you'd be trapped on this side of the tunnel. You must be close to the boat."

"I see," he responded, the first light of a desperate hope beginning to gleam in his eyes.

"Nicky, what have you told the Martens?" I asked, hating to ask the question, but needing to know.

"You have no right to question my word, Carlos. You know we all swore to secrecy. They have guessed much, but I have admitted nothing."

"I'm glad you haven't forgotten that vow. As long as we admit nothing, our enemies may suspect, but they can never be sure."

"I know, I know." Nicky replied.

Now completely dressed and ready to leave, I asked him, "Do you have any questions?"

"No questions, I'll be ready at nine."

"Arrivederci," I said.

"Ciao, Carlos," he replied softly.

Chapter Thirteen

Nicky did not leave the room once he found himself alone. He needed time to think—to analyze the conversation. "Maybe if all goes well I could be free in Miami very soon," he tried to assure himself. Best of all, by then Elena would also be there. Too good to be true, he thought. It's almost better not to hope. Then he remembered that he was going to have to leave her that very evening. Despair flooded him. He could not lose her. He began trying to remember every detail of her appearance—picturing her as she looked when she went out to ride—her smooth, tanned skin, her flat stomach, her firm breasts so beautifully defined beneath the close-fitting riding clothes. Suddenly, she was so real in his mind that he felt he could reach out and touch her. He became aware of every inch of his body clinging to the soft pajamas.

He jumped out of bed, severely annoyed with himself. I must not think about her as if she were some cheap pick-up, he thought. He stripped off his pajamas and hurried into the shower, but the trickles of warm water running down his body made things worse. He switched to cold. Gasping for breath, but still feeling frustrated, he roughly toweled himself dry and began to dress, the awakened desire of extreme youth absolutely refusing to yield to moral principles.

The sound of Dr. Marten's engine starting up out on the driveway startled Nick out of his trance. He went out onto the terrace, hoping to stop the doctor and tell him about his plans, but he was too late; the Cadillac was already turning onto the dirt road. Nicky stayed out on the terrace, enjoying the gentle warmth of the early morning sunlight. The sound of birds attracted his attention toward the forest. Suddenly, it occurred to him that within a few hours he would be leaving Julio alone behind those trees. Nicky went back into his room, grabbed a sweater, and hurried down the stairs, almost bumping into Mercedes who was on her way up with a tray of cafe negro. "Señor Nicky, I was bringing you a pot of coffee. Aren't you going to have breakfast?" she asked, straightening the cups and pitchers on her tray.

"Not now, Mercedes, but I'll be back soon."

"Perhaps some coffee?" she persisted.

"Later Mercedes," Nick replied without stopping. She watched in amazement as he bolted down the stairs and disappeared out the porch door.

He ran across the back field and then through the forest. Surprisingly, he had no problem finding the site. Between two tall trees, now covered with pine needles and new vegetation, lay the unmarked grave of his friend. The sun's rays filtering through the trees created a peaceful, almost weary effect. But the brutal memories were still fresh, in no way subdued by the quiet surroundings. Nicky knelt and, touching the ground with both hands, said in a low voice, "Don't watch me die, you asked me. But I did watch and without being able to do anything to help you. When you died, something in me died too, and nothing will ever change that. Now I'm getting ready to leave, but if I make it, someday I'll be back for you. Adiós, Julio. God bless you and God forgive both of us."

Nicky got up slowly, staring at the grave. He found it almost impossible to leave, as if his friend were asking him to stay. Finally, he forced himself to turn and to walk slowly back toward the house. The gentle sunlight warmed his shoulders but not his heart.

Chapter Fourteen

Outside a private room on the second floor of the military hospital, a guard stood watch twenty-four hours a day. A sign on the door—NO VISITORS, AUTHORIZED PERSONNEL ONLY—left no doubt about the importance placed on keeping all activities concerning the room's occupant as confidential as possible. At about 1000 the ward's head nurse, Amelia Rojas, a tall, hefty woman in her forties, was about to enter the room as part of her daily rounds. The militiaman, by now familiar with the staff personnel allowed in the room, had never interfered with the nurse. But this morning, for some unknown reason the G-2 guard had made some radical changes in his orders. "I'm sorry, nurse, but you can't go in now," he said to Amelia, barring the door with an outstretched arm.

"What do you mean I can't come in? You know who I am, and if you've had a lapse of memory, check your access list and you'll see my name on it." Amelia was shocked that anyone would try to tell her what to do in her own ward. After a few weeks of caring for Raul, she had come to know him well and to respect the courage with which he had resisted the G-2. Now, she was determined to make sure that he was all right, but the guard absolutely refused to grant her access to the room.

"I'll just see about these new orders," she said indignantly as she reached for the phone on the desk by the door. Before she had a chance to dial, she heard muffled choking noises coming from the room, followed by a loud crash. Catching the militiaman by surprise, she threw the phone straight at his chest and while the startled man reached out to catch it, she burst into the room.

Raul, looking more dead than alive, was lying with half his body hanging out of bed. The IV bottle lay broken on the floor while the needle and tubing remained attached to his arm. A G-2 man in uniform was standing next to the bed, straightening his clothes and wiping blood from his mouth with a dirty handkerchief.

"You murdering animal! Get out of here!" Amelia shouted at the man as she pushed the alarm button by the bed. With practiced skill, she positioned Raul on his back and started the cardiopulmonary resuscitation procedures. In less than thirty seconds the Cardiac Emergency Team, composed of the duty resident and three nurses, arrived with a cart stocked with ready-to-use resuscitation drugs.

The G-2 man finally left the room grunting, "So much fuss for one dirty contrarevolucionario. What's the big deal? He's going to die anyway."

Using the tube still attached to Raul's arm, the young resident injected a cardiac stimulant. Then feeling the carotid artery on the side of Raul's neck, he announced triumphantly to Amelia, "I've got a pulse, and he's breathing on his own. Good job, Amelia!"

Later, Raul, now stable and making a hugh effort to talk, said to Amelia, who had remained at his side, "He tried to suffocate me with a pillow. If it hadn't been for you . . ."

"Don't worry; you are fine now, and I'll make sure that this doesn't happen again, ever, on my ward."

"No, you don't understand," Raul said with great effort. "I heard him today on the phone telling someone, 'I don't give a shit what the orders are! This hijo de puta is not going to see tomorrow's sun—talk or no talk."

Exhausted by what she had just been through and now horrified by Raul's revelation, Amelia began to sob uncontrollably.

"No, stop it," Raul pleaded. "They'll come in. Listen, listen to me."

Wiping her tears, Amelia responded, "I'm listening. What is it? What can I do? Oh, dear God."

"I'll tell you. Come closer; I don't want them to hear. Don't you worry about that G-2 sadist; he acted on his own out of sheer hate. Just wait until his boss hears that he almost killed the one person with all the answers. They might even suspect him of being a counter-revolutionary."

"Do you think that Fidel knows what is going on with you?"

"You can be sure that Castro is calling all the shots himself. He wants me to get strong enough to be able to tolerate the torture that will be coming for sure. His people will not let up until they get all the information they want out of me."

"And then what?" Amelia asked resignedly, studying his face.

"Then, they'll kill me, but not a minute before."

"Perhaps I could slip you out of the hospital and find you a place to hide until things cool down," she suggested as if wanting to believe her own words.

"You are an incredibly brave and wonderful person, Amelia, but you know and I know that there is no way out."

She didn't answer. Instead she signaled him to be quiet. After a few seconds of eerie silence, she alerted him, "There is somebody outside the door."

Suddenly Raul felt faint as if he had been drained of energy. Before he could say anything, Amelia had placed an oxygen mask on his face and lowered the position of his head.

"Just a momentary dizzy spell," she reassured him. "Too much has happened."

Slowly he regained enough strength to pull her close. Into her ear he whispered, "Tonight on your last round, this is what you should do."

She closed her eyes while she listened. When he was finished, she straightened up and in a choked voice said, "I'll do it."

◆ ◆ ◆

Two days later Tony Capó received a letter with no stamp and no return address. It read:

My dear friend Tony,
When you read these lines, I will be dead. Don't feel too bad; thanks to a brave and generous person, my death will be fast and

painless. Best of all, I'll deny these monsters the pleasure of murdering me. They tried today and almost succeeded. I don't have much time left to write.

Don't give up our fight and tell the world about them.

Raul

Chapter Fifteen

When Nicky returned to the house, Elena was still asleep. A good thing, he thought, since it saves me from having to explain why I went into the forest. He sat down on the back porch and waited for her to join him for breakfast. Following his morning ritual, Nicky turned on the radio, hoping to hear some news acknowledging that Raul was alive and under custody. Instead, he was bombarded by twenty minutes of blatant propaganda. Finally, Elena appeared dressed in riding clothes: brown leather boots, tan breeches, and a white silk blouse. The sight of her changed his mood drastically.

"I have never seen a more beautiful rider," he greeted her half-jokingly as he pulled back her chair. Before she could sit down, he wrapped his arms around her waist and whispered in her ear, "Have I told you today that I am crazy about you?"

Elena felt herself trembling as he held her. She only hoped that he was not aware of the effect he had on her, at least not for the time being. Aloud, she said in a tone of mild reproval, "I'm glad to see you so cheerful. For me, this will be a sad day of good-bye."

"What do you mean by a sad day of good-bye?" Nicky asked releasing her and turning to look into her eyes. How could she know? He wondered in astonishment.

"Today they are coming for Monarca. Dad was finally able to sell him—if it could be called a sale; it was more like a giveaway."

"Oh, I see," Nicky replied, hiding his relief. "I'm sorry, Elena."

After Nick had finished his second cup of coffee, Elena rose from her seat and said resignedly, "I thought you might like to take Monarca over some jumps before they come take him away."

"I would love to, but maybe I shouldn't be out of the house that long," he answered without much conviction. Just the thought of riding had caused his spirits to rise.

"I'll saddle him up and call you when he's ready," Elena answered, ignoring Nicky's mild objection. "There is no one around for miles. Why shouldn't you enjoy yourself?"

"O.K., but I'll have to set a short course. Maybe you could warm him up while I do that."

"I will. I can't wait to watch you ride."

"And I can't wait to be out there," Nicky said happily. "I've been wanting to ride Monarca since I first got here. I'll go change. I hope Marco's boots will fit me."

"They will. But don't take too long," Elena said with a smile.

Still elated and filled with a momentary optimism, Nicky ran up the stairs. He found Marco's boots and put them on. A perfect fit! I have never seen Marco, but somehow I feel I know him after wearing his clothes and sleeping in his room for so long, Nicky thought. He looked at himself in the mirror and grinned, delighted at the prospect of outdoor exercise, something he had been deprived of for weeks. Then he saw his pistol lying on top of the dresser, and the sad reality of his situation overwhelmed him once again. I must not deceive myself, he thought. My days of being carefree are over forever. There were grim lines around his mouth as he positioned the holster on his belt and slid the pistol into place. He untucked his shirt to hide the weapon and walked slowly down the stairs to join Elena.

When he walked out into the ring, Elena was already riding, sitting the trot. Nicky went to work immediately setting a short course of eight jumps, the highest a triple of four and a half feet.

As soon as she saw that the course was ready, Elena dismounted and led Monarca to Nick. "Well, here he is," she said with a smile. "Let's see how you two suit one another."

Nick mounted and walked Monarca briskly around the ring, concentrating on the horse's movement. After a few minutes he moved into the trot and marveled at the rhythmic smoothness of the powerful animal's stride. By the time Monarca eagerly took the signal and burst into a canter, Nick was convinced he was riding a remarkable animal. The horse already seemed to be looking over the jumps as if he were anxious to try them. Nick began by taking him over a few cavalletti and a couple of small jumps, being careful to control Monarca's speed and to place him perfectly before each obstacle. Within a few minutes Nicky had realized that the horse would need a little restraint to offset his eagerness to try each fence.

When Nick decided that Monarca was ready, they negotiated all the jumps, including the triple, at an easy canter and then repeated the jumps to approximate a regulation course. After they had finished, Nick was sure that he had never ridden a finer horse, and he could better appreciate Elena's sense of loss.

Elena had been sitting on the white rail fence, watching Nicky with delight and admiration as he was obviously getting the very best out of Monarca. She watched him canter once around the ring after the final jump, his hands quiet, yet in perfect control. With Nick, Monarca no longer was trying to rush the jumps. She waved at Nicky and then nodded in agreement when he shouted to her, "This is some horse."

A little out of breath from the unaccustomed exercise, Nick stopped in front of Elena's position on the fence. "Not bad for our first day together, huh," he teased.

"Not bad? Where in the world did you learn to ride like that?"

"I had a good tutor. Do you know Raul de Leon? He taught me a lot."

"I don't know him, but I've heard of him. Now I see why he has such a fine reputation."

"Señorita Elena," Mercedes was shouting from the back steps of the house. "Get the phone. You have a call."

Elena hurried into the stable and picked up the receiver of the wall phone. Nick removed Monarca's saddle and walked the horse slowly toward the stable. By the time he entered the barn, Elena was saying, "Very well, I'll relay the message. Adiós." She hung up the receiver and turned to take the saddle from Nicky.

"What was that all about?" Nicky asked.

"It was your friend Carlos. He said to tell you that he won't be able to come tonight, but that he'll be here tomorrow night at eight." She replaced Monarca's bridle with a halter and leadline and affectionately stroked the horse's neck.

Nicky watched her, painfully aware that she had no idea of the real meaning of the message she had just relayed. "One more day of grace," he said softly.

"One more what?" she asked, looking up at him.

"Come, I'll tell you while we cool off Monarca," he said, reaching for her right hand.

They walked slowly, Nicky looking down and speaking almost in a whisper; Elena holding back her tears and looking pleadingly at him as if searching for a different answer.

Chapter Sixteen

The cruiser *Cuba*, ex-flagship of deposed president Fulgencio Batista, was an old ship launched in 1911, overhauled in 1937, and later completely reconstructed in 1956. After Fidel's takeover, mainly due to a lack of four inch ammo and of spare parts, the *Cuba* had spent most of her time tied alongside a pier in Mariel. She was used as a training ship for midshipmen and was manned and maintained by a skeleton crew. The officer complement, except for the commandante, was composed almost entirely of academy instructors. I had been delighted when I had been tapped for the billet of first lieutenant/gunnery officer. The responsibilities were not grueling, and I loved the Old Lady.

After leaving Nicky, I had gone to the ship to take care of some paperwork, but mainly to stay out of sight. I needed time to arrange for Nicky's move from Tarara, but during breakfast, the assistant operations officer, Lt. J.G. Roberto Santa Cruz, had handed me a chit requesting that he be allowed to trade duty with me. His wife had just given birth to a baby boy, and wanted to spend the day with his family. The request had already been approved by the senior watch officer and the executive officer. In other words, I had been told to make the swap.

Trying my best to sound sincere, I said, "No problem, Roberto, I'll be glad to change duties with you. My best to your wife and congratulations on the new navy brat." Mentally I groaned, "There goes my plan to get Nicky out of Tarara tonight."

"Thanks, Carlos. My wife will love you for this," Roberto replied smugly as he presented me with a huge cigar tied with a blue ribbon.

"Don't mention it," I told the proud father. He asked permission from the outgoing command duty officer to leave the ship and departed with a silly, self-satisfied expression on his face. I made a firm resolution on the spot that when my time came to pass out cigars, I would not look too jolly or trade duty with some poor bachelor.

No sooner had Roberto left, than I hurried to my stateroom where I picked up the phone and dialed the Marten's number.

♦ ♦ ♦

Nicky and Elena had agreed not to mention his impending departure and to make the most of their last day together. A soft ocean breeze was blowing through the upper terrace which was partially protected from the weather by a handsome green awning. Dressed in dark blue slacks and a pale yellow sweater, Nicky was stretched out on a lounge chair, listening to the beautiful music of Lecuona, Cuba's best known composer.

"Here, Nicky, I've brought you something to keep you warm," Elena said as she walked out onto the terrace carrying a tray holding glasses, a bottle of wine, and a frosty pitcher of freshly mixed daiquiris.

Nicky got up, took the tray from her and set it down on top of a wrought-iron table. "Do you know what I was thinking while you were downstairs mixing the drinks?" he asked.

"No, please tell me," Elena answered softly.

He turned away from her and poured the drinks slowly before replying. "I was thinking that I was going to see you in just a few minutes, that I couldn't wait for you to come back, and that I hated whatever you were doing because it was keeping you away from me." Leaving the drinks on the table, he turned to face her, his eyes filled with undisguised longing. She moved close to him, resting her head on his shoulder. He held her, and neither of them moved. The faint smell of her perfume, the softness of the evening, and the music all had an almost hypnotic effect on him. Staring at the distant ocean he whispered, "If only time could stop right now—if this moment could last forever." He felt her tears.

The ringing of the phone broke the spell, and reluctantly Elena went inside to answer it. Her voice flowed out onto the patio, and Nicky listened to the one-way conversation.

"Hi, Daddy."

"No, we won't. It doesn't matter how late you are; we'll wait for you. This is a special evening."

"No, I'll tell you later. Hurry home."

"I love you, too."

"I'm going to be jealous," Nicky smiled when she returned to the terrace.

"I love you both, but right now, what I really want to do is to dance with you."

"And there is nothing I'd rather do," he answered, putting down his drink and taking her into his arms. They danced close together, oblivious to their surroundings, both trying to forget that there would be a tomorrow. When the music stopped, Elena lifted her head from Nicky's shoulder and looked straight at him. In the uncertain light of the early evening she could almost believe his eyes were filled with promises.

Excited by her nearness and her sense of complete abandon, Nicky kissed her not as he had before, but with a surge of passion. His hands explored her back, and he began to unzip her dress. She shivered, clinging to him with a kind of desperation. Suddenly, she seemed to him so young, so vulnerable and trustful that he felt unclean. The thought of betraying the trust of those who had risked everything to provide him with a haven revolted him. With great tenderness, he took her hands, kissed them, and said, "I don't want you to remember me this way."

They stayed together on the terrace long after the darkness fell.

Chapter Seventeen

I was taking a quick shower before dinner when the quarterdeck called me over the intercom. Dripping water, I climbed out of the shower, wrapped a towel around my waist, and stepped into my stateroom. I depressed the quarterdeck lever on the intercom box and said, "Quarterdeck—Lieutenant Dumas."

"Lieutenant, you have a call from Mr. Capó."

"Put him through."

"Aye, aye, sir."

Tony wouldn't call me here unless he had important news, I thought. I picked up the receiver and said rather anxiously, "Tony, how are you?"

"Not so good, Carlos. I just received a letter from Raul—his last."

After a pause during which I desperately tried to digest the news, I finally responded, "I understand. Can you come over here? We need to talk."

"I'll be there within a half hour."

"I'll see you soon, then. Adiós." Staring fixedly at the bulkhead, I slowly lowered the receiver back into its cradle. Tony's words were still echoing in my brain like some kind of dismal refrain.

An hour later I was sitting on my bunk with Raul's letter in my hands. Tony, looking even more serious than usual, stood staring out at the bay through the porthole.

"Tony," I said quietly, "there isn't anything here for us anymore. If we stick around much longer, we'll be here to welcome Alberti, Vasquez, and the rest when they land somewhere on the island."

Before Tony could answer there was a knock on the door.

"Come in," I said.

The messenger appeared with a large tray of hors d'oeuvres, two rations of coconut dessert with cream cheese, and coffee. "Permiso," he said as he entered the room and deposited the tray on a table. "Lieutenant, the OOD sends his respects, and he asks me to tell you that he believes that you can hardly afford to miss any meals."

"Thank you, Velez," I said, smiling in spite of myself, "but if I were the OOD, I wouldn't brag quite so much about never missing chow. By the way, would you mind taking the tray to the fantail. We'll be there in a couple of minutes."

"Not at all, Sir," answered Velez. He picked up the tray and left, chuckling under his breath at the latest round of good-natured quips between OOD and myself.

"What was that all about?" Tony asked as the door closed behind Velez.

"Oh, the OOD is a veteran warrant officer, a nice guy from the old guard. He's given me a hard time about being too thin since I first reported aboard, and I haven't missed too many chances to comment on his expanding waistline either. He's retiring next month—that is to say, they're retiring him."

"Typical. Little by little they'll get rid of all the old blood. But why did you send the tray to the fantail?" Tony asked.

"Because the last thing I want is to give the impression that I'm holding some kind of secret meeting with a civilian in my stateroom. Besides, the fantail is about the nicest place on the ship. Come on, let's go."

"Before we leave, let me tell you that I've been thinking along the same lines as you—that it's time to join the liberation forces in Miami before it's too late to get out."

"Agreed. And considering how desperately those thugs in G-2 were trying to get information out of Raul, it's imperative to get Nicky out of Cuba as soon as possible—before we lose him too."

"Well, the house has been ready for him since yesterday," Tony replied. At the mention of Raul's name, his face had gone dark and now he spoke with obvious effort.

"If all goes well, I'll bring him at about 10:00 P.M. Is that O.K. with you and Cathy?"

"Of course," Tony replied flatly. He was staring at the deck and even when he spoke, he did not look at me. "Someday, Carlos, someday I will see them pay for what they did to Raul. I won't forget." When he finally looked up, the spasm of hatred had passed, but there was still a dangerous edge in his voice when he said, "Well, then, let's go put in our appearance. We certainly don't want to be taken for conspirators, now do we?"

The next morning after being relieved of my duties as CDO, I got in my car and headed for the Naval Academy, driving as fast as the traffic permitted so as to be on time for my classes. As always, the view of the ocean with its amazingly clear waters delighted me. But this time my enjoyment was mixed with a sense of loss for I knew that the day was rapidly approaching when I would have to leave all this behind. With a touch of cynicism I reflected that it really didn't matter—the way things were changing it would soon be more painful to stay.

Someone once said that every nation has the leader it deserves. I hoped that was not the case with our country. We had the great misfortune to go from Batista to Castro—both dictators and, as such, both undesirable. Yet, Fidel's despotism, wanton cruelty, and giant ego made Batista look like a choir boy.

Fortunately, we Cubans could look back and be proud that most of our other presidents had been freely elected by the people—Estrada Palma, Menocal, Grau, Prio. It was regrettable that outside our country there was a general misconception that the Cubans' only choice was between a dictator of the right or a communist one. But, we could never lose faith in the future; much good had to be said of any country that could produce a leader of the stature of José Martí—the humanist whose ideas of social justice and human rights were 100 years ahead of his time; Martí, the poet, the patriot, the man of the people who wrote, "Among the poor of this earth, I want to throw my lot."

When I entered my classroom, Midshipman Diaz was still there collecting his books. As soon as he saw me, he came to attention and said cheerfully, "Buenos Dias, mi Teniente."

"Buenos Dias," I replied. "But why haven't you left for your next class? You're going to be late."

"It's my study period, Lieutenant. Besides, I thought you might be interested in knowing that our mutual friend, ex-Midshipman Delgado, has been dismissed from the academy."

"Oh, yes?" I said, startled by the deep feeling of satisfaction that this news had evoked in me. "How come?"

"Academic incompetence. It seems that he was failing almost all of his classes."

"Well, it looks like our superintendent hasn't dismissed all of Captain Driggs' standards to accommodate our new masters." Captain Guillermo Driggs had preceded Comandante Pinto and had been perhaps the most admired and respected of all the superintendents in the history of the academy.

"Apparently not," Diaz replied, his youthful face radiating an obvious sense of justice and delight.

"Apparently not what?" questioned the voice behind me. Lieutenant Nodal had walked into the classroom just in time to catch Diaz' remark. He tossed his cap onto my desk and looked at Diaz with curiosity.

"Apparently there are not enough pictures of the Soviet frigate *Kynda* to go around, Sir," Diaz answered with considerable presence.

"Diaz," I quickly interjected, "is very interested in anti-ship missiles, and we were discussing the SS-N-3 Shaddock missiles which according to last week's briefing, constitute the main battery of the *Kynda* class frigate."

"Well..." Nodal replied, "I wouldn't dig much into that subject. That briefing was only intended as a general overview of the latest accomplishments of our Soviet friends and not to lead to discussion of details that are undoubtedly classified." He was staring at Diaz as he spoke, apparently not quite sure of the young midshipman's intent.

"Aye, aye, Sir," Diaz replied calmly. "Now, if you will excuse me, I must go to the library."

"You are excused," Nodal replied rather caustically.

After Diaz had left, Nodal said, "That midshipman—what's his name?"

"Diaz," I replied.

"Diaz, eh? Well, I never quite know what to make out of him."

"Oh, he's all right. But what brought you into my classroom?" I asked, trying to steer the conversation away from Diaz.

"More important things for us than any Shaddock missile. We are going to headquarters to pick up a check for $20,000."

"To spend on the French Riviera?"

"Very funny! But strangely enough, you're fairly close—at least geographically. We're going to spend it on underwater equipment—Italian, of course."

"Of course," I replied with amusement, thinking that we might as well buy Italian equipment since we couldn't get American supplies which were undeniably superior. "It's about time," I added. "Maybe we can get some decent underwater lights."

"I wouldn't complain much. We've been getting everything we've asked for. Just look at your wrist."

"Well, I can't complain about the Rolex. Maybe you're right," I said, deciding not to mention the really necessary equipment we had been lacking for the last year. "When are we going?"

"As soon as you finish your last class."

"And what about lunch?"

"We'll eat at headquarters."

We could hear the midshipmen filing up the stairs.

"Well, I'd better get ready," I said. "I'll look for you at about 1100."

"Come to my room," he replied, picking up his cap and leaving the classroom.

At 1200 we were slowly approaching headquarters, fighting our way through the noontime downtown traffic with Miguel at the wheel of his rusty Oldsmobile. He had played it smart and was wearing the hideous, but cool, green uniform that had replaced the khaki, irrationally condemned because of its association with the Batista regime. Having lacked Miguel's foresight, I was perspiring and itching in my 100% wool blues under the midday sun of Havana. As we entered headquarters, Miguel said, "Let's eat before attending business."

"Fine. I'll tell you, I haven't eaten here in quite awhile, but I'd be willing to bet that they'll serve coconut preserves for dessert."

"In our navy," Miguel replied as he returned the salute of the guards posted at the main entrance, "that's one bet I would never take."

As we left the elevator on the fourth floor, I glanced out of the large paneled windows, and I couldn't help but grimace at the contrast I saw out in the bay. The hammer and sickle emblem on the stack of a Soviet ship entering the harbor had come directly in line with the open arms of the statue of Christ which stood on the hill that dominated the entrance to the bay. The optical illusion lasted only a few seconds, but it left me with a strange feeling of emptiness.

When I turned my attention back to Miguel, he was staring at me intently. "Anything funny going on?" he asked.

"No, more sad than funny," I replied with a touch of irony.

"Attention on deck!" shouted the master-at-arms, announcing the arrival of our Chief of Naval Operations, Comandante Castiñeiras, who had just entered the room. As he approached us, Castiñeiras said, "At ease, gentlemen." Then smiling, he added, "Have you fellows started your Italian lessons yet? I understand you'll soon be visiting that beautiful country."

"No, Sir," Miguel replied, "but Carlos is fluent in that language thanks to the years his father served overseas."

"Oh, yes, how could I have forgotten? Well, I hope to see both of you on the twenty-eighth."

"Yes, Sir, we'll be there," Miguel answered for both of us.

"Very good," said Castiñeiras and with a rather ambiguous smile still on his face, he turned away. We came back to attention as he walked into the elevator, followed by his master-at-arms, two junior officers, and two bodyguards.

I followed him with my eyes until the elevator door closed behind him. Somehow it was difficult to imagine this intelligent and articulate naval officer with the impeccable military bearing as a part of the frowzy gang that surrounded our "Maximum Leader."

Later, as Miguel and I sat in the wardroom enjoying our coconut dessert, he suddenly leaned forward and said in a confidential tone, "We are not only going to La Spezia for training, but we are going to acquire all that would be needed to knock out a couple of U.S. Navy ships in Guantanamo—should the occasion ever arise."

"Congratulations," I said. "It appears that you've finally convinced headquarters that Underwater Demolition Teams are the way to go for a small navy like ours."

"I don't know about the rest, but Castiñeiras is all for it, and he's the one who counts," Miguel replied with sincere enthusiasm.

"That's for sure," I answered. To Miguel, this is just a naval exercise—a game—a challenge. He has no concept of the consequences of such an action. What a shame, it is going to be hard to make a case for him if Castro is overthrown.

Miguel's next remark shifted me away from my unpleasant thoughts. "About the twenty-eighth," he continued, "perhaps you would like to come with Eloisa and me. You wouldn't want to be late for the CNO's wedding."

"Thank you. No, I certainly wouldn't want to be late," I replied in a mocking tone.

"Well," Miguel said defensively, "it's just that I know you kids from El Vedado can't find your way around in downtown Havana."

"I can't argue that," I said mildly, reaching for the coffee server. As I was about to pour us both a second cup, I saw Comandante Pinto with a stern expression on his face heading toward our table. I quickly put the coffee server back on the table and prepared to rise, but the superintendent motioned for Miguel and me to remain seated.

"Please keep your seats, gentlemen," he said. Then with great sadness in his voice he added, "One more of us has made the disgraceful jump. Teniente Alberti has defected."

Chapter Eighteen

With a shaking hand, Nicky knocked on the door of Dr. Marten's bedroom. He was barefooted, his shirt was untucked, and his face was contorted with distress.

"Please come in," Nick heard the doctor say.

"Dr. Marten, I'm sorry to disturb you just a few hours before leaving your home, but I wonder if you could help me," Nicky said after entering the bedroom.

The doctor, who was getting dressed—just finishing buttoning his shirt—pointed to a chair and said sympathetically, "Sure Nicky, go ahead and sit down and tell me what's the matter."

Nicky sat on the chair, leaning forward with his hands clasped together. "The problem is that I don't know what's the matter with me, but I feel like I'm losing my mind."

"How? Tell me about it. I'm listening."

"For reasons too hard to explain, perhaps out of guilt, I have this terrible emptiness inside. It's like being completely alone in the world. I don't believe anyone could understand what I'm going through—or even care. Just look at my hands," he said, holding up trembling hands which were clammy with perspiration.

"Do you know how you would feel if you were falling from a building but never hitting the ground—just endlessly falling? That's how I feel right now. I have an anxiety in me, a pressure in my chest. I can't understand any of it, but I'd rather be dead than go through this."

Dr. Marten walked quickly to his wardrobe and picked up his professional bag. From it he pulled a syringe and a small bottle containing sodium pentothal. "Nicky," he said, "lie down on the bed. This shot will make you feel better right away, and then you will sleep for awhile." As he spoke, Dr. Marten aspirated the liquid from the bottle and moistened a ball of cotton with alcohol.

"But what about when I wake up?"

"Then the crisis of depression that you are going through will he over, and I'll prescribe some medication that will prevent a recurrence. Now pull your sleeve up."

Within a minute, Nick's expression began to relax and his agitation subsided. "I feel fine, Dr. Marten. I can't believe it. Thank God you were here. I would rather face a firing squad than go through that again." Nick then fell into a glorious sleep.

Dr. Marten pulled a chair close to Nick's bedside and watched him rest. After a minute, he checked his pulse, and pulled the covers over his young patient. Then he sat quietly, trying to sort out what this new development might mean—for Nicky—and for his daughter.

◆ ◆ ◆

About 2030 I was finally on my way to Tarara. Luckily, the traffic was unusually light and the drive a familiar one, for my mind was completely occupied with the shocking news of Alberti's defection. I remembered how he had asked me to make the necessary derogatory remarks, but not to bad-mouth him too much. Whatever the reasons, I had not been able to say a word; I had committed the unpardonable sin of remaining silent. Now I realized with great bitterness that not to have freedom of speech was bad enough, but to be unable to remain silent without attracting stares of suspicion and disapproval was infinitely worse.

At 2105 I pulled into Marten's driveway, parked my father's Mercedes, and walked to the front door. Before I had a chance to ring the bell, the heavy front door opened. "Carlos?" asked a tall, distinguished-looking gentleman, obviously Dr. Marten.

"Yes. Dr. Marten?"

"Just Marcelo. Welcome to my home," he said, shaking my hand warmly. "Please come in."

"Thank you very much," I said as I walked into the foyer. "Nick has told me of the courage and kindness of both you and your daughter. We could never begin to repay what you have done."

"Please, say no more. I have been honored to have Nicky in my home. I only wish that I could have met both of you under more pleasant circumstances," the doctor said as he closed the front door.

"Is Nicky all right?" I asked, alarmed by the tone of immediacy in his voice.

"Not quite. But let's go into my study, and I'll explain before you go upstairs to see him."

"Please excuse me, Doctor, but no preambles. I need to know what is the matter."

"I understand. Earlier this evening, Nick had a severe attack of reactive depression. These reactions usually occur in response to separation, death, or emotional upheaval."

"I think Nick qualifies under all those categories."

"Yes, I'm afraid he does."

"But how is he now?"

"I've had him under sedation for several hours. He is over the attack and almost back to normal. The problem lies in the possibility of recurrence."

"Is that likely to happen?"

"It's a distinct possibility. But let's go see him. I think you are the only one who can provide the hope and assurance he so desperately needs at this time."

"Exactly what do you mean, Doctor?"

"He must be reassured, true or not, that he'll be leaving Cuba soon—that the situation he finds himself in is temporary and that the end of it is near."

"I understand. Could I speak to him alone?"

"I was about to suggest it."

When I reached the top of the stairs, Nicky and Elena, holding hands and looking somehow subdued, were just coming in from the terrace.

"Elena," Nick said, smiling as he saw me approaching, "this is Carlos. Carlos—Elena."

"How come you never told me how stunningly beautiful she is?" I said, taking the hand Elena offered.

"Because I know your type."

"You are very kind, Carlos," Elena responded, giving Nick a look of mild reproval. "Nicky really thinks you are something special."

"Well, he has his lucid moments once in awhile."

"I think I had better leave you two alone now. Nicky still has to finish packing. You are taking him away with you, aren't you?" she added, trying to sound casual but betrayed by the redness of her eyes.

"Taking him away sounds too final. He is coming with me, yes, but not too far away. And there's always the telephone."

"Would he really be able to call me?" Elena asked, her eyes lighting up.

"Of course, I will, " Nicky answered for me. Then, taking her face gently in his hands, he kissed her softly on her trembling lips.

An hour later we were on the road, driving in complete silence, each of us wrapped in thought. After awhile, Nicky turned from staring out the window and asked, "Why are you driving your father's car?"

"Because Mercedes are the preferred cars of our socialist friends in high places, and we are much less likely to be stopped and questioned in this car."

At the mention of questioning, Nicky looked back to check the road. Immediately, his body tensed and he reached for the BAR I had concealed under the seat. "I think we have company," he said curtly.

"You can put that rifle down," I answered. "We do have company, but it's the invited type. That's our friend Lieutenant Quesada."

"For the love of God, Carlos, why didn't you tell me we'd be followed?" Nicky said almost shouting.

"I was going to, but Arturo joined us sooner than he was scheduled to. Relax, Nicky; it's just an extra precaution. I didn't want you to get the idea that there was anything to worry about."

"Next time, please let me worry. Now tell me, are there any more surprises along the way?"

"None planned."

"Thank you."

Escape from Castro

"Prego."

We drove along the waterfront, practically reversing the route that had taken Nick to the ambush. One out of three, I told myself. He had been the lucky one—at least so far.

After awhile, Nicky started to look more relaxed. He seemed to be absorbed in the splendor of the Havana coastline, lit up for the night. The old-fashioned Cuban songs playing on the car radio added to the soothing effect of the pleasant drive along the waterfront. Still, ever so often, Nick would look back to see if Quesada was still there.

"Is he taking us all the way?" he asked, as if reading my thoughts.

"No, he'll turn around after we cross the Almendares River. Tony will be with us the rest of the way."

"One more precaution?"

"That's right. This way, Quesada doesn't know where I picked you up, and, of course, he won't know where I'm taking you."

"That's good."

"He doesn't even know who is in the car with me. That's better for him, and for us too."

"Carlitos, I owe you, you know that," Nicky said, turning toward me.

"I don't know any such thing. Listen, Romeo, you'd better pay attention to your starboard side." We had just stopped at a red light alongside a convertible driven by a rather unattractive, but obviously wealthy woman in her forties. She was having difficulty dividing her attention between the traffic and Nicky. With his dark hair almost covering his ears and his boyish good looks, he appeared more like a movie idol than the traumatized soul he really was. I pressed the gas pedal and left Nick's admirer behind.

"What a shame," I said. "Maybe she would have liked to adopt you."

"She's probably impressed by your uniform."

"Oh, heck, she'll have to settle for Quesada."

"Speaking of Quesada," Nicky said, looking back, "he just turned around."

"Someday I'll thank him for this," I said. "And there is Tony, your host for the next few days, by the way."

107

"I like Tony a lot, but let's make it as few as possible. I can't wait to get out of here."

"It might be sooner than you think."

Fortunately, the rest of the ride to Tony's apartment was uneventful. We entered the building, apparently without drawing any unwanted attention, and were soon safely inside Tony's front door. While Nicky unpacked, I briefed Tony and Cathy on the crisis of depression that Nicky had suffered, and we agreed not to tell him about Raul's tragic end. We did tell him about Alberti's defection, and that cheered him up considerably.

Cathy had canceled all her piano lessons for the next few days, claiming a flu virus. In addition, we all now went through a long list of security precautions, including codes which determined when to answer the phone, emergency exit procedures, and even instructions for Nicky not to play the radio or flush the toilet when alone in the apartment. I had brought Dago, our German shepherd, as insurance against anyone sneaking into the apartment without being heard.

In spite of all these measures, the whole thing made me nervous. In this police state that Castro has made of Cuba, you can never be sure of anything or anyone, I reminded myself as I lay in bed in Tony's guest room. When it had been time for me to leave, Nicky, trying hard not to sound anxious, had suggested that it might be a good idea if I slept in the apartment for a night or so. Considering Nicky's depressed state of mind, I didn't argue.

After a restless night, I woke up before my alarm had a chance to go off. I lay in bed, mentally going over the plans for our escape on the *Sirius*. Although I deeply regretted the delay caused by Quesada's request that we help him with his ambitious plan, I owed him more than one favor, and I could not say no. I had lied to Nicky when he asked why we couldn't just get on the *Sirius* and go, using the excuse that my parents were not quite ready to leave the island. In fact, they had been waiting impatiently to leave for sometime.

I heard the alarm clock go off in Tony's bedroom and looked at my own—0600—time to get moving. In the other bed Nicky was beginning to stir. Looking at him now, I couldn't help remembering how fast he had reached for the rifle in the car when he felt threatened. So far he has killed three men, I reminded myself. What a complex person he is. There are some facets of his personality that I don't think even he recognizes. And I'm afraid if he came face to face with them, he wouldn't be too pleased.

Now awake, Nicky lifted his head and said with a smile, "Have they sounded reveille yet?"

"Not yet, but you are going to like the plan of the day."

"Yeah? Tell me."

"We are going to the Miramar Yacht Club for breakfast and to show you the *Sirius*."

"Do you think it's safe?"

"I think so, but we have to go regardless. It's important that the militiamen that G-2 has posted in the boathouse get used to seeing you with me and around the boat."

"I see."

"But before we leave, you are getting a haircut. Cathy has volunteered to do it."

"And why is that? I like it the way it is. After all, I'm not in the academy any more," Nicky protested loudly.

"Is this a convincing enough reason for you?" I opened the drawer of the night stand, pulled out an ID card, and tossed it to him.

"How in the world did you get hold of my old ID card? I had to turn it in to headquarters when I resigned."

"And who do you know in headquarters who would do something like steal ID cards?"

"Who else? That Quesada really gets around. Couldn't we get him out with us?"

"I'm afraid not. Anyway, Arturo doesn't need us; he has his own plans. They are going to remember him for a long time."

By 0800 we were already out of the apartment. The morning was crisp and clear, and Nick's spirits were high in spite of the haircut. It was Saturday, the beginning of a weekend without duty, and my own spirits were soaring at the thought of some freedom. I was looking forward to surprising Nicky by taking him out on the *Sirius* instead of merely looking at it tied up to the pier. My only hope was that nothing would spoil our day.

As I started the engine, Nicky suddenly turned to me and said, "Carlitos, do you think we could stop at the school's chapel before going to the club? I really want to see Father Nazario."

"I don't see why not. It would do us both good to see the Father."

The traffic was light and people were driving fairly slowly—for Havana. Something about the weekend had a way of slowing down the pace a little. I parked in front of La Salle Academy, the fine Catholic high school from which both Nicky and I had graduated, and said to Nick, "You go on ahead. I want to take a quick look around the block before I go in."

"That's what I like about you," Nicky grinned. "You never let your guard down."

"I try not to," I said, "Now stop talking and get moving."

"I'm on my way," Nicky answered, and he walked briskly into the school. Noting that he paused several times to look around him, I thought with amusement that I was not the only one to keep up his guard.

There was nothing unusual going on around the school. The students were already in the classrooms, and the only traffic consisted of the school buses lining up in preparation for taking the students home when the Saturday half-session ended at noon. Not wanting to get caught in the confusion of the break between classes, I decided to go in and hurry things up. I was crossing the main yard when I saw Father Nazario coming out of the chapel, looking tall and robust in spite of his fifty-five years. He had spotted Nicky who had stationed himself just outside the chapel door, and now he opened his arms and exclaimed, "Nicasio, my son," as he enfolded Nick in an affectionate bearhug. Nicky hugged the Father with sincere affection, and the two of them walked off slowly into the garden, talking in low voices. I was glad neither of them had seen me approaching. Deciding that I would visit Father Nazario another time, I headed back to the car to wait for Nick.

After one and a half hours, I had digested every scrap of the newspaper when Nicky finally returned and took his place in the passenger's seat. "The Father wanted to see you," he said. "Why didn't you come in?"

"Oh, for no reason. Today was your turn; I didn't mind waiting. But what took you so long?"

"We chatted awhile, and then I went to confession and communion."

Escape from Castro

"Still—you were gone too long," I said as I started the engine and headed for the club.

"Well, it takes a long time to cleanse your soul when you have blood on your hands," Nicky answered slowly, staring out his window.

"You know better than that, Nicky, " I answered, startled by the pain in his voice.

"Do I?"

"Yes, you do," I said forcefully.

He turned and looked at me, not bothering to disguise the anxiety on his face. "What I know is that we stalked them like wild animals. They never had a chance."

"Neither did the hundreds of innocent people they have sent to the wall. Or those who are tortured to death daily by the G-2."

"But I am not one of that gang."

"No, you are not. You risked your life taking theirs. They were armed and brutal. If you had been unarmed and defenseless, they would not have hesitated to gun you down."

"No one detests their cruelty and hypocrisy more than I do, but the next time I face them, it will be in combat, as the military man that I am. Ambushes—never again!"

Chapter Nineteen

Early the next morning after saying good-bye to her father before he left for his office, Elena went to feed Monarca whose sale had been delayed. She hoped that her outdoor tasks would help ease the deep sorrow and pain she was feeling since Nicky's departure. Once she had finished grooming Monarca, she let the horse out into the pasture and headed for the house. The minute she opened the back gate, she heard Suki barking with the unmistakable ferocity he reserved for strangers who approached the property. Elena quickened her steps as her anxiety sharpened.

Three G-2 men armed with long weapons had left their official sedan by the front gate and walked quietly toward the main entrance. Their hope of arriving without being detected had been thwarted by Suki's sharp senses. "Perro hijo de puta!" burst out the youngest one as he pounded on the front door with his right fist.

◆ ◆ ◆

Not far from his home, Dr. Marten crossed a G-2 sedan speeding toward Casablanca. Looking through his rear view mirror, he noticed that the man in the back seat had turned his head and was staring at him. His muscles tensed, waiting for the G-2 sedan to turn around and give chase. But it didn't happen.

The two cars going in opposite directions were soon out of each other's sight. Dr. Marten turned on the radio in an effort to relieve some of his anxiety, but only official propaganda and loud martial music were being bombarded from the stations polluting the serene countryside. Annoyed, he was reaching to turn off the dial when all at once the realization of what was happening struck him like a bolt of lightning. The G-2 sedan was heading for his home, not for Casablanca! Intense fear, the Cuban Revolution's secret weapon, drained the blood from his face but sharpened his protective instincts. "To get my daughter, you pigs will have to kill me first," he shouted as he applied the brakes, made a 180 degree turn, and slammed his foot down on the gas pedal.

◆ ◆ ◆

Elena entered the living room and saw Mercedes desperately trying to calm down Suki. She motioned Elena to come close and in her ear she whispered, "Don't worry, Señorita, I took care of the upstairs, and no one could ever tell that we have had company."

"Good thinking, Mercedes, and don't you worry either. We can take care of ourselves. Now answer the door while I lock up Suki. I'll be right back to deal with these people."

"I only wish the doctor could have been here now," Mercedes murmured under her breath on her way to the foyer.

The agent in charge, a middle-aged, rustic looking man, greeted Elena and flashed his ID card. It read: Sergeant Arsenio Espinosa, Military Intelligence/G-2.

"Señorita, I have orders to search every house, barn, and building in this area regardless of who lives in it or any objections that are raised." Espinosa's voice underneath the authoritative tone was almost apologetic.

"No objections," Elena replied, "but I would like to accompany you while you search *my home*."

"Absolutely. Where shall we start?" The sergeant hoped he did not show the effect that Elena had made on him. He had been taken aback by the poise and courage of one so young... and so guilty. He turned to his assistants and directed them to search the barn and the grounds. He alone would search the inside of the house.

In Marco's bedroom after a few minutes of perfunctory search, Espinosa held up a pair of Marco's riding breeches which he had found on the closet floor. "Whose are these, may I ask?" he began.

"Those are my son's. Now, what are you doing here?" answered Dr. Marten who now stood just outside the bedroom door.

"Daddy, this is Sergeant Espinosa," Elena quickly interjected. "He is just complying with his orders to search all the houses in our area." With her eyes and tone she desperately tried to convey a message, "All is well so far."

"Doctor, if your daughter will excuse us, I would like to clarify our reasons for being here."

"The sooner, the better. Elena, would you please ask Mercedes to bring us some coffee out on the porch."

"Doctor," Espinosa interrupted, "let me meet you there in a few minutes. I must talk to my men. I'll be right back." With these words, he was out of the room, leaving Marten and Elena alone.

Elena embraced her father and with her head on his shoulder began to sob uncontrollably. He took her face in his hands and gently wiped her tears. "I'm so proud of you, Elena—the way you handled yourself," he said in a low voice.

Making an effort to stop crying, Elena was finally able to speak. "Oh, Daddy, I'm so glad you came back."

He kissed her on the forehead and said reassuringly, "Come on, now. We must be strong. We don't want Espinosa to believe we have a reason to be nervous. Remember, God is with us. Nicky has not been out of this house for twelve hours, if that doesn't tell you something. . . ."

Elena raised her eyes and studied her father's face. "Daddy," she asked at last, "are we really going to get out of this mess?"

"Just watch," he replied, wishing he could believe his own words.

After ordering his subordinates to return to the car, Espinosa joined Dr. Marten on the porch, pulled up a chair, and sat facing the doctor. He finished the offered espresso and without any preambles, leaned forward and asked, "Doctor, does the name Orlando Santiago mean anything to you?"

Marten's eye twitched involuntarily and for a few seconds he just gazed outside, his face expressionless. Then he broke the silence in a low, tired voice. "No, Sergeant, I can't say that it does," he lied.

"That's too bad because, you see, Santiago remembers you very well." The sergeant lowered his voice to a near whisper. "Doctor, you don't have to react in any way to what I'm going to tell you. Just use the information I'm about to give you as you see fit."

His expression unchanged, Dr. Marten listened in silence as Espinosa continued. "You took care of my nephew Orlando after he was shot while trying to leave Cuba in a small boat. I will always be indebted to you, and I will try to help you if I can. The real reason that I am here today is because the G-2 is hoping that if we harass you enough you'll make a mistake and lead us to bigger game. My men have just finished tapping your telephone lines. Don't waste any time—you don't have it to waste. Leave!" With that, the sergeant rose and left Dr. Marten staring after him.

Chapter Twenty

The Miramar Yacht Club, located in the residential area of Miramar about ten miles west of Havana, had a fine boathouse and all kinds of sports facilities. Nevertheless, since we were in the cool month of February, we found the club almost empty—just a few people playing squash and a couple of boat owners socializing or taking care of their boats. We skipped the locker room and went directly to the pier, hoping to avoid any well-intentioned but dangerously curious friends. No sooner had we set foot on the pier than we were confronted by the militiaman on duty, a stocky, grubby-looking individual of about thirty who was suspicious of all club members, especially those who owned large boats. Luckily, he recognized me and remembered that I was a naval officer—not that my position inspired any great trust, just that he apparently reasoned that I might have enough clout to get him in trouble if he hassled me. Whatever the reason, I was seldom subjected to the questioning and harassment that had become the steady diet of most of the civilian club members—at least whenever they wanted to take their boats out. I made a quick, casual comment that Nicky was an ensign, and we proceeded toward the end of the pier where the *Sirius* was tied up.

"Is that the one?" Nicky exclaimed with a mixture of disbelief and delight in his voice.

"That's it."

"Permission to come aboard, Sir," he said with a wide grin.
"Permission granted."

We both climbed aboard the *Sirius*, and I turned the key in the ignition and started the two powerful inboard engines. Nicky could not stop smiling. "Come take a look at this," I said, pointing to the gas gauge which indicated "Full."

"Carlos," Nicky said, "do you realize that we are standing on freedom? Right now we could take off, and with this sea condition, we would be in Key West for supper."

"And we will soon. Just give me a little time. Go ahead and take in the lines; we are going for a short ride."

"Aye, aye," Nick replied, looking at me with shining eyes. We pulled out of the basin at low speed, the engines protesting like two thoroughbreds trapped behind the starting gate, desperate to take off. We had a sea condition three on the Beaufort scale—that is to say that crests beginning to break were seen amid white caps. We headed northeast and opened up to a speed of about thirty knots.

"What's our top speed?" Nicky asked, shouting over the roar of engines. He was obviously exhilarated by the sight of the open sea and the realization that the end of his odyssey was in sight.

"Thirty-eight knots," I replied.

"I can't believe it! They don't have anything that can come close to this, not even our PT boat, the R-42."

"You're right on that score. But look up!" I shouted. I had just spotted a Cuban Navy PBY flying at a relatively low altitude, evidently patrolling the coastline.

"Yes, I see it."

"If we were to continue on this course for awhile . . . No, wait! Look, he's headed this way. Hold on, Nick, we are returning—pronto." I changed course as rapidly as I could without making the change too obvious. The PBY made a low sweep, flying over us so closely that we could see the pilot checking us out with his binoculars. The noise of the plane's engines was deafening.

"Do you think they were able to identify us?" Nick asked anxiously.

"I don't think so. Wait, look, they're coming in for a second

Escape from Castro

pass. Hurry—hand me that lantern," I yelled, pointing to a powerful flashlight on the bulkhead. "Now take the wheel."

As soon as Nicky had taken over the steering, I rushed outside and, leaning against the forward part of the cabin, I pointed the light directly at the aircraft. In Morse Code I began transmitting N...A...V...Y. The sluggish, awkward-looking reconnaissance craft came roaring over, no higher than five hundred feet above us. After a couple of minutes, it banked to port and steadied itself on a reverse course, straight back to us.

Sweat streaming down my face, sickened at the thought of losing our craft, I turned around and shouted to Nicky, "Start zigzagging and get ready to jump!" At that very minute, the PBY tipped its wings, acknowledging the message. With unspeakable relief, we watched the aircraft climb steadily at a normal angle.

"They're heading toward Havana," Nicky said.

"That's fine with me. By the way, those were some of Alberti's gang. As long as they can get away with it, they'd be the last ones to stop anyone from fleeing the country."

"That's reassuring," Nicky answered, not sounding at all convinced.

"Of course, if they get specific orders or if we put them on the spot, they would have no choice but to sink us."

"At least," Nick remarked, "a PBY wouldn't be very effective at night." He had already begun to relax and was enjoying steering the boat now that the crisis was over. I was still gasping mentally at the thought of just how close we had come to losing our only transportation out of Cuba. I sat down on the bunk behind the wheel and made an effort to unwind, hoping to salvage the rest of Nicky's afternoon of freedom.

"Well, Nicasio," I said with a feeble attempt at humor, "now maybe you can see why we couldn't make it to Key West for dinner tonight."

As we approached the club, we sailed between two large government "fishing" vessels, each about one hundred and fifty feet long. They had, as usual, strategically positioned themselves about three miles out from the main yacht clubs. Both vessels were loaded with radar and sophisticated communication equipment. I took the wheel from Nicky and steered with one hand, using the other to reach for a pair of powerful binoculars which I handed to Nicky. "Take a look at those two skunks," I suggested. "We'll have to go past them when the time comes."

Peering at the vessels through the binoculars, Nicky remarked, "They must have ordered the PBY to take a look at us."

"Probably, but they are not very worried at this time of day. They know that it would be suicidal to try to sneak out in broad daylight."

I slowed down. The wake of the *Sirius* would not be a welcome sight to the owners of the small sailboats moored in the waters close to the club. We headed straight for the gas pump to top off. Although we had used very little gas, every gallon was going to count when it was time to make our move.

Once we had pulled alongside the pier, Nicky checked the boat from fore to aft. Sounding like a kid with a new toy, he commented, "Prowler, huh? Not bad." Then, he added with great satisfaction, "No, not bad at all!"

"They're built in Miami and although they're supposed to be very expensive, we got this one for an excellent price."

"There's nothing in Cuba today that you couldn't buy for an excellent price," Nicky replied. "The whole island is for sale."

"And for good reasons. Come on, let's go have some lunch," I said as I locked the cabin.

"I would like to be served on board," Nicky said, sitting on one of the bunks and pretending to read a newspaper.

"In Key West," I answered. "In Key West."

We sneaked out of the club through a side gate by the boathouse, stopping to talk to no one. Instead of going to a regular restaurant, we decided to stay out of sight by trying our luck at a small diner near Marianao Beach. There we ate well for little more than what we would normally have spent on tips. Over coffee, I said to Nicky, "Remember Lourdes, the stewardess who lives on First Avenue?"

"Of course I do. She is beautiful. But what about her?"

"I promised to call her today. How would you like to go over to her house for awhile?"

"I would like it a lot better than being locked up alone in Tony's apartment. The question is, how would she feel about your bringing a friend?"

"Leave that to me," I answered, thinking that I had been

wondering exactly the same thing. I got up from the counter, located the diner's phone booth, and dialed Lourdes' number.

Lourdes told me that she was leaving the next day on a flight from Havana to Miami and New York. After some arm-twisting, she agreed reluctantly for me to bring Nicky along, but she let it be known that she had expected an evening for two, not three. Regretfully, that would have to wait. After hanging up, I made the call that I had really needed to make. On the other end of the line a muffled voice, probably someone speaking through a handkerchief stretched over the receiver, said "Hola."

"May I speak with Arturo?" I asked.

"Who is calling?"

"A friend."

"Hold on." In the background I heard someone say, "I think it's him."

After a long pause Lieutenant Quesada answered, "Who is this?"

"Tyrone Power. Who the heck do you think it would be? You said to call at 1400."

"Carlos! We were just talking about you."

"I was afraid of that."

"Nothing to fear, comrade," he said sarcastically. "We have a good game of dominoes going; why don't you join us?"

"When?"

"Now."

"I'll be there shortly. Give me an hour to tie up some loose ends. Adiós," I said.

When I turned to leave the booth, I was startled to see Nick standing by the door. "All arranged," I said brightly.

"Who were you really talking to?"

"What do you mean?"

"You know what I mean. You weren't talking to Lourdes; the tone was all wrong. You don't fool me."

"Let's go to her house: she's expecting us right away, you wise guy," I replied with a laugh, deciding to bluff my way through.

On the way to Lourdes' house, Nicky was in a quiet mood, something for which I was deeply grateful. I needed to figure out a way to go see Quesada without causing Nick to become suspicious. I was also hoping to avoid infuriating Lourdes who would not only lose her evening for two but would also be saddled with an almost complete stranger in the bargain. To make my dilemma worse, I knew that Nicky should not be left alone for long; Dr. Marten had stressed the importance of keeping his hopes and his spirits high. A recurrence of Nick's depression could be disastrous given the present circumstances. Tony and Cathy were seldom in their apartment and normally that would have made it the perfect place for Nicky to hide, but now, enforced solitude was the worst possible environment for him.

"Boy, aren't you a slow driver," Nicky remarked, breaking my train of thought.

"Only because we don't want to be stopped for a small infraction and wind up having to answer a lot of unwelcome questions."

"At this rate you're going to get stopped for causing a traffic jam."

"I'll take my chances," I said patiently. "You know what Tony's contact in the G-2 said. No one is looking specifically for you. Your name is on the list of those who would not be allowed to board a plane, but so are the names of thousands of other military and ex-military personnel who would never be granted an exit visa."

"Then why are we so careful?"

"Because like Tony's contact said, if you were stopped for any reason, you would be questioned about your place of employment, where you live, and where you have been during the last few weeks. Before you knew it, you'd be detained until all questions were answered."

Nicky sighed and looked away. "I'm pretty much a pain in the neck, aren't I? Why do you put up with me?"

"I wish I knew. Anyway, here we are," I said as I pulled up in front of Lourdes' house.

"Something just occurred to me," Nicky said, giving me a sudden look of disapproval. "What about Thais?"

"What about her?"

"Aren't you kind of engaged to her?"

"Nicky," I said in exasperation, "Lourdes is just a beautiful woman whose company I happen to enjoy. Nothing serious."

"You sound so innocent," Nicky said, still eyeing me suspiciously.

"I never realized that you were such a puritan; I think it's a recent development," I laughed. We got out of the car and started up the long walkway toward her house. Lourdes, looking radiant in a long hostess gown, had just appeared at her front door. "It's been a long time, Carlos," she called to me in her low, musical voice.

"Too long," I murmured before I kissed her. Nicky, looking rather embarrassed, had come up behind us.

"Lourdes, you remember Nicky, don't you?" I asked. It was difficult to remember my social duties with Lourdes so close, but I was acutely aware of Nicky's awkward position; after all, I'd gotten him into it.

"Of course I remember him," Lourdes replied, her genuinely kind nature overriding any earlier feelings of annoyance. "It's good to see you again, Nicky."

Nicky took the hand she offered and said, "I hope I'm not imposing."

"Nonsense! I'm delighted that you were able to come. Such a big house," she made a sweep with her arm that encompassed the oversized living room, "needs people to keep it from feeling like a museum."

How can she afford this? I wondered as I once again admired the spacious, tastefully decorated room.

After one drink and a hastily muttered excuse that I needed to drop off some reports at the ship, I beat a rapid retreat, leaving Lourdes at the door—the expression on her face an interesting combination of injury, anger, and suspicion. Nicky looked even worse.

Lieutenant Arturo Quesada lived in a condominium a short block from the ocean and not far from the American Embassy. After I had identified myself through the intercom, Arturo unlocked the entrance door electrically from his apartment. I took the elevator to the fifth floor, and the door opened into Arturo's foyer where he was waiting for me. He was wearing a militia uniform with a 9 mm Browning pistol in the holster. Smiling, but obviously tense, Arturo put his left arm around my shoulders and said as he held out his uniform shirt with his right

Escape from Castro

hand, "It's good to see you, Carlos. Don't mind these rags."

"I don't mind them although they're not exactly your style," I replied.

"Come, before we get down to business, I want you to join a few mutual friends in a toast." He opened the doors leading to the dining room. Standing behind a table covered with maps and notebooks and also dressed in a militia uniform, stood Lieutenant Luis Calderon, Commandante Pinto's political advisor. He greeted me with a nod and the slightest hint of a friendly smile. At his side, wearing a militia uniform and a mischievous grin—now stretching his hand across the table to shake mine—was Midshipman Diaz.

After the moment of mutual astonishment had passed, greetings were exchanged. Arturo passed around cups of cafe negro, and we quickly got down to business. Even before a word was uttered, I realized that we had been summoned for a briefing concerning a plan that was *about* to be executed. I did not like the fact that I had never been consulted during the planning stage of the operation. In some ways I could understand their reasons; complete secrecy meant no chance of indiscretions that might compromise the action. Still, understanding the reasons did not make the situation more palatable.

Somehow the modus operandi doesn't match Arturo's personality, I thought. My suspicions were promptly proven correct with Quesada's opening remarks. Standing at the head of the table, he spoke in a businesslike tone. "We are here to listen to Luis Calderon's plan for what we believe will be a blow with international repercussions to the government of Castro. If any of you feel for any reason, that you cannot take part in this action, we will understand. There will be no criticism or comments, now or ever. We will, however, ask you not to leave this apartment until the action has been completed." Looking at his watch, Arturo said, "It is now 2100. Everything will be over in three hours. If all goes well, Calderon and I will defect after this mission is over. Our destination—Miami—to join the Brigade that is presently being formed. Carlos, and you Jorge, are welcome to join us."

"And I wish you would," Calderon interjected.

"I thank you both for your offer, but I have my own plans. God willing, I'll join you in the very near future," I said.

"I, too, am grateful for the offer, but I'll finish at the academy first, unless something goes wrong tonight," Jorge said, sounding very mature and sure of himself.

Quesada walked around the table, touched Calderon on the shoulder, and said, "It's all yours."

Calderon stood up and took Arturo's place at the head of the table. He was a tall, imposing man with broad shoulders and large hands, and his heavily lined face and sparse dark brown hair made him look older than his thirty-two years. For a brief moment, he did not speak but only stared into space. When he finally broke the silence his voice was low, but the tone was sharp. "As you all know, tomorrow the Soviets will open their industrial exhibition at the National Museum of the Arts in downtown Havana. Fidel himself will welcome visitors from the majority of the Third World Nations."

"The academy staff has been requested to attend in civilian clothes; the Executive Officer will be there with a roster just to make sure," I interrupted.

"Yes, I issued those orders," Calderon replied. "But if we are successful tonight, and we will be, there will be no opening tomorrow or for a long time." He began to explain the details of his plan. Tension filled the room. None of us spoke or even moved as we listened. When Calderon had finished his explanation, I was impressed by the extent of groundwork which had gone into preparing this operation. The years Calderon had spent in the Plans and Operations Department followed by his training in Naval Intelligence had paid off. We had just witnessed the results of an organized military mind working with absolute dedication from a privileged position. I rose from my seat, shook his hand, and said, "I am in."

Diaz followed suit.

Chapter Twenty-one

I don't know how many times we went over every single detail of the plan before Calderon was satisfied that each of us knew exactly what his particular mission entailed. The blueprints of the National Museum of the Arts were spread out on the dining room table next to several photographs of the museum's main floor which showed the Soviet machinery and equipment already in place. A red X marked each of our targets for destruction: two automobiles and two tractors.

Standing by the table, I looked out onto the balcony and watched the lights of the automobiles travelling along the Malecon, Havana's beautiful oceanfront drive with its hotels and high-rises overlooking the ocean. Habaneros in search of pleasure, indifferent to our struggle—to what was going on in this room, I thought irrationally. The authoritative voice of Calderon broke through my thoughts. "I think that you will agree with me that every aspect of this operation has been planned with painstaking attention to detail." He paused, and there was an immediate positive response from all of us.

Calderon continued, his tone as cool and businesslike as if he were giving a lecture at the academy. "If I have made a mistake, it could cost all of us our lives. No one in this group will be taken prisoner. We all know the reason: few people leave the G-2 house alive, and those who do wish they hadn't. Only last week during a trip to the Isle of Pines, I witnessed atrocities against political prisoners which are unsurpassed by the most barbaric governments in human history. With these two eyes," Calderon said, pointing to his eyes with his index finger, "I witnessed scenes that made me sick to my stomach—and I mean that I actually vomited from the stench and the hellish spectacle. I was unfortunate enough to be there for the political prisoners' "shower." The sadistic militiamen who act as guards stood on the chain link ceiling of the cells and emptied buckets of urine and excrement over the sleeping inmates. Some of those prisoners have a crust of old excrement and sweat in their hair that drives them insane with the foul odor and the itching. They plead for water, but they are given none. They have barely enough to drink—not one drop can be spared to wash the filth from their bodies."

"And just who are these prisoners, you ask yourselves. Well, they are ex-officers from Fidel's own army, student leaders, and ordinary citizens whose only crime is the failure to embrace communism. In spite of their sub-human conditions, these men refuse to be sent to camps for political rehabilitation. They continue to prefer torture, degradation, and even starvation to the joy of following the party line. Because of this situation, for us there can be no compromise; tonight we will accomplish our mission or die trying."

Calderon paused for a few seconds before concluding, "I have nothing else to say except that we'll be leaving in about fifteen minutes. Unless there are questions, let's adjourn and enjoy the fresh coffee that Arturo just made."

As we filed into the living room, I moved next to Calderon and said to him in a low voice, "Luis, I must make a phone call. You are welcome to listen, but I must make it."

"Carlos, if I didn't trust you, you wouldn't be here. In fact, after that night at the academy, you would have been in quite a different place."

"So it was you who pulled me out of the claws of the G-2!"

"Not entirely, I wouldn't have been able to do it alone. Commandante Pinto and Miguel Nodal are the ones you should be grateful to. But we can discuss that affair some other time. Go and make your call; there isn't much time."

I went into the study, picked up the telephone, and dialed

Lourdes' number. She answered on the first ring, her low sexy voice edged with anxiety.

"Lourdes," I said, speaking quickly to cut off any reaction on her part, "I can only talk for a couple of minutes. Please listen carefully."

"I'm listening, Carlos. What is the matter?"

"Take care of Nicky until I return. If I don't make it back by morning, please drop him at Tony Capó's apartment. He can give you directions."

"I'll be glad to, but tell me . . ."

"Please don't ask me any questions. Hopefully, I'll see you tomorrow, and I'll explain everything then. But, how is Nicky?"

"He talked to his girlfriend on the phone for a long time, then he had a few drinks. Apparently, the G-2 searched the houses in the area where she lives. She and her family didn't have any problems though."

"Thank God for small favors—actually, not that small."

"I agree. Right now, Nicky's asleep on the sofa. Should I wake him up?"

"Yes, yes, but please hurry."

There followed a brief pause which seemed like an eternity. Finally, Nicky's anxious voice came over the line, "Carlos, where are you?"

"Nicky, listen to me. I only have a moment. Call my cousin and tell him to be ready to leave tomorrow evening. If I am not back before dawn, go with him. He is a fine yachtsman and a courageous man."

"Carlos, what are you talking about? What's happening?"

"Nicky, calm down. I'll explain everything tomorrow . . ."

"I'll never forgive you for this. You—my only friend. I had no secrets from you . . ."

"I must leave now. Adiós, Nicky," I said with anguish in my voice. I hung up the receiver and hurried to join the others who were already gathering at the front door.

◆ ◆ ◆

Lourdes excused herself and once in the privacy of her bedroom, made a phone call.

"Armstrong speaking," the autocratic voice came strong after the second ring.

"Michael, it's Lourdes. Can we talk?"

"Yes."

"I might need to send two or maybe three packages as early as tomorrow."

"We will be ready. Can you tell me some more?"

"Not at this time, perhaps later tonight."

"I'll be here," Armstrong replied.

◆ ◆ ◆

The four of us rode the elevator down to the building garage. Luis had somehow managed to "borrow" two blue sedans from the SIN (Naval Intelligence Service). Calderon and Quesada took the first car—Luis at the wheel. They were carrying the C-3 plastic explosives, detonators, one PRC 10 radio, and one 30 caliber BAR automatic rifle. Following them in the second sedan, Jorge was driving with me at his side. We had the second PRC 10 and another BAR. Luis drove at a moderate speed, and Jorge followed closely, never allowing more than one vehicle to come between us. Illuminated by the dashboard lights, his face registered a tension I had never seen before. He turned to me and forcing a smile, said, "Carlos—you don't mind if I call you Carlos, do you?"

"No, of course not. Besides it wouldn't be the first time, would it?"

"No, I guess not. Anyway, I'm sure glad you decided to come along."

"I wish I could say the same thing about you, Jorge."

"What do you mean?" he interrupted, giving me a hurt look.

"I mean that I would have liked to see you graduate before getting into this type of activity. It's too risky."

"Oh," he exclaimed, looking relieved.

"Heck, since it's too late to worry, I'm glad you're here, too. But if we pull this one off, I want you to promise me that it will be your *last*."

"At least until after graduation," he replied, keeping his eyes glued to the road as we entered the heavy traffic of central Havana.

I sat restlessly as we struggled our way through the congested streets. As always, I hated every minute before the action and longed to put an end to the talking and get on with it. Finally, Luis parked on Zulueta Street, and we pulled next to the curb about thirty feet behind him. "Jorge," I said, "you know your instructions. Stay in the car and give us a radio check two minutes after we enter the building."

"Roger. Good luck," he said.

"I'll see you." I got out of the car without looking at him and followed Arturo and Luis who were already approaching the side door of the museum. The street was deserted—just as Arturo had said it would be. He had parked in the same spot at this time for three weeks in a row to determine the traffic conditions. "He did his homework well," I muttered to myself as I joined the others.

A militiaman armed with an AK-47 was standing by the door. We walked together—Calderon in the center carrying a large, heavy bag which contained the explosives and the firing assemblies. Arturo was at his left with the PRC 10 in his hand, and I stood on the right carrying a BAR with the safety in the off position. The militiaman, a clean-cut young man about Jorge's age, saluted us and then unlocked the huge door.

"Si, mi Comandante," the militiaman replied as he swung his AK-47 over his right shoulder and brought his watch close to his face. "I'm ready."

"The time is now 2305," Calderon said.

"Sir, you have exactly twenty minutes," the young man replied. He came to attention, held the salute for a split second while looking Calderon directly in the eye, and left without saying another word. This look of mutual understanding and secrecy was most understandable under the circumstances, but somehow it left me feeling apprehensive.

We went in. Quesada stayed by the door, ready to alert us of anything unusual.

On the main floor of the exhibit we found an unexpected bonus: right at the center show place was one of the most sophisticated members of the newly developed battle tanks, the T-55. We honored it with two charges of C-3 plastic explosive. I jammed them under the gun barrel at the edge of the turret, straightened out the prima cord leads, and attached two firing assemblies to the leads. This procedure we called "dual priming the charges." It was like an insurance policy: if one firing assembly didn't go off, the other would.

"Well, that should take care of this one," I said, more to myself than to Calderon.

"Carlos," Calderon said abruptly, "let me have the remaining firing assemblies. I can easily handle the rest by myself. You had better go to the front door and stay there for cover."

"But don't you..." I started to object. Then I cut my protest short. Calderon was in charge—no room for dissension. "Aye, aye, sir," I said as I picked up the BAR and hurried toward the front door of the museum, neither understanding nor really agreeing with the change in plans.

I slid open the door. In the semi-darkness I could see the foyer, elegant and imposing. All quiet, I thought, but not for long if our work goes well. The time dragged by slowly in the uneasy silence. I wished I could have been setting the explosives instead of standing this idle watch.

From my post I had difficulty seeing Quesada, but I had no problem following Calderon's moves. "Waiting, waiting," I mumbled to myself, "how I hate it." One more time I checked the BAR to make sure that I had a round in the chamber.

We knew that there was another militiaman standing watch at the main entrance. The one working with us was to see that his comrade wouldn't enter this part of the building before 2330. Both men were scheduled to be relieved at 2345 after making the final rounds. I heard Quesada whistle one, two, three times—the signal indicating immediate danger. My heart began to pump faster as the adrenaline flowed into my system. Calderon had just finished checking our work on the tank and was signaling me to join him. I motioned for him to go ahead and leave—not to wait for me. Then, I began running toward the rear door. I saw Quesada leave, then Calderon.

They were out: I had to rush not to hold them up. As I ran, I heard hurried steps resounding on the marble floor. I didn't look back. Just as I burst through the door, I heard a series of small caliber shots echoing in the huge main floor. As the door started to close behind me, I felt my back on fire; I had been hit.

Stumbling forward, I lost my footing and fell. All my instincts were shouting, "You have only a couple of seconds to react. Do it! Now!" Motivated by raw anger and the sheer terror of being captured alive, I rolled onto my back and as soon as the door swung open, I squeezed the trigger of my BAR. I saw the dark shadow of a man clutching his abdomen and then falling backward. The ceiling, the door, the whole building seemed to come straight at me and all went black.

When I opened my eyes, I was bouncing on Calderon's shoulders. Suddenly the bouncing stopped; we had reached one of the SIN sedans. Calderon shoved me into the back of the car, and I heard him shout, "Take him to the condo." The car took off. As I lay in the back seat, I could feel the blood oozing from my wound. My back felt wet, and I was already getting cold.

Not more than a minute after we had left, we heard a series of loud explosions coming from the museum. "He did it; he really did it!" I heard Jorge exclaim. Then, glancing back at me, he asked, "Carlos, how are you doing? Can you hear me?"

The deafening sounds of firetrucks and police cars heading toward the museum made it impossible to communicate. "I'm okay," I said at last. "Drive carefully."

"I will, I will. Just hold on. We'll get you to a doctor in no time at all."

"Call Tony's brother, Dr. Rene Capó. He's one of us."

"Will do. I'll pass the word through the PRC. But how are you—really?" he asked, his voice heavy with concern.

My lips were dry and I felt weak, but I had decided that my condition was not immediately dangerous. I was struggling to keep my self control; I had heard of people falling into shock just out of fear and anxiety. At least I did not feel any more blood coming out of the wound. I didn't have to worry, I reassured myself; I was not going to bleed to death. I lay very still so as not to reopen the wound and watched the street lights rushing past as we traveled toward the condo—and safety.

"How are you Carlos? Tell me! Tell me!" Jorge kept repeating. Then I realized that I had answered the question to myself, but not to him. I must reassure the poor kid, I thought. "Fine Jorge, fine. I promise you. Look, I'm going to sit up."

"No, please. Stay down. I believe you," he shouted.

"O.K., O.K.," I replied, grateful not to have to make the effort. By now I could feel a salty tang in the air and I knew we were driving along the coastline. We were finally on the Malecon, away from the downtown traffic. We're going to make it, I thought. We're really going to make it. I asked, "How are we doing, Jorge? How much longer?"

"We're doing great, Carlos. We'll be there in no time at all," came the reassuring voice.

"That's good, but don't hurry. I'm fine." This time I was lying. I had started to bleed again and was feeling dizzy. Suddenly I remembered my conversation with Nicky. I must tell Jorge, I thought, in case I pass out.

"Jorge, Jorge," I called, making an effort to shout. He was listening to the G-2 radio station and did not hear me. I called again, "Jorge . . . Jorge."

Finally he responded, "Yes, Carlos. What is it?"

"Call Nicky . . . at . . ."

"Yes, I'll call Nicky. Where? Where?"

I couldn't think clearly—couldn't remember Lourdes' number.

"Call Nicky," I tried again. "At . . . at 11117. Tell him not to move until he hears from me."

"Sure thing, Carlos."

"Repeat the number . . . please . . . the number."

"11117. I never forget numbers."

"That's it . . ." I mumbled as my eyes closed and my body went limp.

Chapter Twenty-two

I opened my eyes slowly. A cool ocean breeze was blowing in through an open window, causing the curtains to move in rhythmic waves. The house was still very quiet, and the light flowing into the room was soft and pale. It must still be very early in the morning, I thought, just a little after dawn. Or was it evening? I couldn't be sure.

I felt disoriented, but physically strong. I made a visual search of the room. It was almost empty—just the bed I was lying on, its sheets stained with my blood, and a mattress on the floor beside the bed. I heard the bedroom door opening and lifted myself gingerly, turning just enough to be able to see the door. Diaz was trying to push the door open with his left foot while using both hands to support a heavy tray. I tried to get up to assist him, but he yelled, "Stay in bed. I can manage." Once inside the room, he dumped the breakfast tray on the foot of the bed, turned to me with a smile and asked, "How is my patient today?"

"I'm fine, but where am I and what time is it?"

Jorge checked his watch and answered, "0550, and we're not at the Hotel Nacional, but at least we're close to it—at Quesada's condo. Don't you recognize it?"

"I never went into the bedroom," I replied shortly, in no mood for extreme cheerfulness.

"Well," he said, helping me into a sitting position with my back cushioned from the brass headboard by several pillows, "first things first." He picked up the tray and dropped it ceremoniously on my lap. The aroma of fresh coffee and the fragrance of newly-squeezed orange juice did wonders for my irritability. Diaz, as usual, was chattering away, and I divided my attention between him and the contents of the tray.

"Be sure to drink all the juice," he was saying. "Dr. Capó told me to make sure that you took plenty of liquids and that you ate as much as you could."

"Jorge, stop the nonsense and tell me what's going on," I said as I spread jelly on a roll.

"Aye, aye, Sir. As soon as you start drinking your juice."

"You punk! Well then pour me a glass." I took the glass from him and gulped the juice, enjoying every drop.

Jorge made himself comfortable on the edge of the bed and, helping himself to most of the coffee, began a narration of the last evening's events.

"When we arrived about 0130, Calderon and Quesada were already in the apartment waiting for us."

"How did you get me up here?" I interrupted.

"Easily. I put you in the elevator right from the garage."

"And who called Lt. Capó?"

"Quesada did, and get this, when they were only a few blocks from the museum, they stopped at a cafe and Quesada got out and made the call to Dr. Capó."

"That must have taken a lot of nerve," I remarked and then added, "Where are they now?"

"Those two took off as soon as they found out that you were going to be O.K. Thanks to their call, Dr. Capó arrived here just a few minutes after we did. He brought all kinds of instruments with him and started to work on you right away. He took a bullet from your left shoulder blade and said that you had been lucky— that the bullet had not touched any vital organ."

"Lucky? One out of four gets hit and that's lucky?"

Jorge refilled his cup and paying little attention to my remarks, continued, "I have to agree with Capó. The bullet had gone through the door before it struck you so it had lost much of its force. Still, it lacerated a couple of blood vessels and chipped some part of the scapula that he called the acromion, or something like that."

"You know, maybe you should have been a doctor," I said sarcastically.

Again ignoring me, he said, "You haven't heard it all. He called the academy and told the officer of the day that you had suffered a bad fall, had broken two ribs and that he was placing you on two weeks of convalescent leave."

"Well . . . that's more like it! Now I might agree that, after all, I was kind of lucky. Two weeks was more than the time I needed to get ready to leave. "Jorge, please hand me my clothes," I said, pointing to the pile of neatly folded clothing on the floor by the wall.

He shook his head. "First you finish your breakfast—then I'll help you get into your civvies and we can get out of here."

"You are too much, you know that?"

"Am I really?"

"Yes, you are. But tell me, did you call Nicky?" I asked, feeling guilty.

"Of course I did. He's fine but mad as hell. Your friend Lourdes insisted that he stay in her apartment until you could pick him up. He wants to talk with you as soon as possible." He got up from the bed and began to gather my clothes.

"Is there any more coffee?" I asked.

"Sure thing," he said, lifting the coffee server and pouring the last few drops into my cup. Looking slightly embarrassed, he offered, "I'll get more. I guess I didn't bring enough."

"I guess," I replied, amused. "But don't bother to get any more; you've drunk enough for both of us."

As soon as I had finished struggling into my clothes, I put my right arm around his shoulder for support, and we took the elevator down to the garage. "I brought the car inside before you got up," he said.

"I'm glad you did." Pointing to a dark corner of the garage, I asked, "Aren't those the SIN sedans that we used last night?"

"They sure are," he replied as he opened the passenger door and helped me get in. He walked around the car and pressed the electric switch to open the garage door. "How is the back?" he asked as he slid behind the wheel.

"My acromion is fine," I teased him. Outside the dark underground garage the sun, strong as it was, felt good. I was glad to be leaving Quesada's apartment; lingering there had made me irritable and nervous. I put on my sunglasses and rested my head on the back of the seat.

"Are you O.K.?" Jorge asked, momentarily taking his eyes off the road. "I really am," I replied, thinking that I was the one who should be worried about him. He was going back to the academy, and I feared for his life. Aloud I said, "Jorge, why don't you come with us to Miami?"

"I'd love to, but I have to finish school first. As you know, we are anything but rich, and a diploma is all I'll be able to count on."

"I wish you'd think it over. It's much too dangerous to try to continue at the academy."

"Tomorrow," he replied with his usual confidence, "we'll know where we stand. Perhaps I'll be forced to accept your generous offer."

Thanks to the light early Sunday morning traffic, we reached Fifth Avenue in no time at all. Jorge stopped at the red light just a few blocks from the G-2 horror house. An old man was tottering slowly across the street. "Come on, old fellow, let's go," Jorge said impatiently.

"It sure is a bad place to fiddle around," I agreed.

"A G-2 sedan is a couple of cars behind us," Jorge said, looking through the rearview mirror. The light changed to green just as the old man finally made it across the street. We moved cautiously.

After a few blocks, Jorge said tensely, "They are still with us." It was close to 0800 and the traffic was becoming slightly heavier as we approached the Miramar parish.

"Jorge, pull in," I said. "We are going to mass." He turned at the last minute, hoping that the G-2 would not have enough time to react. He was wrong.

We got out of the car, I was making a tremendous effort to walk normally and Jorge was smiling and pretending to be engaged in an animated conversation with me. Suddenly, he waved; he had spotted an aunt and uncle in the crowd. Somewhat bewildered, but obviously delighted with Jorge's extemporaneous display of affection, his relatives joined us as we walked into the church. Out of the corner of my eye, I watched the sedan double park across from the parish.

It was impossible to concentrate on the mass, and naturally we missed communion. Only yesterday morning, Nicky had told me that it was hard to cleanse your soul when you had blood on your hands. Today, that remark had taken on a new meaning.

When the mass was over, we were careful not to leave the church too soon. We mingled with the older crowd. Jorge kissed his aunt and uncle good-bye, and I shook hands with them as I surreptitiously searched the street for the G-2 sedan. It was gone! Thank God for big favors, I sighed.

We drove to Lourdes' house without further complications, and I waited in the car while Jorge rang the bell. For the longest time there was no answer, and I was beginning to worry when Nicky finally answered the door. He motioned Jorge inside the house and came toward the car alone. Opening the door, he bent down to look at me appraisingly. Even the sunglasses did not hide the relief in his eyes.

As he helped me out of the car, he asked with deep concern, "Carlos, are you all right?"

"Yes. And are you pissed?"

"Not any more."

"Good." I took support on his arm, and we walked slowly together into the house. Nicky helped me to lie down on one of the heavy rattan sofas in Lourdes' spacious, elegant living room. The room opened onto a manicured back yard surrounded by a high stucco wall, and as I enjoyed the view, I relaxed for the first time in many long hours.

Jorge had gone directly to the kitchen to fix something to eat so Nicky and I were alone in this peaceful setting. He pulled up a chair next to the couch on which I was lying and said, "Tell me how bad your wound is."

"Not bad at all—really."

"May I see?"

"There is nothing to see. I'm wrapped in bandages."

"Then I'll look at it when it's time to change the dressing," he insisted.

"Be my guest," I answered, suddenly feeling tired. I closed my eyes and was barely aware of someone covering me with a light blanket before I sank into a deep, welcome sleep.

Chapter Twenty-three

Still adjusting his necktie and shaking his head in disbelief, Dr. Marten walked out of the men's room at the Jose Martí International Airport in Havana. He had been ordered to strip off his clothes and submit to a thorough search before leaving Cuba. The search had been bad enough, but as he was leaving the room, a militiaman had pulled his gold watch off his wrist. No gold or precious stones will leave Cuba, he had been told. They can have that too, he thought, as he paced nervously outside the lady's room where Elena was being searched.

The two militiawomen in charge of searching the female passengers were both middle-aged. The older of the two, a tall, rough-looking woman with a brusque, almost masculine manner, pulled the curtain which divided the room into two cubicles. Looking maliciously at Elena, she said in a low, menacing tone, "Girl, take off your clothes, and I mean all your clothes, and lie down there." She pointed to a high table of the type used for medical examination.

Struggling to maintain her composure, Elena obeyed as the militia woman stared unabashedly. The sight of the young woman naked, so beautiful and innocent, sent an electrifying shock throughout the brutal woman's body. She felt an irresistible desire to subjugate her by force and then touch her at will. The risk of getting caught didn't seem to matter; in fact, it aroused her more. Under the guise of searching her for hidden valuables, the militiawoman began to fondle Elena's body. Horrified and repulsed, Elena screamed and tried to sit up, only to have a huge hand clamped over her mouth as the brutal woman pushed her backwards onto the table.

At the sound of the struggle, the other militiawoman pulled open the curtain and said in a voice that trembled with restrained anger, "Marta, you stop that. Have you no shame? Can't you see she is just a child?"

"Child? No child is built like that." The depraved woman turned to Elena and jeered, "Get dressed, little girl, and get out of here."

Shocked and humiliated but determined to hide her ordeal from her father, Elena left the room with quiet dignity.

"Are you well, Elena?" Dr. Marten asked, alarmed at the unusual pallor of his daughter's face.

"Fine, Daddy, just fine. I'm just a little nervous. Come, let's get in line."

"One last check point to go through and we'll be on our way," Dr. Marten said, putting his arm around Elena's shoulders. "I'll bet your mother and brother are already at the airport waiting for us."

"I only wish Nicky could have left already," Elena said, her eyes filling with tears.

"Don't worry, he'll be out soon. You'll see," Dr. Marten said reassuringly.

"Oh, Jesus, help us. Please help us," Elena prayed as they approached the G-2 checkpoint.

"Your passports," demanded the uniformed G-2 agent without taking his cigar out of his mouth.

"Here they are," Dr. Marten replied, handing him the documents.

Slowly, the man ran his dirty finger down a long list of names, stopping occasionally to wet his thumb before flipping a page. At last he looked up at Dr. Marten and said with obvious hostility, "Your daughter can board the plane. You . . . Marten . . . step aside."

Elena could not believe that what she feared the most was now upon her. At a signal from the G-2 agent, two militiamen had stepped forward and aimed their weapons at her father. "No," she screamed, "you can't take him." Arms reached out to restrain her. She felt her legs folding beneath her, the building seemed to be rolling around, and then darkness.

When she opened her eyes forty minutes later, she was in a plane flying over the Straits of Florida. "My father," she screamed in panic. "Where is my father?" Then the terrible memory flooded over her. "Oh, my God," she sobbed, "they've taken my father."

Chapter Twenty-four

The ringing of the phone woke me up. I looked at my watch and I couldn't believe it—it was almost 5 P.M. Nicky, who was sleeping on a chair with his feet propped on the couch, jolted upright. After three rings, the sound abruptly stopped.

"Who could that be?" Nicky asked.

"We'll know soon; they'll call again."

Within a minute the annoying sound began again. Nicky handed me the phone, and I picked up the receiver and listened without saying a word. On the other end of the line Lourdes' voice sounded worried.

"Carlos, is that you?"

"Of course."

"My flight will be leaving Miami in a few minutes; I just called to ask you a favor."

"Just ask."

"I have a friend who is going to drop by my house tonight, and she doesn't know a soul in beautiful Havana. Would you introduce her to some of your friends?"

"I'd be glad to. What's her name?"

"Judy... Judy Anderson. I'm sorry, but I have to run. I'll see you soon."

"I hope so. Bon voyage," I said.

"Who was that?" Nicky asked.

"Lourdes. She's sending a friend, probably another stewardess, with a message. It has to be extremely important for her to go through all this trouble."

"When is she coming?"

"Tonight, but where is Jorge?" I asked.

"Sleeping in the bedroom after eating everything he could find," Nicky replied.

"Before we send him back to the academy, we must make sure that the G-2 doesn't suspect him."

"He called his home; his parents said no one has asked for him."

"That's a good sign," I admitted, "but not enough. I'll try to find out more. I'm worried that Lourdes' call might have something to do with last night's outing."

"Shall I wake him up?"

"No, he needs his sleep. Let's have something to drink."

"Would Manzanilla be okay?" Nicky asked, pulling a bottle of Spanish sherry from a wood-carved portable bar.

"It'll do just fine." I sat down on the couch and watched Nicky pour the amber liquid into two crystal glasses. "How have you been feeling lately?" I asked, trying to sound casual.

He finished filling the glasses and replaced the bottle in the bar before answering. "Do you mean the kind of depression I suffered at the Marten's?"

"What else?"

"I think it was a freaky, isolated letdown of my strength. I won't even discuss it. It won't happen again."

"Fine, but I am still going to give you the sedative injection that Dr. Marten prescribed."

"I don't care one way or the other. Speaking of the Martens, they left this morning on a PanAm flight to Miami. They might even have been on the same plane with Lourdes."

"That would be quite a coincidence, but they would never guess that they have mutual friends."

"Complicated friends."

"I'll say, but here . . . to friends," I said, raising my glass.

"To good friends," Nicky replied, touching my glass with his own.

After I had finished briefing Nicky about the last evening's events, I picked up the phone and called my home. My mother answered.

"I was hoping it would be you, Carlitos. I don't know why, but lately you have been constantly in my mind, even more than usual."

"Nothing to worry about, Mamy. I'll be home for dinner tomorrow night. And, by the way, tell Dad to start making the arrangements for our vacation."

"Well, that's good news."

"It sure is. About tomorrow's dinner, I might bring a friend with me."

"Who?"

"You'll see; it's a surprise. I can only tell you that it's someone you like."

"Come early, if you can. Oh, I almost forgot—Lieutenant Nodal has been calling you since early this morning."

"I'll call him back now. If anyone needs to get in touch with me, I'll be either here or at Tony's, but don't give out the numbers. You call me."

"Of course."

"Hasta mañana, Mamy."

"Hasta mañana, mi hijo."

I put the phone down, and for a brief moment I stared despondently at the tile floor.

"You look distraught. Who are you supposed to call right away—Lucifer?" Nicky asked.

"Almost, although at times I don't know."

"Who, for crying out loud, who?"

"Miguel Nodal."

"He *is* Lucifer," Jorge said, coming out of the bedroom yawning and stretching his arms.

"I'm not so sure at times," I answered.

"I am sure, and worse than being Lucifer, he doesn't like me," Jorge retorted.

The doorbell sounded—loud and menacing to our ears.

"Jorge, see who it is. Nicky, get ready," I whispered. I pulled the BAR from under the couch and handed it to him. Under the pillow, I was holding my .45.

"Who is it, Jorge?" I asked.

"A pretty thing in a PanAm uniform."

"Nicky, you go into the bedroom. Jorge, let her in. We are expecting her."

Jorge opened the door and escorted a tall slender blond woman into the living room. She had high cheek bones and incredibly blue eyes. She was undoubtedly the loveliest woman I had ever seen. Looking at Jorge, she said, "Carlos Dumas?"

"I am Carlos," I said, standing up and leaning on the sofa for support. "Please join us."

She walked toward me and extended her hand. "I am Judy Anderson," she said, as her eyes considered me thoughtfully.

I smiled, took her hand and said, "Lourdes called to tell me that you were coming. Could I offer you a glass of sherry before you tell me what our friend has in mind?"

"Yes, please. It has been a grueling day," she replied, her excellent Spanish flavored with an oddly appealing American accent. She sat in front of me, her hands on her lap, holding the glass that Jorge had brought her. She can't be much older than twenty-one, I thought.

"Carlos," she said gravely, "I have bad news for your friend Nicky."

"Would you mind if I call him to hear what you have to say?"

"Not at all. This isn't my usual route, and I'll be leaving in a few hours—not to return. I'm not afraid of getting involved."

"No need to call me," Nick said as he came out of the bedroom. He went directly to Judy and asked, "Is Elena all right?"

"She is," Judy replied, "but not so her father. Lourdes was the stewardess on the plane on which Elena left Cuba this morning. Her father was not allowed to leave, and Elena fainted when she saw the militiamen leading him away. When she started to regain consciousness, she was given an injection of some sort of sedative and then carried aboard the plane."

"Where is her father now?" Nicky asked in a choked voice.

"We don't know for sure, but Lourdes thinks he was arrested by the G-2."

Jorge had been standing behind Nicky, and now he placed a hand on his friend's shoulder. "Judy," he asked, "how in the world did Lourdes make the connection between Nicky and Elena?"

"When Elena regained consciousness, Lourdes tried to help her, for she was very close to total emotional collapse. It was when she learned Elena's name that Lourdes remembered Nicky

Escape from Castro

talking on the phone to his girlfriend... Elena. It wasn't difficult to figure out the rest." Distress stamped on her face, Judy reached for her glass and took a sip of Manzanilla. Nicky picked up the bottle and began to refill her glass, but she placed a hand over it and said softly, "No thank you. I must be back to work in just a few hours."

Making an obvious effort to keep his voice steady, Nicky asked, "Could you tell me what happened when she arrived in Miami?"

"Lourdes stayed with her until she was reunited with her mother and brother. I witnessed that meeting, and it was an incredibly sad scene." She got up and said in her charming accent, "Now I must go."

I got slowly to my feet. I hated for her to leave and I hated myself for being so selfish. Throughout her account of the Marten's ordeal, I had kept thinking how much I would love to have the chance to know her better. I couldn't help but feel extremely attracted to this beautiful woman whom I would probably never see again.

Judy offered me her hand but changed her mind and kissed me on the check instead. She turned to Nicky and embraced him. There were tears in her eyes when I opened the door and watched her go.

After Judy left, Jorge went to the bedroom to make a few phone calls, hoping to clarify his situation. He did not have much time left to decide whether or not it was safe to return to the academy. A wrong decision could very well be fatal to him—and probably to us too.

Nicky sat leaning forward, his hands covering his face. He had not changed positions since Judy's departure. "Here," I said, handing him a cup of espresso, "Freshly made."

He lifted his head and took the cup. "I did this to them, you know," he said. "It was my staying at their house that did it."

"You don't know that, Nicky. In fact, if that were the case, the G-2 would have apprehended Elena too. As soon as Jorge is finished on the phone, I'll call Tony's contact in the G-2. He must know something by now."

"The phone is all yours," said Jorge, obviously having overheard my remark as he walked into the room. "I just hope you have better luck than I did; I wasn't able to find out a thing."

After an hour of trying to reach Tony's contact, we still had not tracked him down. I finally gave up trying, afraid to make the agent too conspicuous. Instead, I called Tony and told him that before the day was over, we needed to know where Dr. Marten was being held and why. It was not an easy assignment, but Tony took it on gracefully, saying that he would get back to us as soon as possible.

It was very late in the evening when he called, but he had what we wanted—a report straight from the G-2 headquarters. Dr. Marten, it seemed, had been accused of counter-revolutionary activities by several of his students. In addition, a neighbor's son had reported him for refusing to place a pro-communist bumper sticker on his car. There was no connection to anything else, Tony had emphasized.

Nicky had followed the conversation on the bedroom extension, and now he came into the living room—relief written clearly on his face. Standing by the patio door and looking out onto the garden, he said, "I guess you were right, Carlos. It looks like I wasn't the cause of his arrest. But now what? What can we do?"

"Now," I replied, "we'll try to help him—although at this point, I can't see how. Tony's contact says that friends of Marten's have been inquiring about his whereabouts, and G-2 is denying his arrest."

"That's sure isn't a good sign," said Nicky, turning around to look at me.

"No . . . no, it isn't," I replied.

Chapter Twenty-five

Just a few blocks away from Lourdes' home in Miramar, the Calvary of Dr. Marten was taking place. When Elena's plane was landing at Miami International Airport, her father, his hands handcuffed behind his back, was being escorted through the main gate of the Political Police Headquarters at Fifth Avenue and Fourteenth Street. After being forced to turn over his wallet and all the contents of his pockets, Dr. Marten was thrown into a small cell in the back of the building. The cell had low bunks attached to the wall and a toilet behind a partition. Its only occupant, a young student leader, stuck his head out of his rack to see who the new arrival was. This young man, Emilio Carrero, had been accused of conspiring with the imperialists against the Marxist-Leninist government.

In the beginning Emilio had been a strong supporter of the Revolution, especially after his father, a personal friend of Fidel, had been killed in the Escambray Mountains during a surprise raid of the rebel camp by the Batista forces. Emilio, a brilliant student in his sophomore year at the University of Havana School of Mechanical Engineering, had been able to leave the country and go into exile in Costa Rica. After the triumph of the Revolution, he had returned to Cuba and assumed a prominent position in the University of Havana Student Association. His public statements against communism had infuriated Castro to the point of threatening him personally—first with expulsion from the University and later with prosecution. But Emilio, a slim young man in delicate health, was not easily intimidated. He had continued to alert his fellow students to the unequivocal signs of communist infiltration in the higher levels of government.

Finally, one morning at about 0400, he had been arrested at his home. When his terrified mother had pleaded in tears with the G-2 agents, she had been assured that Emilio would be questioned and then returned home in a matter of two or three hours. Two weeks later, she had not even been notified where her son was being held.

Now, after two weeks of solitary confinement, Emilio welcomed having a cellmate. As the door clanged shut behind Dr. Marten, Emilio jumped off his bunk and extended his hand to the new prisoner. "I am Emilio Carrero," he said with a warm smile.

The doctor shook his hand and responded, "Marcelo Marten. I have seen your picture in the newspaper several times."

"I'm afraid that the next time you see my picture in the paper, it will be under a different heading," Emilio replied resignedly.

Close to midnight, a militiamen came to Dr. Marten's cell in the G-2 house and transferred him to a very small soundproof room. A two-way mirror above a sink covered most of one of the walls. Dr. Marten was stripped of his clothes and left waiting— alone and cold. As a medical doctor, he knew only too well that this favorite communist tactic of keeping prisoners naked was one of the most effective of the psychological weapons used to demoralize and break the spirit of political prisoners.

For two long hours he waited, agonizing, as he tried to figure out why he had been arrested. Finally, he heard loud steps approaching the interrogation room. *At least I don't know Nicky's whereabouts,* he thought. *That's one piece of information they won't be able to get out of me, if that is the reason that they have arrested me.*

Three men, a G-2 official and two militiamen, burst into the room. It was the G-2 agent who spoke. "You have been accused of being an enemy of the State. You are known to be conspiring with the imperialists to destroy our Revolution."

"That is just not true. I have contributed great sums of money to the Revolution at the time when it was needed the most."

"You have, eh?" the agent questioned cynically.

"Yes, I have. And what have I done to be humiliated like this? Who has pressed charges against me?"

"You refused to have a revolutionary bumper sticker on your Cadillac, didn't you?" the interrogator asked, ignoring the protests and stressing the word 'Cadillac.'

"That was not a revolutionary sticker I refused. It was a pro-communist one that read, 'If Fidel is communist, put me on the list.' Well, I will not be put on any list of communists," Dr. Marten replied with bitterness. He had just realized that his accuser was undoubtedly Gilberto, the farmer's son, the same young man who had been the object of his wife's affection and generosity over the years. He had received gifts of money, special presents on holidays, and all of Marco's outgrown clothing.

"You have also been accused by students who say that you use your podium at the University to preach pro-imperialist ideas," the G-2 man shouted at him.

"If I made any comments they were against the evils of communism, and those are many."

At this point, the interrogator rose to his feet and shouted, "Basta, basta. Take this tool of the imperialists away."

The next morning a newspaper was delivered to Dr. Marten's cell. On the front page of *Revolucion* he saw his own picture next to one of Emilio. Under the photographs the caption read, "Agents of the imperialists caught conspiring against the State."

At 0900 both Dr. Marten and Emilio were shoved into a van and driven to La Cabaña, a fortress constructed in the 1700s on a rocky hill at the entrance to Havana's bay. There, Fidel's firing squads were kept busy in the fortress's deep moats seven nights a week.

Dr. Marten and Emilio were taken to a receiving station where they were issued prisoner's uniforms with a large "P" stenciled on the back. They were told that their clothes would be returned to them when and if they were released. It was common knowledge that the guards distributed the prisoners' clothing among themselves as soon as the political prisoners left the room.

On their way to their assigned galera, large rooms once used by the Spaniards to store ammunition and food, now converted into cells, they crossed the central patio to the stares and shouted insults at the common prisoners. Emilio noticed that one inmate, who was wearing a T-shirt decorated with a picture of Fidel, was attempting to make eye contact. Emilio stepped up the pace in an effort to catch up with Dr. Marten a few feet ahead of him. The escorting guard, an older man who was annoyed at being rushed, pushed Emilio back with his baton and barked, "What's the fucking hurry, punk? You'll be here for a long time, that is if you're lucky enough not to end up in front of the firing squad."

Just before they arrived at the galera, the inmate, who had been following them, held his crotch in his hands and said in a low, mocking tone, "Hey, baby-face, don't be scared, I'll be gentle tonight." Then he broke into a sadistic, toothless laugh.

Emilio's body tensed, more from disgust than fear. He knew very well that the political prisoners were kept apart from the common criminals. It was the army defectors who suffered the horrors of sexual assault before being returned to their units. The Fidelistas hoped the panic created among the new recruits would reduce the ever rising number of deserters.

Once inside the galera, Emilio loosened up as some of the political prisoners came to offer assistance and comfort. It was then that Dr. Marten and Emilio learned of the courageous way that the political prisoners faced the firing squads. In the middle of the night, they were told, the guards came to take away those who were going to die. The sound of the iron gates opening and closing would announce who had been taken out never to return. In the silence that followed the closing of the last gate, cries like "Viva Christ King" or "Down with Communism" would ring out in the night, only to be drowned out by the barrage of shots fired by the squads.

Lately, the soldiers had begun gagging or taping the mouths of those about to be shot. They feared that the executioners would be affected by the incredible testimonials of courage and faith that their victims shouted out with their last breaths of life.

Among the political prisoners who came to greet them was a young black man with an air of dignity and strength who came forward, shook Marten's hand, and said, "I'm not a bit surprised to see you here, Doctor. You never looked to me like one who would fit their mold."

Dr. Marten looked inquisitively at the young man, trying to place him.

"Don't worry, Doctor, there were so many of us in your pathology class, and I wasn't one of the brightest. It's hard to remember one of the crowd."

"Don't pay any attention, Dr. Marten," a blond political prisoner whom the others called the Americano said. "Dr. Rivera is a very special person. There's no one among us who is not indebted to him."

Uncomfortable at his friend's praise, Dr. Rivera shifted the attention back to the newcomers. "Doctor, I heard about your son's arrest. What happened to him?"

"After they harassed and tortured him for two days, I was finally able to pull him out of the G-2."

"And where is he now?" Rivera asked with concern.

"He is out of the country."

"Good for him. Times are changing rapidly and for the worst."

"You bet they are," interrupted the blond man. "I'll tell you something hard to believe, but it's the gospel truth . . ."

"Not now, Americano," said Rivera. "We're about to have company." He signalled with a discrete movement of his eyes toward the two guards closing in on them, their bloody batons poised to strike. "Hurry, let's split up before they get here." The prisoners quickly moved off in several directions.

"What the hell is going on here? You bastards think this is your old country club? Break up this damned meeting before I break your heads," the taller of the two guards yelled as he pushed around a couple of the older political prisoners left behind because they were too old and out of shape to move fast. Dr. Rivera stood his ground, untouched. Even the guards seemed to have a special respect for him.

Finally the guards, satisfied that the so-called meeting had been dissolved, went on about their business of making the lives of the counter-revolutionaries as miserable as possible.

Marten and Emilio joined Dr. Rivera and the Americano and headed for the filthy dining hall and the daily ration of watered down spaghetti. None of them spoke much, afraid of being overheard by the many stool pigeons anxious to make points.

That evening the Americano ate his last meal; Emilio and

Dr. Marten never got to know what he had called the gospel truth. In the early hours of the next morning the guards came for him. The Americano refused to be blindfolded and was riddled by bullets next to his friend, Dr. Rivera.

◆ ◆ ◆

When night fell, Emilio said, "Doctor, you had better take the lower bunk and try to get some sleep. It has been a long day." For Emilio, sleep was a long time in coming. He had not been assigned a defense counselor as Dr. Marten had, a sure sign, he now thought, that he would be one of those dragged out to the wall in the middle of the night.

At about 0200, Emilio was jolted awake by the sound of the metal gates being pushed open. He felt his heart begin to beat so rapidly that it seemed about to jump out of his chest. Soon he heard the sound again—the gates were being slammed closed. He then relaxed, and his heart slowed down a little. He thought of the courageous patriots about to face the firing squads and felt ashamed of his fear. Holding his rosary in his hands, he prayed in a low, choked voice, tears streaming down his cheeks, "Jesus mio, give me the faith to resist and the strength to die with courage."

Emilio lived to see another day.

Chapter Twenty-six

I spent the night on the couch and Nicky and Jorge slept in the bedroom. I had felt very tired and not wanted to move. We had set the alarm for 0430. Convinced at last that he was not suspected of any wrong doing, Jorge had decided to return to the academy. Nicky was going to drop him at the terminal so that he could catch the early morning bus to Mariel. Liberty for the senior class expired at 2200, but Jorge's liberty had been extended to 0630 to allow him time to prepare the boats for Monday's regatta.

As usual, I woke up before the alarm had a chance to go off. I lay awake going over the day's plans, trying to reassure myself that all would go well. The fifteen minute ride to the terminal worried me the most. At this early hour, a car with two young men in it might easily arouse the suspicions of an overzealous G-2 patrol. Even a routine search could lead to complete disaster. But there didn't seem to be any other way, so I decided to keep my misgivings to myself.

As I was about to wake up Nick and Jorge, I heard them talking in the bedroom, followed by the sound of water running in the bathroom. It looks like I'm not the only one who doesn't need an alarm clock, I thought as I got stiffly to my feet. I heard Jorge laughing as if he were getting ready to go to the beach. With his light-hearted personality, he was the perfect companion for Nicky in these difficult times. I was amused and gratified by the close companionship that had developed between the two of them.

At 0530 Nicky left to get my car, and I walked Jorge to the door. Standing on the porch, we shook hands. Without letting go of my hand, Jorge looked me straight in the eyes, and suddenly we both realized the terrible chance we were taking. "I'm risking not only my own life, but yours and Nicky's as well. I have no right to do this. I'll stay if you think I should," he said with doubt in his voice.

"You'll do exactly what you have planned; we can take care of ourselves. But later if you change your mind, remember that wherever I am, there will be a place for you. I wanted to look after you, but it turned out to be the other way around on more than one occasion." As I spoke, I watched his face turn pale. He started to speak, then changed his mind, and looking away from me with difficulty, he turned and walked to the car.

After Jorge got in, Nicky stuck his head out the window and shouted, "I'm taking him all the way to Mariel."

"Nicky, don't!" I yelled, raising my right hand to signal a stop. If they heard me, it didn't make an impression on them, and before I knew it, they were gone. I rushed inside the house to get ready to follow them in Lourdes' car. "I won't sit here while they take all the chances--wound or no wound," I said out loud to myself. Picking up Lourdes' car keys and my pistol, I opened the door and was about to leave the house when the phone began to ring. Two rings—then stop—a call from home. I thought of ignoring the call, but it suddenly occurred to me that my parents would never call at this extremely early hour unless they had very important news for me. Resignedly, I picked up the receiver and dialed home.

My father's anxious voice answered on the first ring, "Carlos?"

"Yes, Dad. What's the matter?" I asked, too worried and too much in a hurry for niceties.

"Son, Lieutenant Nodal just called and left a message for you to call him immediately. He said there is a state of emergency and that he had been given orders to get in touch with you right away."

"Don't worry, Dad. We have one of these alerts every other day. I'll take care of it," I replied, trying to sound positive.

"Carlitos, this sounded different. Call him, and when you can,

Escape from Castro

let us know about you," he said in a voice filled with concern.

"I will. Tell Mamy not to worry. I still plan to be there for dinner tonight. Adiós."

"Adiós and please be careful," he replied.

I hung up and quickly dialed Nodal's number. He answered with an abrupt, "Hola."

"Miguel, what's going on?"

"Lots of things, Carlos, and none of them good. Please don't ask me any questions this time and do exactly what I tell you. Forget about your fall, get in your car, and report to headquarters right away." His voice was edgy, but not without an underlying friendliness.

"Not to ask questions, that's difficult, but I'll do as you say."

"All right, I'll tell you as much as I know," he replied.

That he'll never do, I thought as I listened carefully.

"There is a general recall—just in the Navy. It looks like some of our so-called shipmates have been doing some backstabbing to the interests of the Revolution."

"Anyone I know?"

"Your blond friend—among others," he answered coldly.

I stood motionless, the receiver still in my hand, the dial tone echoing in the quiet room. They are heading straight into the lion's den; they are as good as dead, I thought with a despair I had never known existed. I need to think and think fast, I said to myself, coming out of the initial impact enough to hang up the phone. But what . . . what to do? They would be heading up the road to the academy in less than twenty-five minutes. "I must act now," I said out loud with terrible desperation. Then I shouted, "Of course! Carlos, you moron, why didn't you think of it before?"

I grabbed the phone and dialed information. The operator seemed to take forever, but finally the monotonous voice on the other end of the line replied, "Chief Alberto Miranda's number is 371 642."

"Thank you," I said and before the operator could answer, I hung up and dialed with fingers made inept by frantic eagerness.

The call was answered by a cheerful female voice. "Chief Miranda just left for the academy."

"How long ago?"

"No more than a minute or two ago."

"Please, this is Lieutenant Dumas. Could you go outside? Maybe he hasn't left yet. This is terribly important."

"I'll be glad to try," she answered.

I looked at my watch. The second hand seemed to be telling me, "Hurry! Hurry! There isn't much time, and I can't stop."

"This is Chief Miranda," said a friendly voice.

"Thank God!"

"What? What did you say?"

"Nothing ... nothing. Chief Miranda, this is Lieutenant Dumas. Listen carefully. Go to the intersection of the academy road and the highway. Wait there for my car—the Opel. You will recognize the passengers. Tell them to go back immediately—that it is a matter of life and death—theirs. I can't say anymore—except that I'll be in debt to you forever if you do what I have asked you."

"You don't need to say anymore, Lieutenant. As always, I am at your service. Adiós."

"Adiós, y gracias," I replied. I put down the receiver, feeling utterly exhausted. My back was wet with blood; the physical exertion must have reopened the wound. One more thing to worry about, I thought. Broken bones from a fall do not produce blood. I would have to stop that bleeding before reporting to headquarters. I went to the bathroom and was searching the medicine cabinet for bandages when I heard the front door being opened. I took out my pistol and got ready for the worst.

"Carlos?" I heard Nicky's familiar voice calling me.

"Where are you?"

I stepped into the hall and saw Nicky heading into the bedroom. "Nicky! I can't believe it. Where is Jorge?" I said, still stunned by this incredible good fortune.

"He's outside in the car. I'm afraid I forgot my ID card. Don't worry, we'll be on our way in a matter of minutes."

"No, you won't!" I exclaimed. "Call Jorge inside right now. The G-2 is after him."

"What? Do they know about the National Museum?" Nicky asked.

"Don't waste time asking questions. Bring him in, and I'll explain to both of you at the same time. I must leave almost immediately."

After Jorge and Nicky had come in and closed the door behind them, I told them about my conversation with Nodal. They sat silently for a moment, and then Jorge, sounding almost casual, said, "You know, I really didn't want to go back to the academy. I should be grateful that they made up my mind for me . . ." He was interrupted by the ringing of the telephone.

"Let's answer it; we have nothing to lose," I said as I reached for the receiver. I immediately recognized Quesada's voice on the other end of the line. "Arturo!" I said. "I thought you'd be . . ."

"Well," he broke in, "I *have* been kind of slow in leaving. But I called in case you had changed your mind about coming with me to visit my Uncle."

"When are you leaving?" I asked, wondering what in the world was keeping him in Cuba—away from his uncle—Uncle Sam.

"Right now. If you'd like to join me, be at my place as fast as you can."

"Give me thirty minutes."

"Thirty minutes? You've got them, but if you don't make it, call our friends and ask to speak to the cultural attache. His name is Armstrong. Just tell him that I sent you. I must go now," he said and I heard the phone click.

Before I could speak, Jorge asked, "Was that Arturo Quesada?"

"It sure was, and he has your ticket to freedom. He is leaving and has room for one more, and that's you."

"But how is he going to get out?"

"I don't know how he is getting out, but I do know how he *isn't,* and that is by the airport."

"I'm ready; I trust his judgement," Jorge said eagerly.

Then it occurred to me that Jorge might believe that I didn't want him to come with us, and I felt guilty. Speaking with a strain of urgency in my voice, I said, "Jorge, you're hot, and you will be taking a terrible chance every hour you remain in Cuba. I really believe that Quesada is your best bet, but it's your decision. You always have a place with Nicky and me on the boat."

"I agree that this is my best bet. I already told you that I'm ready for whatever Arturo has planned," he replied, sounding impatient.

"Then let's go. Give me the keys," I said to Nicky.

"Wait," Nicky exclaimed, turning me around to get a better look at my back. "You have blood all over your shirt."

"The jacket will cover it. If we don't leave immediately, Quesada will be gone. I'll go home, change bandages, and get into uniform after I drop Jorge off. Nicky, you stay here," I ordered as Jorge and I rushed out the door.

But when I reached the car, Nicky was right behind me. "I asked you to stay here," I said without much conviction.

"And I say I won't. Give me the keys. I'll drive unless you want the wound to open all the way."

"Oh, hell, let's go," I replied as I surrendered the keys.

◆ ◆ ◆

The morning traffic was already getting heavier, and Nicky was driving as carefully as possible, taking no chances. If only we could make it on time, I thought, at least one of us would be on his way. As for now, I sure didn't like traveling with three of us in the car: too many, too conspicuous—asking for trouble. We crossed the Almendares River and entered the El Vedado district. Just a few more blocks, I thought. I wanted to tell Nicky to speed it up, but I knew that would be stupid.

We had been traveling in disconcerting silence for too long. This is no good, I thought. "Jorge," I said confidently, "as soon as you get to the United States, if that's where you are going, try to get word to us that you have arrived safely."

"Sure, Carlos, and don't worry, I'll be careful. You too—please don't linger around here. Get out while you can. I'll be waiting for you."

"There's Arturo," I said, spotting Quesada sitting in an outdoor cafe across from his apartment building. "Let's ignore him," I cautioned. "He's seen us. We'll drop Jorge off around the corner." Quesada's not as foolhardy as he might seem, it occurred to me. He's in the ideal spot—blending in with the crowd and with a perfect command of the entrance of his building.

We rounded the corner and pulled to the side of the road. "Be careful with Lucifer," Jorge said, referring to Nodal. Then he got out of the car and started to walk toward the cafe. We waited to make sure that he was not followed. Just before disappearing around the corner, he turned to wave to us, his face illuminated by the usual engaging smile.

With a strange feeling of emptiness and once again in near silence, we drove to my parents' home.

"How is your back?" Nicky asked, as we entered Calle A and began the rather bumpy ride over its cobblestone surface.

"It's fine. I think I've stopped bleeding. And how are you doing?"

"Much better now that Jorge is with Quesada. He's such a character. I sure hope he makes it. Do you think he will?"

"I wouldn't have let him go if I didn't think that the odds were good. He and Quesada will be following Calderon's plan, and that's about as much of a guarantee as you can get." As we approached my home, I added, "Don't bother to pull in. I'll be leaving right away."

"Look," Nicky said, pointing to the empty garage, "the Mercedes is out."

"Good. That means my parents aren't home. They must not know about my wound. Come on, let's go in."

Nicky and I went straight to the living room where I picked up the phone and dialed Chief Miranda's number. I asked his wife to send word to him that there had been a change in plans and that he should not wait for my car.

As I was hanging up, Lucila came into the room, drying her hands on her apron. "Oh, it's you," she said, sounding rather disapproving. But when she saw Nicky, her frown melted into a smile. "Señor Berrocal," she exclaimed, "it's been a long time."

"Much too long," Nicky replied.

"Lucila, Nicky is going to be with us for a couple of days," I said. With obvious pleasure in her voice, she answered, "I'll make sure to arrange your bedroom so that he'll be comfortable."

"I wish you were that interested in my comfort," I told her jokingly. What was it with this punk, I asked myself, that he had such an effect on people?

"Don't pay any attention, Lucila," Nicky said. "You know how he loves to gripe. Come on, Carlos," he added as he grabbed me by the right arm and steered me toward the stairs.

"You have to change and hurry out of here, or you'll be late."

As we walked up the stairs, he whispered to me, "The blood was beginning to show through your jacket."

"As long as it doesn't happen while I'm in headquarters...." I answered.

A half hour later when Nicky and I walked out the front door, I was feeling comfortable and dry. He had done a fine job of changing the bandages, and luckily my uniform concealed the dressing completely. By the time I climbed into my car, I was already perspiring. In spite of an overcast sky and a fairly stiff breeze, the high humidity was making the morning sticky and unpleasant.

"Are you sure that you don't want me to drive you to headquarters?" Nicky asked.

"I'm sure. I'll be back as soon as I can. If I don't call you within two hours, you must go back to Lourdes' place immediately. If something happens to me, call my cousin as we have agreed."

"Be careful, Carlos. I agree with Jorge; Nodal is not to be trusted," Nicky said as I rolled down the window, wishing that I had air conditioning in my Opel.

"Just remember that he warned us about Jorge. That phone call undoubtedly saved Jorge's life and probably ours. The question is—did he warn us intentionally."

"He is complicated, isn't he?" Nicky replied.

I started the engine and reached for my sunglasses. Before pulling away, I said, "I'll be able to tell better about him before this day is over."

"Ciao, Carlos. Buona fortuna."

Chapter Twenty-seven

In order to avoid the heavy downtown traffic, I drove to Navy Headquarters via the Malecon. My mind was restless, filled with more apprehension and uncertainty than I wanted to admit. Over and over, I thought about the close comradeship between Nodal and myself that had survived in spite of our political differences. There was no denying that a special type of bond existed between the members of a Navy Underwater Team, brought on, I suppose, by working in hostile and dangerous environments. I remembered the many times we had shared bread at his table and mine. Could the poisons of communism and ambition have finally taken their toll, and was he now setting me up? I honestly did not know.

Even the weather seemed threatening. A strong north wind was whipping up the surf, producing huge waves that kept rolling over the seawall and drenching the passing cars with salt water. I turned on my windshield wipers and prayed that the weather would improve in case we had to get out soon. The *Sirius* just couldn't take this kind of punishment. As I approached headquarters, I noticed an unusually large number of official vehicles in the traffic around me. I parked on a side street and started to walk toward the main entrance. A sailor, overtaking me on the sidewalk, saluted sharply and said, "By your leave, Sir."

"Very well," I replied returning the salute. "Do you know what all this bustle is about?" I asked.

"Yes, Sir. Fidel Castro is inside visiting with Comandante Castiñeiras."

"Thank you," I answered, thinking only that this was going to be an interesting morning. I only hoped it would not prove to be too interesting.

The duty guards at the main entrance, dressed in their warm, but sharp looking uniforms, presented arms as I climbed the steps and entered the quarterdeck. I reported to the officer of the day and was immediately directed to the Operations and Plans Office. The minute I stepped out of the elevator onto the fourth deck, I noticed an unusually high tempo of activity. The passageways were crowded with unfamiliar army types carrying automatic weapons and talking in low voices. The operations duty officer spotted me in the crowd and came over. "Stick around," he said in an impersonal tone, "Comandante Castiñeiras is having a small ceremony in his office the minute Castro leaves the building, and he wants you to attend."

"Roger," I replied, turning around to see who had just placed a hand on my shoulder.

"Oh, it's you," I said stiffly.

"Relax, Carlos. You look pale and tense. That must have been quite a fall," answered Miguel Nodal.

Regaining my composure, I replied, "Not half as bad as it could have been. I may not be looking my best, but you surely are. I haven't seen you in blues in a long time. What's the occasion?"

"You'll see in a few minutes," he replied. Before I could ask him to explain, someone shouted, "Attention on deck." As we all stood at attention, Castro and Castiñeiras came out of the operations conference room, followed by a handful of army and navy officers. I did a double take. I couldn't believe my eyes. Was I hallucinating? Among those following Castiñeiras, dressed in full uniform and smiling confidently, was Luis Calderon.

Castiñeiras gave the order, "Carry on," and everyone relaxed and the humming of low voices once again filled the room.

Miguel turned to me and said, "I believe Castro is coming this way."

"Hell yes, he sure is," I muttered. Castro was without a doubt walking toward us, his cold, expressionless eyes fixed on mine.

My throat felt dry. I tried to swallow, but couldn't. My distress must have been apparent, for Miguel threw me a hard look and asked, "Are you all right?"

"Of course," I heard myself answer in a surprisingly confident tone. Then, before we knew it, he was standing next to us.

"Como estan ustedes?" Fidel asked Miguel and me.

"Fine, Comandante," Miguel replied after we had both returned to attention with a soft clicking of our heels.

"Perhaps some day soon, we will make another fishing trip, but this time we will stay on the north coast," Fidel said to me. Then, with an ambiguous smile, he added, "Only not too far north." Before I could answer, he was gone, now escorted by Castiñeiras and the usual entourage. Calderon stayed behind, absorbed in conversation with Comandate Pinto. I didn't think that he had seen me, but as he passed close to us, he looked in our direction, and with the faintest trace of a smile on his face, gave me a subtle wink.

"What was all that about fishing trips?" asked the operations duty officer. He had always been rather aloof, but was now obviously consumed with curiosity. I ignored the question, but Miguel decided to answer. "Fidel was referring to a fishing trip that Carlos and I took with him on a forty foot yacht—about a year ago."

"How come? How did it happen?" questioned the persistent fool, utterly fascinated that we had once been fishing with our great leader.

"We were in Barlovento checking over the confiscated yachts when Fidel showed up and asked if the yacht we were on could be ready for a fishing trip that evening..." As I listened to Miguel satisfying the duty officer's curiosity, some of the experiences of that trip began flashing vividly across my mind. It was during those days at sea, living at close quarters with Fidel, that I realized that I could never fit into Fidel's Cuba. He had been very friendly to me, so it wasn't anything personal. Yet, by the end of the trip, I had a clear idea of how Castro planned to use his socialist beliefs to suffocate all freedom in Cuba.

Fidel had been scheduled to begin the fishing trip at about 2100, but he had not shown up until 0200 the next day. He brought with him Oswaldo Dorticos, the appointed President of Cuba;

Celia Sanchez, his girlfriend/advisor; a few bodyguards, all very young; and a professional photographer. We sailed around the western tip of Cuba and headed east—never farther than a few miles from the Cuban southern coast. One of our coast guard cutters, the CG 107, commanded by another anti-communist young officer, Ensign Luis Pino, remained in sight at all times. Fidel tried unsuccessfully to catch a swordfish, but didn't seem to mind at all when his luck failed. He joked a great deal, fired his automatic rifle at anything he could find in the water, and talked constantly against the Americans and about his plans for a new Cuba. Had I been uneducated or politically naive, I might well have fallen under the spell of his magnetism and been convinced by his anti-imperialist harangue. But I knew better. Under the jovial exterior lay one of the most vicious murderers the world had ever known.

"There goes Castiñeiras. Fidel must have left," I heard Miguel tell the Operations Officer, interrupting my recollections. We followed the CNO to his spacious and elegantly furnished offices. Castiñeiras was already at his desk looking over some documents. At his side stood his aide, Lieutenant Arguelles. Also present were Comandante Pinto and Calderon, who were engaged in conversation in a corner of the room.

As we entered, Castiñeiras lifted his eyes from the papers and said, "Please make yourselves comfortable." He waited a moment as his aide closed the door behind us then continued in his usual crisp, direct style. "We have gathered here for a happy occasion. In these trying times for our Navy and our Revolution, nothing gives me more pleasure than rewarding those who demonstrate true faith in our future. It is my pleasure to promote Lieutenant Luis Calderon and Lieutenant Miguel Nodal to their next higher ranks. Lieutenant Calderon, front and center..."

After the conclusion of the short ceremony, we left Castiñeiras, Comandante Pinto, and Lieutenant Arugelles going over some pictures of a Soviet OSA missile boat. Calderon had invited Miguel and me to have lunch at La Zaragozana to celebrate. I accepted, but asked to be excused briefly to make a necessary phone call. I had suddenly realized that over two hours had passed since I had left Nicky. As I dialed the number of my house, I only hoped he would still be there. Before the first ring had stopped, someone picked up the receiver, but did not speak.

"Nicky, is that you," I asked.

"Yes, of course. Carlos, is everything O.K.?" Nicky replied after recognizing my voice.

"Everything is just fine. This is one time I'm glad you didn't follow my orders too precisely. I'm on my way to the Zaragozana, and I'll be home after that. I am sure that Lucila will fix you something to eat."

"She already did—enough to feed an army. Your parents haven't returned yet and it gets eerie here. Come back soon, if you can," he said.

"I will. Why don't you play the piano for awhile; it'll make the time go faster."

"That's what I've been doing for the past hour, and it hasn't helped. Just hurry."

"I'll be there in no time at all, Nicky. Ciao."

"Ciao," he replied, still sounding a little lost.

I hung up the receiver and joined Calderon and Miguel who were already waiting restlessly by the elevator door.

"I'm ready," I said.

"Let's go then," said Calderon, as we stepped aside to let our new Comandante enter first.

Going down the front stairs, Miguel bumped into an old shipmate. While Nodal was being congratulated for the extra gold on his sleeve, Calderon took the opportunity to draw me slightly aside. Speaking in a low voice, he said, "There goes a friend of ours," referring to a passenger ferry which we could see pulling out of port—on its way to Key West.

Realizing that he meant Quesada, I replied, "Not one but two. Our blond rebel joined Arturo early this morning."

Calderon's face tightened slightly as he took in the news. "Now we really have a reason to celebrate," he said as Miguel rejoined us.

The restaurant was crowded and lively with music, loud laughter, and conversation. Just like old times, I thought, although any astute observer would have immediately noticed the difference in the clientele. The familiar good-natured and cosmopolitan American tourists had been replaced by the unsophisticated, rustic-looking Soviets and their dour friends from the communist block.

Impressed by our uniforms and especially by Calderon's rank, the maitre d' hurried solicitously to find us the best available table. After ordering, Calderon excused himself to make a head call. I decided to grab the opportunity to have a moment alone with him, and as soon as he had left, I rose and said to Nodal, "Miguel, I think Luis had a good idea. I'll be right back."

"I'll be right here," he replied, pouring some more beer into a frosty mug.

When I walked into the crowded men's room, I spotted Calderon washing his hands at one of the basins while talking in a low voice to a tall well-dressed man who was obviously a foreigner. Through the mirror, Luis saw me coming in, and looking startled, he abruptly ended the conversation. He gave me a rather caustic smile and, indicating the foreigner with a movement of his head, said defensively, "I was just giving this gentleman from Argentina directions back to his hotel." Before he had even finished the sentence, the tall man was gone.

Wondering why Calderon had bothered to explain such a mundane matter, I replied casually, "Yes, it's hard enough for us Cubans to find our way around this city, much less for outsiders."

He finished drying his hands and sounding like his arrogant self again said, "True. Listen, I'll meet you back at the table. We'll have a better opportunity to talk later on."

As I walked through the foyer on my way back to join Miguel, I noticed the well-dressed Argentinian standing by the entrance door. The doorman was talking into the phone, and I heard him say, "Yes, please send a taxi with someone who can speak some Russian. I have a customer here who doesn't speak either Spanish or English." With a jolt, I realized that he was referring to the supposed-Argentinian.

I shrugged and kept on walking. Calderon had lied. In the business he's in, I can't completely blame him, I thought. Yet, as I approached our table, the sight of Luis Calderon in his blue uniform with the brand new extra stripe on the sleeve sent a shiver down my spine. His outright lie had shocked me more than I wanted to acknowledge.

I rejoined Miguel and Calderon just as the waiter arrived and began to serve generous portions of fragrant paella. The sight of large white pieces of lobster mixed with chunks of tender pork and chicken breast—all floating in steaming yellow rice—immediately stimulated my appetite. Even all the unanswered questions which were plaguing my restless mind were not going to keep me from enjoying my favorite dish.

Later, while the waiter was pouring cognac into our glasses, Calderon said, "Miguel, I think it would be better if Carlos dropped me back at headquarters to pick up my car. For you, it would mean going in the opposite direction from your house."

"Sure Luis— either way is fine with me," Miguel replied.

"I'd be happy to take you back," I remarked immediately. "I'm ready whenever you are."

We walked together to the entrance of the restaurant and parted company with Miguel after one more round of congratulatory remarks. The parking attendant brought my car to the door, and after placing a tip in his hand, I got myself behind the wheel. Calderon slid into the seat beside me, and we both tossed our caps into the back seat. With all four windows down and the sun roof wide open, we made our way out of the parking area and toward Navy headquarters.

"Now we can talk," Luis said as he loosened his tie slightly.

"First you," I said.

He cleared his throat and began absently unwrapping a large Havana cigar. "It was all very simple," he said in a matter-of-fact tone. "The morning after our excursion to the museum, I received information that I had been selected to take over a newly-created office—Navy Liaison for Political and Intelligence Affairs. There was practically no risk involved. I had the information verified by three different sources. Now, what about *your* plans?"

"I have no plans. I'll keep a low profile, and when the time is right, I'll ask you for a one-way ticket on the ferry," I said, following my rule of never telling anyone anything I didn't have to reveal.

"But you told me you had your own plans for getting out," he replied with restrained irritation. The traffic was getting heavier and the temperature was getting hotter—or was it the conversation? I waited for a green light.

Finally the light changed, and without taking my eyes from the road, I said, "I gave up my plan; it wouldn't have worked. I was planning to take over the cruiser." Two could play at this business of lying, I thought.

"No problem getting you on the ferry. Just give me a week's notice," he said. "Would it be just you?"

"Just me."

He twisted in his seat and gazed at me appraisingly for a second or two. Before he said a word, I knew he was about to bring up the real subject that had brought him into my car. With his arm resting on the back of the seat, he said, "How many people would you say took part in the attack on Fidel, including those not directly involved?" The voice underneath the casual tone was calculating, entrapping.

"I wouldn't know," I said and instantaneously a defense reflex alerted me to a possible trap. Almost without pausing, I added, "Has anybody made an attempt on his life?"

I could feel his stare. He didn't answer.

"Hey, Luis, " I said, "I asked you a question." I turned to face him. "You wouldn't be holding something back from me, would you?"

"Oh, come on," he replied, shaking his head disbelievingly. "It's common knowledge that the accident in the tunnel in which Comandante Rivera was killed was a bloody attempt on Fidel's life."

"Maybe it's common knowledge, but not to me." I knew I couldn't back down from my initial statement now.

"What people do not know for sure is whether Fidel was in one of those cars or not."

"And was he?"

"Yes, and he got out of the mess by a sheer miracle."

"If it was a miracle, it sure didn't come from above," I added.

Luis chuckled and said, "There's my car." Suddenly the smile disappeared from his face. "Remember, Carlos, I will need a week's notice for the ferry."

"I won't forget," I replied. I was glad to see that there was no place to park. I had had enough. I needed to go home and digest all that had taken place.

I double-parked next to his official sedan. "Now you even rate a driver," I said in English as he got out of the car.

"It all comes with the job," he replied, also using English to assure that his driver would not follow our conversation.

"Some job!"

"We will have to get together. I'll call you soon," he said.

"Do that. And, again, congratulations. You really are something else," I shouted as he got into the back seat of his sedan. He smiled coldly.

Chapter Twenty-eight

Emilio, looking gaunt and pale, was on his knees praying. With both hands he held a wooden crucifix. Lying on his bunk, Dr. Marten was also praying—praying not for himself, but for his young cellmate.

When Emilio had finished, he stood up, reached for the paper bag where he kept his few possessions, and took out a can of pineapple juice. "Dr. Marten," he said, "would you share this juice with me? I've been saving it for days, but I know I won't be alive tomorrow, and I would like to propose one last toast."

"Nonsense, Emilio. That's what you believed the other times, and nothing happened," Dr. Marten replied, trying to sound confident.

"Tonight will be different."

Dr. Marten rolled out of his cot and said, "I don't believe it, but let's drink the juice. It will lift your spirits."

"What shall we toast to?" Emilio asked.

"Not long ago, I joined in a toast with another unusual young man. Like you, he was in a difficult situation."

"Did he make it?"

"I really don't know, but if anyone makes it, he will."

"What was the toast?" Emilio asked.

Dr. Marten lifted his glass and said, "To courage!"

Close to midnight, the sound of the footsteps of the guards echoed metallically through the empty corridors. This time, the sound did not stop until the guards had reached Emilio and Dr.

Marten's cell. The heavy metal door opened and two guards, shadowy and anonymous in the gloom of the hallway, called out, "Carrero, let's go!"

Dr. Marten jumped in front of Emilio and extended his arms to prevent his young friend from joining the would-be executioners. With tears in his eyes, he called out, "My life for his."

At the first hint of opposition, the guards had burst into the cell, and now the man in charge, a burly, young militiaman, reached out and shoved Dr. Marten violently against the wall. Bleeding badly from a nasty wound on the back of his head, Marten staggered forward, fell against the guard, and wrapping an arm around the man's thick neck, whispered, "Save his life and I'll make you a rich man."

Chapter Twenty-nine

Finally alone, I felt an overwhelming sense of relief. I turned on my car radio and stepped on the gas; I needed to get away. The long hours of constant tension had taken their toll and my back and shoulders were aching almost unbearably. As I drove, the pain and tension slowly began to fade, only to be replaced by a deep sense of sadness and loss. I passed the Hotel Nacional and watched the part of the city where I had been born glide past me. The time of leaving was very close, and the uncertainty of ever being able to return weighed heavily on my soul.

I pulled into tree-lined Twenty-First Street, almost deserted, and then turned onto A Street and into my own driveway. As soon as I got out of my car, the coolness of the evening, the scent of the pine trees, and the soft sound of music flowing down from the terrace made me feel good—almost as if I had gotten away with something. And come to think of it, maybe I had. By the time I walked through the foyer, I was feeling almost optimistic. I started up the marble stairs, taking them two or three at a time, until a sharp pain in my back reminded me that my wound was still too fresh for unnecessary exertion.

Out on the terrace, the record player was playing old Cuban songs. Nicky, looking relaxed in a burgundy cashmere sweater, was leaning against the wrought iron rail, talking to my mother. She was in her favorite lounge chair, her legs covered by a comforter, and she was obviously enjoying Nicky's company. "Carlitos," she said, "how many days since I have seen you?"

I sat down next to her on the lounge chair and embraced her. "Too many," I replied.

"Then why are you so late?" Nicky interrupted.

"Has he been making a pest of himself?" I asked, ignoring the question.

"He?" she said, looking up fondly at Nicky who immediately came over to her, took her hand, and kissed her on the cheek. "You see what I mean? He is a joy. Someday he'll make some lucky woman very happy."

"Well, I'll drink to that," I said, getting up and heading for the portable bar. "Maybe when he has someone else to check up on all the time, he'll give me a break. Daiquiri anyone?"

"No thank you. It's getting too cold out here for me," my mother replied as she rose slowly to her feet. "Nicky, don't pay any attention to him. He loves to tease you."

"Don't you worry, Maria Luisa, I never do," Nicky answered as my mother, still smiling with amusement, went inside the house.

Once alone with Nicky, I said, "We are getting out of here in less than three days. On the Thursday flights to Miami, there are always some seats reserved for members of the diplomatic corps. My father has been told that all the state department needs is forty-eight hours notice, and he will be giving that notice tomorrow."

Nicky lifted his glass and said, "Thank God!"

"Let's go inside. So much has happened today. You're not going to believe half of it," I said leading the way to my room.

By the time Nicky was through changing my bandages, I had finished briefing him on the day's experiences—being careful not to omit a single detail. I had taken pains not to add any comments or impressions that might influence his assessment of the situation. I needed an unbiased and intelligent analysis of the whole Calderon affair, and I trusted both Nicky's mind and his instincts.

Sitting on the bed, leaning forward as if to catch every word, he had listened to me with total absorption. Now he looked at me, his eyes alive with intelligence. "Carlos," he said, "I know what I'm about to say doesn't make any sense, and I hope that I'm mistaken, but I think that Calderon is a traitor and that I'm his target."

There was no longer any doubt. My scheme had worked; I had given him the pieces, and he had put the puzzle together. I was sure that he was right, but there was nothing to gain by making him more nervous.

"Perhaps, Nicky, perhaps," I said. "But he risked his life to save mine just a few days ago."

"Did he? Think twice. After so much ado and such careful preparation, all that was accomplished was to blow up a couple of vehicles and to delay the exhibition for a few days. By the way, isn't it kind of odd that the only target that wasn't destroyed was the tank?"

"True, but what about the shoot-out? He, himself, could have been killed," I replied, playing the devil's advocate.

"Obviously it was just unexpected interference by some gung ho militiaman, not by the G-2."

"Well, the main thing is that regardless of whether he is not, we are going on the assumption that he is a Judas. We'll leave no later than Thursday."

A knock on the door was followed by Lucila's stern warning: "Dinner in ten minutes."

"We'll be there Lucila," I answered.

"Well, I'm headed for the bathroom," I told Nicky.

"I'll be down in the living room," he replied. "I promised your mother that I'd play something for her."

"Good, I'll see you in ten minutes."

"You'd better, or Lucila will get you," Nicky answered, smiling and trying to sound casual. I knew that beneath his calm surface the undercurrent was turbulent. I must give him that sedative tonight, I decided, even if I have to tie him down to do it. I walked into the bathroom, undressed, and filled the bathtub. The hot water soothed me and washed away my problems—at least for the moment.

Chapter Thirty

At about 0400 Dr. Marten was awakened from a troubled sleep by the sound of hammering vibrating through the thick walls of the prison. The guards were closing the wooden coffins of those who had been executed during the night. Dr. Marten knew that the coffins would soon be loaded aboard a truck and then dumped into an unmarked grave in Colon Cemetery. He did not move but only closed his eyes again to pray for the souls of the dead ... and to thank God for Emilio's life.

When the light of a new day woke him up from a fitful sleep, he heard Emilio tossing in his bunk. Dr. Marten got up and stood for a moment looking down at his young friend. He realized that Emilio was slowly awakening from a restless sleep and decided it was better to let him finish waking up by himself. His practiced eye automatically noted Emilio's physical deterioration: the deep purple shadows under the eyes, the gaunt, tense face—unshaven, yet almost bare of whiskers, the emaciated body which was beginning to look almost like that of a child. If he continues like this, the doctor reflected sadly, they won't have to shoot him. He'll die on his own.

Finally Emilio opened his eyes slowly. "Are you all right, son?" Dr. Marten asked.

Emilio sat up and buried his head in his hands for a moment. When he looked up at Dr. Marten, his face seemed lit from within. "I have never been better," he replied, "for I have learned the true meaning of courage and compassion."

"You are too generous, Emilio. I was only an instrument of God's will. Every night within the walls of this fortress, those who refuse to surrender to communism show the true meaning of courage to their assassins—they teach them how to die."

"Dr. Marten, I only know that thanks to you, I can see the light of today's sun. I was as good as dead. It's like being born again . . . but look at the blood stains all over your bunk," Emilio said, interrupting himself abruptly as he realized for the first time how badly the doctor had been hurt in his defense. He then threw his arms around Dr. Marten and embraced him in an emotional silence.

After he had regained control, Emilio asked the doctor, "What in the world could you have told the guard to make him spare my life? Please tell me. I must know."

"I simply told him that if he saved you, I would make him a rich man. But it wasn't so much what I said that made it work as what I did."

"And what was that?" asked Emilio.

"I placed a thousand dollar bill in his hand."

"A thousand dollars! But where did you get it? How did you do it?"

"Emilio, come, let's sit down," said Marten, sitting on his bunk and propping his back against the wall. His head ached almost unbearably, and a momentary wave of dizziness had just overtaken him. He did not want Emilio to realize his condition, so he paused as if collecting his thoughts. Finally, he continued speaking, but in a tired voice that was little more than a whisper. "I must tell you, Emilio, that I am a very rich man and that I intend to buy my way—and yours—out of here."

"But how?" Emilio asked, his eyes widening with astonishment.

"You already know about the thousand dollar bill that I gave to the guard. Well, I have two more where that came from, and outside these walls, I have access to all we might need."

"But that's impossible! We have been searched stark naked."

"If anything happens to me, those bills are yours. I have them taped to my body with surgical tape—right under my testicles."

"Dios mio! I never heard of such a thing."

"Luckily, neither have the guards."

After a moment, Emilio struggled to speak. "Dr. Marten . . . I only wish I could thank you, but I can't find the words. A few days ago, you didn't even know me, and now . . ."

But Dr. Marten shook his head and motioned for silence, and Emilio realized that words were not necessary after all.

That same day during a gathering of the political prisoners, Emilio and Dr. Marten learned that Emilio had been assigned a defense counselor. They also learned that one of the two guards who had made the rounds the night before had been found stabbed to death.

"Which one?" Emilio asked with apprehension. Before anyone could answer, Dr. Marten said to him in a low voice, "The one without a thousand dollars."

Emilio sat down, feeling sick. "Animals," he said. The reason for the murder was only too obvious—greed. The stronger, more brutal of the two had decided against having a witness, especially one with whom he would have to share his good fortune.

Chapter Thirty-one

Jacinta prepared us a fine dinner, and even though it was not a paella, the company was infinitely better. Although my parents were both delighted with the idea of leaving on Thursday, I could sense that my mother was already worrying about me. She knew very well that if I were caught trying to leave the island that I would undoubtedly end up in front of a firing squad. My father was also worried, but in a different way. He had seen action a couple of times during his years in the Army, and now he thought of my escape as a kind of military adventure. I had managed to convince him that taking the *Sirius* to Key West was a relatively easy thing to do—practically without risk. Now I only hoped that time would prove my optimistic deceit to be true.

Coffee was served in the living room and at my mother's insistence, Nicky sat down again at the piano. He began playing some of the beautiful music of Franz Lehar—amazingly well, considering his lack of practice. Nicky's mother had been a fine concert pianist, and thanks to her years of coaching, Nicky really was an accomplished musician. Absorbed in the music, I missed the ringing of the telephone, but Lucila answered it in the pantry. She came softly into the living room and whispered to me that I had a long distance call. As quietly as possible, I slipped out of the room and made my way into the pantry.

"This is Carlos Dumas," I said into the receiver. "Do you have a call for me?"

"One moment, Sir," the operator answered in English. "You

have a person-to-person call." In the background I heard the operator say, "Go ahead, miss. Your party is on the line."

"Carlos, how are you?" Lourdes' familiar voice was asking me.

"I'm fine. Missing you. When are you coming back?"

"That's why I'm calling. I'll be in Havana tomorrow evening, and if you still like my cooking, I'll see you at my house at 7:00. ... No, better yet at 8:00. Can you make it?" The obvious tension beneath the casual words left me no doubt that this was no ordinary dinner invitation.

"I'll be there. I like the cooking almost as much as I like the cook. See you at 8:00. Ciao, bella."

By the time I returned to the living room, my parents had retired for the evening. My father's arteriosclerosis and his advanced years were draining him more and more of the tremendous energy which had once been his trademark. Even though his health was deteriorating rapidly, the secretary of state had asked him to postpone his retirement for awhile. Like the rest of the government, the state department had lost the majority of its experienced personnel since the Revolution.

Nicky, still sitting on the piano bench, was reading the newspaper. When he saw me coming, he put it down and said, "Your parents said to wish you buenas noches. Your father suddenly felt very tired, and they decided to go on upstairs. But who was on the phone?"

"Lourdes. She'll be here tomorrow, and she wants to talk with me—that is with us. I believe it's important."

"I wonder what it's all about. Maybe Jorge has gotten in touch with her. What do you think?"

"I really don't know. I'd rather wait and see than go crazy trying to figure it out. Let's go upstairs. I have everything ready in the bedroom to give you your injection."

"Do I look that bad?"

"No, actually you look very healthy. I don't think you'll ever have any more problems, but we can't take the slightest chance. The next couple of days are going to be very demanding, and we must be prepared," I said, trying not to show the effect that Nicky's reaction had on me. I had expected him to put up a strong fight against the sedative. God knows what was going on inside his head.

"Well, if you don't mind, I'll finish my brandy first," Nicky said, reaching for his glass and burying his head in his newspaper.

So much for my worries; that sounds more like him, I thought.

The next morning after breakfast while my parents were making their last minute preparation for the trip, Nicky and I drove to the club. The north wind had abated considerably, and the sun was making an appearance between the clouds. As I drove, Nicky read the weather forecast in the newspaper. "It looks good," he said, putting the paper down and turning on the radio. "They're predicting several days of sunshine and warm temperatures. For us—only two more days... if only Dr. Marten had not been arrested..."

"At least he's been assigned Dr. Aramis Tamargo as his defense counselor—a sure sign they're not planning to seek the death penalty. It's a small consolation, but it's something."

We soon arrived at the club, parked on a side street and headed directly for the boat house. The *Sirius* was out of the water, her canvas cover snugly in place and her tanks full. "Everything seems to be on track," I said to Nicky.

"Except that we have a new, unfriendly-looking face among the militiamen guarding the club," he replied, gesturing discretely in the direction of a surly looking young man who was arguing hotly with one of the club members.

"That could be a problem," I agreed, "but I'm afraid there's nothing we can do about it. Come on, let's get over to Lourdes' place. We still have to lay down the track."

"I'm driving this time," said Nicky, trying to get the keys out of my hand.

"What if they stop us for some reason? When we get to Miami, you can do all the driving," I replied while keeping a firm grip on the car keys.

He shrugged, put on his sunglasses, and slid into the passenger's seat. "In Miami," he said, "we won't have enough money to buy a bicycle, let alone a car."

"True, but it's going to be wonderful to live without fear—car or no car. Besides, we'll get a car within a week or so—you'll see," I said.

We circled around Lourdes' house a couple of times to make

sure that everything was normal, and after the second pass, we pulled into her driveway. "While you were lingering over lunch with your friends yesterday," Nicky said sarcastically, "I played around with the course to Key West. It's a pretty straight forward track. Let's see if you like it."

We went inside and spread out the chart on the dining room table. Nicky had done a good job—no need for any corrections. After compensating for variation and for the Gulf current, he had come up with two courses. First, we would head straight north at 357°. After one hour of cruising at the top speed permitted by the sea conditions, we would come to 027° true, heading straight for Key West.

Nicky put his divider down on the table and looked up at me. "If we leave at 1800," he said, "we should be in Key West no later than 2300."

"I agree," I replied. "Let's just hope that the weather forecast turns out to be accurate."

"Carlos, while we wait for Lourdes, do you think we could call Tony and ask him to check with his G-2 contact about Dr. Marten's status?"

"I don't want you to be in suspense waiting for a reply, so I didn't mention to you that I called Tony from the club. We should be hearing from him any time now. I told him to call us here."

The sound of the key turning in the front door startled us, and we both jumped to our feet. Lourdes appeared at the door, and I had never seen her looking so nervous and distracted. She kissed us both and taking my hand, said, "Come, let's sit down. We must talk."

"It sounds bad," Nicky muttered.

"Very bad indeed," Lourdes replied. "Calderon is a double agent—a communist."

Nicky and I looked at each other for a split second. Then, turning to Lourdes, I asked, "How do you explain that a few days ago he participated in an armed action during which he saved my life? And later he arranged the escape of Lieutenant Quesada and Midshipman Diaz?"

"Just token concessions—a small price to pay to gain credibility with the highest echelons of the anti-communist forces

Escape from Castro

in both Miami and Cuba. Fidel has two primary goals, and he is willing to pay *any* price to achieve them."

"What are they?" I asked.

"The first," Lourdes replied, "is to obtain information about the composition of the forces that are being trained to invade Cuba. And, of course, he is after anything related to landing plans, etc., etc. The second goal, and the one closest to his heart, is to identify, track down, and capture the man who staged the bold attempt on his life. That's where Calderon fits into the picture. Ironically enough, he has already been rewarded for the attack on the museum—he'll be promoted to comandante very soon."

"He already has been. But tell us how you know all this . . . who do you really work for?" Nicky asked, visibly upset and eying Lourdes with undisguised suspicion.

"Nicky, this is no time for a third degree. It's enough to say that Lourdes works for an agency of the U.S. government, and that I can vouch for her," I said hastily.

"It's all right, Carlos. He's entitled to an explanation. Nicky, going back to your question, I know much more than what I have just told you. You must have read about the recent defection of a very high ranking KGB agent in London."

"Of course—everybody has," Nick replied.

"The defection was made public two weeks ago. What was not disclosed was the fact that this agent had been working for us for the last six years. The amount of detailed information that we have gained from him is mind-boggling. In addition, we have the cooperation of some members of Fidel's inner circle. There is practically nothing that Fidel plans or carries out that we don't know about. For example, we know that he recently almost died of apoplexy when he found out that one of his own G-2 sadists in charge of interrogating the only witness to the attempt on his life was responsible for the witness' suicide."

From the corner of my eye, I saw Nicky's face grow somber, but he did not say a word. "Do you know that man's name?" I asked.

"Yes, but I am not authorized to divulge it," she answered. "The important thing for you to know at this time is that Calderon is convinced that you—Carlos—were involved in the assassination attempt. That's why you were invited to the museum masquerade—so that he could secure your trust and later your conviction."

"That explains his interest in my plans for leaving Cuba," I said.

"Warning you is the reason for my visit. Calderon's orders are clear: he is to continue to try to pump you for information, but above all, he is to make sure that you never leave the country."

"Well, he's in good shape, then, because I intend to stick around long enough to bury him and his bearded friend," I said vehemently, getting to my feet. "Traitor! Stinking traitor—to have pulled that one on me. I could kill the bastard!" I shouted.

"Carlos, please sit down. You'll open your wound," Nicky said while looking at me questioningly, not able to comprehend my words. He was obviously wondering about our plans, but he had the presence of mind to remain silent.

"Let me tell you more about the bastard, as you called him," Lourdes said, unperturbed by my outburst. "His father is a Commy from the old guard. Luis had a hard time getting admitted to the Naval Academy for that very fact."

"Then why did the Navy let him in?" Nicky questioned.

"His uncle on his mother's side is—of all things—a priest, and an influential one at that. He interceded for Luis."

"One more question, Lourdes," I said, sitting down next to her. "Does Fidel know that Calderon is stalking me and why he is doing it?"

"He does. Someone very close to him masterminded the whole affair. Fidel is paranoid about the attack. It was just too close. Now he's afraid that it could be repeated at any time—unless he finds the culprits. Even worse, he's afraid that if the whole thing gets to be known that he will lose face and that others will try to emulate the daring act."

"Where does Miguel Nodal fit into this scheme? He was promoted at the same time as Calderon," I pointed out—almost afraid to hear the answer.

"Nodal is just an efficient naval officer. They haven't been able to fully indoctrinate him . . ."

"Lourdes," Nicky interrupted, "if you are finished with your briefing, I would like to ask a couple of questions."

"I'm through. I'll answer as much as I can."

"I don't want to burden you with my personal problems, but could you tell me what happened to Elena after the G-2 arrested her father? You took care of her on the plane, didn't you?"

"Yes, I did," Lourdes replied, looking at Nicky with compassion, "but there isn't anything I can add to what Judy already told you. I did try to call her before I came here, but the family had left for Venezuela."

"Venezuela? To do what?" Nicky asked.

"To take care of Dr. Marten's business. Nicky, I don't know if you are aware that Elena's father is a very wealthy man with more friends and more connections than you or I could begin to imagine."

"As close as she is to her father, I can imagine what she must be going through right now," Nicky said.

"I think she'll be fine. I believe Dr. Marten is a man who cannot be taken for granted. He may surprise us all."

"I didn't know about their fortune," Nicky said, biting his lower lip—a sure sign of stress with him. "I don't think that I could fit in their world. We have lost everything—not that we ever had much."

Lourdes looked at him skeptically. "With a name like Berrocal, you couldn't be that bad off."

"We have the name, but not much else. My father had a good law practice and that was about all. Any luxuries like studying abroad or expensive clothes came from my grandparents on my mother's side. Their money was in sugar mills—there isn't anything left."

The ringing of the phone put an immediate end to the conversation. We all stared at the instrument in silence and with apprehension. After a couple of rings, I picked up the receiver. It was Tony—in a hurry—with the message that he needed to see me. We set a time and place and both hung up. I turned to Lourdes and Nicky, saying, "I'm on my way to Tony's. He's anxious to see me—says we can't talk on the phone."

"Well, I'll turn in right here," Nicky said, making himself comfortable on the couch. "Wake me up when you get back. It has to be important for Tony to want to see you right away."

Holding her shoes in one hand, Lourdes said before heading toward her room, "I'll say adiós now. I have to get up at 0400;

the Pan Am limousine will be here at 0500. Please don't get up when you hear me moving around. I love you both, and hopefully next time I see you, it will be in Miami. Now I'm going to bed."

"Thank you for everything, Lourdes," Nicky said with much feeling. "You're fantastic."

She turned back to him and holding his face in her hands, kissed him lightly on the lips. "And you are beautiful," she said.

He blushed and did not say another word. Standing by her bedroom door, Lourdes turned once again to face us. "Judy has a crush on you, Carlos. What did you do to her?" she questioned with a sharp edge in her voice.

"She has what?" I asked.

"A crush on you. She really does."

"And she told you that?"

"Not in so many words, but my feminine intuition did tell me. I can assure you that she has flipped over you, and from the look on your face, I suspect it's mutual."

I honestly could not think of an answer. Finally, I said, "Well, if you want, you could tell her that she'll hear from me someday soon. Now, I'd better get over to Tony's. Have a good flight tomorrow, Lourdes." The sharpness of her glance seemed to go right through me. I looked over at Nicky as I hurried out the front door. He was still blushing.

Outside the house the air was soft and sweet with the scent of jasmine. The street was dark and quiet under a clear sky filled with stars. I identified the Belt of Orion and, of course, the Big Dipper, its pointers brighter than ever as if they were showing me the way north. North—that's where Judy was. Perhaps she was watching the same stars at that very moment. I walked slowly to my car, thinking of her and wondering if we were to be defeated by the dark forces of communism, what it would be like to grow old on foreign soil.

The minute I rang the bell of Tony's apartment, the door opened. Tony answered dressed in pajamas under a blue robe and looking tired. "Come in Carlos," he said, "I have good news for you for a change."

I sat down in the rocker he had pointed to and said, "I could use some good news. Tell me."

He poured Drambuie into two glasses filled with ice and

handed me one. "Our friend in the G-2 believes that something unusual is going on with Dr. Marten. He and his cellmate are being transferred from La Cabaña to another prison, possibly El Príncipe."

"That's good news," I replied.

"You don't know just how good. It's almost incredible. It shows that someone, possibly more than just one person, is pulling strings for him. That doctor seems to have more connections than anyone thought."

"How do you figure that?"

"Among other things, it seems that he was instrumental in saving the life of his cellmate, Emilio Carrero, a student leader."

I finished my drink and put down the glass. "Tony," I said, "what are you waiting for to get out?"

"Nothing. We have airline tickets. We're flying out next week. What about you?"

"I still don't know," I answered, regretting having to lie but knowing that giving him the details would only endanger him.

"Just let it be soon, Carlos," he answered, looking at me with sincere concern. "Let it be soon."

Chapter Thirty-two

Nicky had only been asleep for a half an hour when he became tormented by his recurrent nightmare. In his dream Julio was once again dying next to him in the forest. Awakened by his agonized screams, Lourdes rushed out of bed and into the living room. Immediately, she realized what Nicky was going through. She sat beside him on the couch and, taking his hands, gently tried to wake him up. "Nicky, Nicky, wake up. It's only a dream," she kept repeating, but her voice seemed to have no power to penetrate his deep, anguished sleep. At last, the screams subsided into low, guttural moans and then into silence. But Nicky had begun to tremble uncontrollably, and cold drops of perspiration were rolling down his forehead. Lourdes was frightened. If only Carlos had not left—he would have known what to do.

On an impulse, she began to rub Nicky's back, his smooth skin trembling beneath her fingers. Finally, he calmed down and seemed to have fallen into a relaxed sleep. She felt warm inside, and following an irresistible urge, she leaned over and kissed him on the back of his neck. The smell of his flesh awakened her sensuality in a disquieting way. She couldn't stop looking at him—his handsome face, almost covered by his black hair, his half-naked body now still beneath the linen sheet. Shame on me, she thought. He needs to be comforted, and I'm ready to climb into bed with him. She gently covered him with the bedsheet. But as she started to get up from the couch, Nicky reached out, grabbed her by the wrist and whispered, "Don't leave me now . . ."

♦ ♦ ♦

I slipped back into Lourdes' house, trying not to make a sound. The living room was dark; only a thin stream of light flowed in through the kitchen door. Nicky was asleep on the couch, and Lourdes was curled up on a chair next to him. She was beginning to wake up, pulling her blanket around her to ward off the night chill. I saw that she was dressed only in a nearly transparent negligee. I looked at her with contempt, and she must have felt my gaze because she stretched and then rose gracefully to her feet. Placing her index finger on her mouth, she whispered, "Shh." She motioned her head toward Nicky and said, "He had a terrible nightmare. Now he needs to rest."

"I'll bet," I remarked caustically.

Coming close to me, she said, "You are wrong, you know. I wouldn't deny it if it happened, but it didn't. He needed company, and I was there. Don't think it didn't cross my mind; it would have crossed any woman's mind. But as unflattering as it may be, it didn't cross his mind. He is as beautiful inside as he is outside. Now you can believe me or not. It's really not important."

"I believe you."

♦ ♦ ♦

The annoying sound of the phone woke me up. Lourdes had left, and Nicky was still asleep on the couch. I reached for the receiver and waited in silence.

"Carlos?" I recognized Tony's voice.

"Yes, Tony, what's up?" I looked at my watch; it was close to 0800.

"I must talk with you. I'll be there in ten minutes," he said and hung up without waiting for an answer. When he rang the bell, Nicky and I were both up and dressed. Nicky was making espresso in the kitchen, and I was pacing impatiently behind the door.

Tony rushed in, smiling and obviously delighted with his

good news. He didn't even bother to say hello before he began the story. "That Dr. Marten has balls bigger than a bull's!" he exclaimed. "He escaped while they were transferring him and his friend from La Cabaña to El Principe prison."

Nicky yelled, "I don't believe it!"

"But listen," Tony interrupted, "that's not all. The best part is that he, his friend, and one of the guards crashed the G-2 sedan through the gates of the Venezuelan Embassy where they are now under the personal protection of the Ambassador."

"What about the other guard?" I asked. "They always use at least two."

"The three of them overpowered the second guard and threw him out of the car at 50 kph. He's now recovering in the military hospital. To pre-empt any violent reaction by the government, the Venezuelans called the AP and UPI and told them exactly what had happened. Their escape made the morning news on American television."

"Incredible!" I shouted.

"But true! Fantastically, beautifully true!" Nicky added, tossing one of the sofa cushions into the air so violently that it knocked some plaster loose from the ceiling.

After Tony left, I said to Nicky, "We'll leave tomorrow. There is no postponement, no turning back. We are running out of time."

"I'm ready to go right now," he answered promptly.

"Unfortunately, we couldn't leave today without compromising my parents. Also, I have to show up at the academy today because I promised to deliver some lesson plans."

"I guess paying a visit to the academy would reassure everyone that you're still around, but please be careful."

"Don't worry; I'll be very careful. We're in the final stretch now, and this is one race we can't afford to lose. By now, Calderon knows that my parents are leaving tomorrow. He also knows that I would never leave before they did because of the unavoidable reprisals. So the real surveillance is going to begin after they leave."

"You're right. But don't forget that since Calderon is a double agent, everybody, including Nodal, knows that the story about your breaking a couple of bones is just that—a story. They know only too well that you were wounded by a militiaman and that you later killed him."

"That may or may not be accurate, Nicky. Men like Pinto and Nodal are strictly Navy. They don't care about—or even understand—this game of double-crossing and intrigue that Calderon plays so well. Besides, they are more useful to Calderon if they don't know all the facts."

Still looking worried, Nicky replied, "You are only useful as long as Calderon believes that he can get information out of you. If he even guesses about your escape plans, he'll make sure you never carry them out."

"True," I said, "but he'll be careful to make it look as if he was trying to help me all the way to the end. He has invested a lot to gain credibility with the top people in Miami. By the way, I have to stop by the hospital to alert Dr. Capó that we have compromised him. He'll have to get out fast—while he still can."

"I almost forgot about him," Nicky said remorsefully.

"But I didn't. Come on, I have to change into uniform," I said, going into the bedroom.

Nicky sat on the edge of the bed while I changed. "Do they know that you have the *Sirius?*" he asked.

"No, my cousin bought it in his name. You know, I might have gained a little extra time by telling Calderon that I was planning to ask him for a place on the ferry."

Nicky jumped off the bed. "That's it!" he exclaimed. "Call him right now and ask him to get you on the ferry that leaves next Monday. That would take the immediate pressure off you."

As I combed my hair in front of the mirror, I quickly weighed the pros and cons of Nicky's idea. "No," I decided, "he would probably become suspicious. The less we do, the better."

Hoping to change the subject and get Nicky's mind off our desperate situation, I remarked, "I sure do need a haircut."

"Get it in Miami. You know you hate haircuts."

"Good idea. I'll do just that." As I picked up my cap, I added, "Nicky, take Lourdes' car and go to Tony's apartment. Park the car inside the garage and stay put until you hear from me. You know the rules—no lights, no radio, no flushing."

"What about piano?" he asked, trying unsuccessfully to sound carefree.

"No piano. Why don't you exercise? With me half crippled, it would be nice to have one of us in good shape."

I opened the door and was about to leave when Nicky suddenly put a hand on my shoulder and asked, "Carlos, are we going to make it?"

"I know we are," I replied.

Chapter Thirty-three

All the way to Mariel, I felt as if I were heading into the lion's den. Added to my apprehension was my growing physical discomfort. Not only was my shoulder aching, but the pain now seemed to be radiating into my lower back and my right leg. When I get to Miami, I thought, I must have that wound checked. I turned on the radio, trying to get my mind off the annoyance of that dull, insistent pain. After a few minutes of music, an announcement came over the air that several agents of the imperialists had crashed thought the gates of the Venezuelan Embassy after attacking and almost killing the escort. The announcement was followed by an interview with the wounded guard's wife and his six year old son. I shook my head and changed the station, only to realize that the same announcement was being transmitted simultaneously on all frequencies.

I turned off the radio and looked out at the ocean to my right. The storm was over. We could easily sail with this type of weather. Small waves were rolling gently over the reefs, and the large cumulus-nimbus clouds had been replaced by the reassuring cirrus type. The wind was no longer strong and from the north, but gentle and from the south. If the weather continued like this, we would indeed sail with Godspeed and following winds.

As I drove up the road to the academy, I passed the superintendent's car on its way out. Commandante Pinto was sitting in the back seat, and he smiled and returned my salute.

I dropped off my lesson plans at the quarterdeck—

accompanied by a note that stated that I was including plans through Friday and that I would be in class as usual on Monday morning. The classes were over for the day, and only a few midshipmen could be seen standing around outside the library. As I walked toward the parking lot by the Merchant Marine Pavilion, I took a last good look at the school grounds. How often had I had my spirits lifted by these quiet and beautiful surroundings. But somehow today everything looked strangely gloomy and austere. Jorge's absence couldn't have that much of an effect, regardless of how cheerful and rambunctious he had always been. I knew that this was farewell to a place full of memories—most of them satisfying and pleasant.

In the parking lot I saw Miguel Nodal's old beat-up car. I made an about-face and walked briskly toward the officer's quarters. I wanted to see him one last time, and it would be a good idea for him to see me. At the same time, I could not afford to linger. I had less than twenty-four hours left in Cuba, and I didn't want any complications.

Miguel was sitting at his desk, his uniform shirt unbuttoned at the top, his feet up on his bunk. Absorbed in whatever he was reading, he didn't notice me standing at the door. Several copies of *Morskoy Sbornik*, the official Soviet Navy professional journal, were scattered on his desk. I cleared my throat. He looked up and smiled, but his eyes remained cool and his voice was reserved, almost sarcastic. "Oh, are you still here?" he said.

"What do you mean?" I replied foolishly. His question had taken me by surprise. How much does he know? I wondered.

"Just that I saw you from my window walking toward the parking lot." He took his feet off the bunk. "But come sit down. I want to show you something—that is if you have time."

"I have time." I sat on the bunk and took the manual that he handed me. It was in English—a complete rundown on the new Osa missile boat.

"Impressive," I said.

"You bet they are. We're also getting some of the smaller, but still effective, Komar type. The Komar can only fire its missiles in the direction it's heading. That's the great advantage of the Osa; they can fire in any direction."

"They're the latest design, aren't they?" I questioned.

"Less than a year old. Isn't that something? We've been close allies to the Americans since the beginning of the Republic, and the best we've been able to get from them has been hand-me-down, obsolete frigates."

"Look at this," Miguel continued with growing enthusiasm as he pointed at a picture of an Osa missile boat. "The Osa has four STYX launchers instead of the two carried by the Komar."

"How many are we getting? And when?" I asked as I recognized how sad but true his remarks about our friends to the north had been.

"I don't have that information, but I'll tell you, if you should be interested, I'm sure you could get one of these."

"I'm interested."

"Are you serious?"

"You don't see me laughing, do you?" There was a short silence.

"No, I guess not."

"I'll tell you what; why don't we meet for lunch on Friday and talk more about it," I said, getting up. He's going to pin me down about tomorrow if I'm not careful, I thought.

"Sure, why not. But, see, you were in a hurry after all. These days you don't seem to have time for anything."

"I was on my way to my car, turned around just to come see you, and you complain that I'm in a hurry."

"O.K., you're right. I'll see you Friday. By the way, how are those broken bones?"

"I could be worse."

"I'm sure of that."

I walked out of the Officers' Quarters thinking that Miguel might not be Lucifer, but he was almost as cunning.

Going down the stairs, I passed Midshipman Quintana, Diaz' sailing crew. He saluted smartly and came to attention. I returned the salute. "At ease, Quintana," I said. "How have you been?"

"To tell the truth, Sir, I'm just marking my time. Have you heard anything about Jorge? Here, it's just like he never existed."

"No, I haven't heard anything specific, but I have the feeling that he is well." Quintana's dark, pleasant features melted in comprehension, and he smiled conspiratorially.

"Good for him," he said.

"I must go now," I answered, thinking that it would not be good for Quintana to have been seen with me. "Keep faith and good luck."

"Good luck to you, Lieutenant," he replied, as if he knew that this was good-bye.

When I arrived at Tony's apartment, it was already dark. From outside, it looked as if no one was at home. I went slowly up the stairs, feeling every step on my not-yet-healed back. I tried unsuccessfully to open the door, but it had been bolted from the inside. I rang three times, then twice, and the door opened. "I was really beginning to worry," Nicky said without smiling. Dago stood next to Nicky, wagging his tail and jumping all over me. Nicky was dressed in shorts and had a towel draped around his neck.

"I came as soon as I could get away from Nodal without arousing his suspicions."

"It figures. Carlos, since there isn't anyone at home in the entire building, I was planning on taking a shower. Is that O.K.?"

"It sure is. I'm planning on doing the same as soon as I get home," I said.

Nicky's face went pale. "On second thought," I quickly added, "Why don't you shower over there too?"

"You don't think it would be too careless for me to go out the last night?"

"Of course not," I replied, avoiding his eyes.

"You really don't believe that, do you?"

"Nicky, you ask too many questions. I really don't believe it makes much difference. Let me call my parents and see how they're doing, and then we'll decide."

"No, it has already been decided. I'm not a child. Just go; I'll be fine. Tony and Cathy might be back early."

I reached for the phone. "I'll call my parents anyway," I said, and as I dialed, I glanced at his reflection in the mirror. He was standing behind me, staring at the floor, and biting his lower lip in distress. During the brief conversation with my mother, she assured me that all the packing and final arrangements had been taken care of, and that she and my father were enjoying a pleasant evening in the company of Luisita Olivella.

"You see, there's no need for us to go after all," I told Nicky. He beamed.

"I'm heading for the shower." I tossed him a towel and said, "I changed my mind. We're going to the movies."

"How come? Are you kidding?"

"Not at all. Movie theaters are the best hiding places in Havana."

"I wouldn't mind that at all," Nicky replied. "I haven't seen a movie in ages."

That night we saw *Tiger Bay*, an exciting adventure film about a young sailor. Unfortunately, the movie had an unhappy ending.

We got back close to midnight. Tony, dressed in pajamas and still half-asleep, answered the door. After a short conversation, Tony went back to bed and Nicky and I headed for the guestroom. Looking exhausted, Nicky went straight to bed. I sat at the desk in the bedroom and wrote Tony a note in our code, explaining our plans and asking him to understand our reasons for not discussing them beforehand. I had no doubt that he would understand.

When I had finished, I lay on my bed staring at the ceiling and wishing I could sleep. I looked over at Nicky's bed. His breathing had become quiet and rhythmic. After awhile, my eyes began to get heavier and finally I fell asleep for what I hoped would be my last night in Red Cuba.

Chapter Thirty-four

When I woke up the next morning, Nicky was sitting on his bed cleaning his .45.

"Good morning," I said, stretching and then getting out of bed. "How long have you been awake?"

"A good morning it is," Nicky exclaimed enthusiastically. "The weather is perfect and so is the forecast. I woke up about an hour ago."

"Is Tony still here?" I asked.

"No, he and Cathy left a few minutes ago. He was going to drop Dago off at the Olivella's. You never told him about our plans, did you?" I didn't miss the slight accusatory tone in Nicky's question.

"No, I didn't, but I wrote him a coded letter explaining our plans. He'd be the first one to agree that it was the safest and best way for us all."

"I still feel bad about not telling him," Nicky insisted as he got off the bed and started to get dressed.

"So do I, but now we'd better get moving instead of moping around feeling guilty. We still have a couple of things to do before we can take off," I snapped at him and immediately felt bad for doing so. I must not allow the stress to affect my actions like that, I thought.

Nicky nodded calmly and disregarding my outburst, said, "Carlos, today we will either be free . . . or dead."

"We agree on that," I replied as we began to gather our

belongings. A few minutes later, we left Tony's apartment for the last time, heading for my parents' home and some painful, although hopefully not permanent, good-byes.

◆ ◆ ◆

About noon, two hours before Luisita was due to come with her chauffeur to drive my parents to the airport, I said to my mother, "Why don't we go to La Rampa Mall for a quick lunch while Dad rests up for the trip?"

"I'd love to, Carlitos. Nicky, will you join us?"

"Maria Luisa, I hope you'll excuse me this time. I just finished eating most of what was left in the kitchen," Nicky answered tactfully, obviously realizing that I wanted a few minutes alone with my mother.

"I understand," she replied. "We'll be back in no time at all."

I drove to the cafeteria with the same feeling of emptiness in my chest and the same sensation of weakness that I had always experienced before a swimming meet. At least some things never change, I thought ruefully.

At the cafeteria, neither my mother nor I could eat. We smiled and made silly excuses about not having much appetite. I found myself just looking at her: the soft gray hair pulled back from her face, the hazel eyes—still so beautiful. Even the sad reality of impending exile could not touch her quiet pride and dignity. Her world—home, friends, customs, everything—would soon be left behind for an uncertain future in a foreign land—all in exchange for freedom. Yet, I could see no regret in her calm, steady gaze.

Finally, my mother ended all pretense of our sharing a normal meal by looking at her watch and saying, "Carlos, we must go." I pulled back her chair, helped her with her coat, and we left—dessert and coffee unordered, plates still piled with food which had been rearranged instead of eaten. We stopped at the cashier, paid our bill, and walked out together into the blinding light of a Cuban afternoon.

Back at the house, we rushed through the good-byes. We all knew what was at stake, and there just wasn't much left to be said. Finally, we walked out into the garden. I hugged my parents and walked quickly to the car where Nicky was already waiting in the passenger's seat. In complete silence, we drove slowly away.

Just a couple of blocks from the house, Nicky suddenly realized that he had left the extra clips to his .45. Controlling my irritation, I turned back.

"Carlos, I'm so glad you came back," my mother said as soon as we walked into the house. "You just had a most urgent call from Tony Capó."

I quickly picked up the phone and dialed Tony's number. "Yes, Tony, what's the matter?" I asked without wasting words.

Switching to English and speaking as rapidly as he could, Tony said, "I read your note. I'm calling you because my brother René needs a favor. I know that it's asking a lot, but if you can talk with him, he'll explain."

"I will, but he has to be here within a half an hour."

"He'll be there," Tony answered.

No more than a minute or two after my parents had driven away with Luisita, Dr. René Capó hurried into the house. Standing in the foyer, René spoke quickly, "Another brother of ours just called Tony from Miami where he arrived this morning. At the airport on the way out of Havana, they tried to arrest my nephew and namesake. It happens that my nephew is only five years old. That order was intended for me."

"René, we owe you. In fact, we're responsible for the jam you're in. You are welcome to come with us, if that's what you want."

"It is."

♦ ♦ ♦

When we pulled into the club parking lot a half an hour later, my cousin Alonso was already there waiting for us. He was not a particularly handsome man, but much younger looking than his forty years, thanks to his athletic build and a generous mop of black hair.

"The *Sirius* is in the water and ready to go," he said as soon as we had piled out of the Opel. "Our biggest problem is going to be getting through the militiaman. He's new and hard to deal with."

Although he had not spoken a word about René's presence, I sensed Alonso's concern and, truthfully, I shared it. Just by not being a club member, René was going to arouse the curiosity of any alert guard. On top of that, René looked like what he was, a surgeon, and not an outdoorsman. We are going to have problems, I said to myself.

Hoping that my misgivings did not show in my face, I reached for a small branch from the shrubbery which surrounded the parking lot. With it, I started to sketch the topography of our plan in the sand. Nicky, René, and Alonso gathered around me, watching and listening attentively.

"If the militiaman sees us all together, he will undoubtedly be suspicious," I began. "Nicky, you'll wait until you see us pulling out. Then work your way out to the end of the jetty and swim out about 100 yards. We'll pick you up outboard the club on our port side—about here," I said while marking an "X" on the proposed recovery spot. "That way, the boat will hide you from any curious eyes back ashore."

"No problem," Nicky answered.

"Alonso, you go back out to the boat as soon as the rest of us go up to change. René and I will walk to the *Sirius* together, and I'll tell the guard that we're headed out for a short fishing trip."

"And what happens if he gives you a hard time and doesn't want to let the boat out?" Nicky questioned.

"I was coming to that. If that's the case, I'll put on my baseball cap. That will be the signal that we'll have to implement a more drastic plan. I'll use the signal only if there is absolutely no doubt that the guard is not going to let us get underway."

"Too bad for him," Nicky said, anxious to get on with it.

"Yes, I'm afraid so. Let's hope it doesn't come to that, but if it does, Nicky—you'll be the one to bail us out. Walk back across the pier that leads to the island where the *Sirius* and some of the other boats are tied up. The militiaman will be distracted—busy arguing with us. It shouldn't be much of a problem for you to head toward the center of the island and then circle back behind and catch him off guard. Just remember, we must try to avoid any shooting in the club. If anybody alerts the aviation, we're in deep trouble—at least until after sunset."

"Understood," Nicky replied curtly.

Escape from Castro

"If there aren't any more questions, let's go change."

"No questions," René replied calmly. After I had erased our sketch, I threw away the branch, and we headed for the clubhouse.

Much to our satisfaction, the locker room was practically empty—as it usually was during the month of February.

Nicky turned to me nonchalantly. "Good thing I wore this baggy shirt," he said. "The pistol doesn't show at all."

"You're right," I answered. "I can't see a thing." I was sure that the pistol he was carrying was Julio's. Anyway why not, I thought. He sleeps with it under his pillow; of course he would have it with him today.

After assuring himself one last time in front of the mirror that the bulge of the weapon was not too conspicuous, Nicky closed his locker door and said, "I'm on my way. Be careful."

"*You* be careful," I replied.

Before going down the stairs that led to the beach, he turned around, grinned, and gave me the thumbs-up signal. Not the slightest trace of nervousness, I thought. He really does seem to thrive on danger.

René, who had been busy changing clothes, came over and asked, "Are we ready?"

"Yes, let's go," I answered.

As we walked down the pier on our way to the island, René kept asking me casual questions about the boat. Just as if he were really going on a pleasure cruise, I thought admiringly. But our conversation stopped in a hurry when we got close enough to the boat to realize that Alonso and the militiaman on guard were engaged in a heated argument.

"Are you two the party he's waiting for?" questioned the militiaman, a stocky man in his late twenties whose blondish hair was already thinning. He spoke sneeringly, not bothering to remove the cigar which was hanging out of the corner of his mouth.

"Yes, as a matter of fact, we are his party. The boat is half mine." As I spoke, I pulled my wallet out of my jacket and showed him my military ID card. "This is Lieutenant Capó, a medical officer and our guest for the afternoon," I added, motioning my head toward René. "Now that you know who we are, may I ask your name and unit?"

After checking my ID card in disdainful silence, the militiaman finally answered, "I am Angel Garcia from the Committee for the Defense of the Revolution—Section 10 in Marianao. My position in this nest of counter-revolutionaries is head of security, and what I say goes. And I say that this boat is not going out this late in the afternoon." By now he was almost shouting, deliberately trying to call attention to what was happening.

"Garcia," I interrupted, "just for the record, you are talking to a naval officer. Keep your voice down. I applaud your dedication to your duties, but there is no need to make a scene. If you give me a good reason why we shouldn't use the boat, maybe I'll agree with you and postpone our outing," I added, doing my best to sound conciliatory.

He took his cigar out of his mouth for the first time during our conversation, spit out some of the chewed leaves onto the pier, and replied patronizingly, "O.K., I'll give you a reason. Last Sunday I was on watch right here, about this same time of day, when I gave permission to a club member to go out fishing. In his bait he was carrying over one million dollars in diamonds. We are still waiting for him to return. This isn't going to happen again—not on my watch."

Sorry, friend, I thought. I put my baseball cap on and looked out toward the foot of the pier. No sign of Nicky. Before I had a chance to take a second look, I was startled by the sound of Nicky's voice—very close. While I had been searching for him in the distance, he had jumped down from the island to the wooden pier where we were standing and had rammed his pistol into Garcia's back. "Get in the boat," he was saying to the militiaman, "That is, if you want to go on living."

There must have been little doubt in Garcia's mind that whoever this was who had sneaked up behind him like some kind of wildcat and was now pushing a weapon into his ribs would not hesitate to pull the trigger. Without turning around, he obediently stepped into the boat. Alonso quickly shoved the militiaman inside the cabin and pulled his Makarov pistol out of its holster. René and I jumped on board, and I immediately started the engines. "René," I shouted, "take in all lines. Nicky help Alonso. Tie the bastard's hands behind his back and connect the line to his feet. Don't take any chances with him."

The two powerful engines roared as we pulled out of the basin, cruising abreast the boathouse. The few members who were sitting outside looked away, pretending not to notice us, but undoubtedly wishing us fair winds.

René, excited and overconfident, exclaimed, "We made it!"

"Not yet, René. Look out there," I said, pointing at the two ENEL ships that guarded the approach to the open sea like two watchdogs. I looked at my watch—1800. Still about half an hour until sunset.

René, unimpressed by the ENEL ships or by my words of caution, went down to the berthing compartment to see how things were going with Garcia.

"Nicky, take the wheel and keep heading toward the beaches," I said.

"Sure, I love to handle her. What a boat!" he exclaimed. "And the weather couldn't be any better. The ocean looks like a lake."

Without replying, I took the binoculars and trained them on the ENEL ships about three miles off our starboard bow. Then I continued my sweep of the waters around us. Not too bad so far, I thought.

For awhile, everything remained quiet and peaceful—much to my satisfaction since I needed the time to concentrate on our next move. Over the sound of the engines, I heard René and Alonso talking down in berthing. I put down my binoculars and took a brief look into the compartment. René and Alonso were sitting on the bunks looking relaxed and unworried. Garcia sat on the deck between them, his hands and feet tied together. He seemed to be trying his best to look conciliatory.

I turned my attention back to navigating. "When we pass El Club Nautico, reverse your course and head back toward El Miramar, always at slow speed," I said to Nicky.

"Aye, Aye," he replied. After a short silence, he asked, "What do you make out of the ENEL ships? Could they really get in our way?"

"About all they can do to us is to alert the air base. All they have on board is a 50 caliber, and its effective range is only about a mile and a half. We're out of their range right now, and with the speed we can make, they... Wait a second.

Take a good look at the sky astern of us," I shouted. Rushing to the stern, I picked up a fishing rod and pretended to be using it.

Nicky turned around and yelled, "What's the matter? What's going on?"

Alonso stuck his head out of the compartment. "Anything wrong?" he asked.

"There!" I exclaimed, pointing toward a Catalina directly off our stern and flying in our direction at an altitude of about 5,000 feet.

"They're probably heading back to the Naval Air Base after finishing a few hours of surveillance," Nicky said.

"You're absolutely right," I answered. "Let's stay on this course until they're gone. As long as we're heading west, they won't bother us." In a matter of a few minutes, the PBY flew right over us at a low altitude but without showing any signs of concern.

After the PBY had disappeared into the western horizon, I said, "Turn around Nicky. I don't like the idea of wasting any more gas fooling around here."

"I agree," he replied and he started a wide turn to port at about twelve knots. Once we were settled on our new course, he added, "After we clear the ENEL ships, maybe we should start heading north. It's getting late and soon the sun is going to take a plunge."

"We will," I answered. "Right now, let's increase our speed a little."

At eighteen knots the bow rose gracefully, cutting the calm, clear water and throwing cascades of white foam to the sides. We were now heading east on a course parallel to Cuba's north coast, about three miles out to sea.

I picked up the binoculars and took another good look at the government spy "fishing" vessels. There was no unusual movement on the decks of either ship. They continued to fish in their previous westerly course, and as we headed east, the distance between us widened rapidly. Still watching the ships through the binoculars, I said to Nicky, "We are now at the starting point of our track, and we're at least five miles away from those guys. This is it! Come left to 357° and open up until we lose them out of sight, then make RPM for thirty knots. We're heading north. Let them see us if they want."

"With pleasure," Nicky answered.

I checked my watch—1840. "At exactly 1940 we must come right to 027°," I told Nicky.

"Are we on our way to Key West?" René asked cheerfully as he came out of the berthing compartment.

"We sure are. You can come up now if you'd like," I replied. "How are things down below?"

"Everything is fine. That character Garcia is telling us now that he isn't really a communist and that he's glad to be leaving Cuba."

"And do you believe him?" Nicky asked.

"I don't know whether to believe him or not," René replied. "He doesn't seem to be afraid. I think he's a lot tougher than he wants us to believe he is. Maybe he figures it would be a long swim back to Cuba, and like a good socialist, he wants to make the most out of the situation."

"Maybe," Nicky replied skeptically.

René shrugged and took a deep breath of the fresh, cool air. He was obviously enjoying being out on deck.

After a while, the sea condition began to deteriorate slightly, now showing some white caps. I turned to Nicky and said, "It's getting dark and we're soon going to need light in the compass and instrument panel. Let me take over the steering so that you can get the canvas on. We shouldn't show any lights for awhile. I'll slow down while you cover the cabin."

"With René's help, I'll have this cover in place in no time at all," Nicky replied. True to his prediction, the cover was in place in a matter of minutes, and we were able to turn on the interior red lights and to resume our high speed. The moonless night sky was unusually dark, and with none of our lights showing, we were a nearly invisible target for any pursuer. Especially, I thought with great satisfaction, since we were heading north instead of following a more predictable northeastern course that would lead us straight to Key West.

By 1930 the seas were getting rougher as the northerly winds increased their velocity, and we were forced to reduce our speed to around twenty-eight knots. Too bad, I thought, with these winds we're going to be using a lot more gas. At exactly 1940, we changed course as planned. Now we were heading directly for the Key West Lighthouse.

Escape from Castro

"What should be our ETA (estimated time of arrival)?" Nicky asked. But before I could answer, we heard Alonso cry out in an agonized, muffled voice, "Carlos, watch out!" The warning had come too late! Garcia, his face pale from sea-sickness and distorted by sheer hate, had burst out of the compartment. In his right hand, he was brandishing his Makarov pistol.

"Our ETA is going to be a lot earlier than you lackeys of the imperialists thought," he shouted, pointing the pistol straight at my head. "Turn back to Havana—now," he said to me.

René who had been dozing on one of the bunks, now started to get up. Garcia caught sight of him and yelled, "If anybody moves, I'll blow his brains out."

"José is lying on his stomach with a knife in his back," Nicky said to me, ignoring Garcia's warning and moving enough to peer down into the berthing compartment.

"That's just to show you bunch of faggots not to mess around with me," Garcia retorted.

For some insane reason I couldn't bring myself to obey his order, and without uttering a word, I continued on the same course.

"For the last time, you son of a bitch, turn back," he said almost hysterically, his eyes bulging and his color turning greenish as a new wave of nausea threatened to overwhelm him. Somehow he managed to spit out a mouthful of vomit and regain some balance.

To hell with you, I thought, and I kept the compass needle steady on course at 027°.

Letting go of his grip on the handrail, Garcia held the pistol with both hands, my face in line with the pistol's sights. His right index finger on the trigger, he held his breath . . .

"For God's sake, Carlos, turn," Nicky shouted. "He's going to shoot you."

"I'm turning," I replied as I turned sharply to starboard and lowered the RPM to an idle. Propelled forward by the violent turn and the sudden loss of speed, Garcia was flung almost on top of Nicky. Both of them were off balance and struggling for the pistol, and both of them were about to go over the handrail. I left the wheel and rushed to assist Nicky who was trying desperately to disarm the militiaman. Hindered by the heavy rolls we were taking, I was a second too late. I heard a shot;

Garcia had managed to squeeze the trigger. The bullet spun Nicky backwards, and in the brief illumination caused by the flash of the pistol fired at close range, I saw the expression of pain on his face. Nicky kept his hold on Garcia, dragging his attacker with him as he went overboard into the dark, turbulent waters. When I reached the stern, they were gone. There was nothing but darkness—no sign of Nicky or Garcia—as if the ocean waiting maliciously for its victims had swallowed them in anger.

With my fists clenched in helpless rage, I screamed maniacally at the ocean, "No, you can't have him." Slipping twice on the rolling deck, I somehow reached the wheel and managed to turn the bow into the surf. René, bleeding from a cut on top of his right eye which he had suffered during the unexpected change in speed, came stumbling toward the wheel. "I just checked on poor Alonso," he said in his customary calm, courageous way. "Amazingly enough, he's still alive. Even though I was able to stop the bleeding, I don't think he has much of a chance. Now, how can I help up here?"

"Still alive?" I answered in disbelief. "Here, René, take the wheel. Keep the boat heading into the sea at minimum speed." Without waiting for an answer, I pulled off the canvas cover, grabbed a flashlight, and climbed on top of the cabin. Shielding my eyes from the weather with my left hand and holding the flashlight in my right, I started a systematic search of the water around us.

Only a very few moments had gone by since he had gone over. Still, he was wounded and without a life jacket, and even though he was a strong swimmer, I knew only too well that if I couldn't find him soon that he would be lost. I had avoided being shot and kept Garcia from forcing us back to Cuba, but, Oh God, at what cost! I was so absorbed in my misery and so numb with cold that it took my brain a few seconds to register the meaning of the words René was shouting.

"There he is! I think I see him," he was shouting.

"Where? Tell me where," I called out, beginning a frantic search with my flashlight. What if it's Garcia that he's spotted, I thought. I was almost afraid to hope.

"To the right of the boat—no more than twenty feet from us," René answered, pointing to the starboard quarter. Nicky's white shirt reflecting the phosphorescent sea water shone in the center of the flashlight's beam.

Looking like a doomed child riding a possessed roller coaster, Nicky raised a hand in a feeble attempt to wave at us as he rode the crest of the wave before being almost immediately rushed down its trough. He was trying desperately to make sure we had seen him. Nicky only had a few moments left, and no doubt, he knew it.

I jumped to the deck and handed the flashlight to René. "Keep the light on him at all times," I shouted; I'm bringing the boat around." René moved aft while I climbed behind the wheel. With surprising speed, I was able to maneuver the craft windward of Nicky, creating an immediate shield against the sea. By this move, I also avoided having him thrown against the hull by the waves.

Looking more in control now that he enjoyed the protection that the boat afforded against the rough seas, Nicky managed to look straight at me and to wave. The line fell very close to him, but his reactions were too slow, and he missed it. I couldn't risk a second try. "There's no time," I said out loud, more to myself than to René. "He's almost unconscious." I secured one end of the line to a cleat and tied the other around my waist.

Just as I was jumping, I heard René shout, "Hurry, Carlos! He's going under."

I jumped in with my legs spread forward and aft and my arms extended, keeping my head out of the water so as not to lose track of Nicky. When I reached him, he was already two feet below the surface and going down. Instinctively, I placed him in a cross-chest carry and swam to the surface. I noticed that my arm which was wrapped around his chest felt unusually warm for these cool waters. I felt around his chest and gasped in horror as I realized that his side was denuded of flesh and muscle—I was touching his bare bones. I called in desperation for René to help us climb onboard, but with the craft about to broach and in danger of capsizing, he had returned to the wheel. Not accustomed to handling the *Sirius*, he gave her too much gas. Instantly, the line became taut and Nicky and I were dragged behind the boat, bouncing on the surface like two giant pieces of bait. I was swallowing water as I struggled to keep Nicky's head above the surface. At the back of my mind was the gnawing realization that the vibrations we were sending out would be interpreted by any large fish as distress signals from an easy prey. The constant trail of blood couldn't be missed for long.

After a few minutes that seemed to last forever, the boat finally came to a stop. Suddenly, I felt a strong tug. I tried to look under the surface, but it was as black as the entrance to Hades. Oh God, no, don't let it end like that, I prayed silently. On every ripple, behind every crest, I imagined the fin of a swift, murderous shark. In the numbingly cold waters, I felt the warm, pulsating flow coming from Nicky's chest. Our jolting ride had started the bleeding once again. Another tug—this one followed by a sharp pull! Then my worst fears rapidly dissipated. Realizing what was happening, René had hurried back to the stern and was pulling us in.

Finally, we reached the leeward side of the boat. As René reached down, I lifted Nicky's arms. Once he had a good grip on Nicky's wrists, René pulled his inert body aboard. I, too, was soon on deck, thanks to René's assistance. I tried to get up, but utterly exhausted and dizzy, I fell to my knees and vomited salt water... and then burning bile. In spite of my wretched condition, I was aware that while René was administering first aid to Nicky, the unmanned wheel was spinning madly. Annoyed at this physical weakness which was now endangering all our lives, I reached for the handrail and with the deck pitching and rolling under my feet, I dragged myself to the wheel. I increased the RPM, and in a short time, we were back on track—the compass needle reading 027°.

René had not wasted a minute; he already had Nicky wrapped in a blanket and lying on the bunk behind me. Making use of our well-stocked first aid kit, he was now tending to Nicky's wound. René was more than just a fine surgeon; he was a friend, an able and courageous one.

I didn't have it in me to ask how Nicky was doing. I feared the wrong answer. Instead, I concentrated on keeping the boat on the right heading. I refused to consider the possibility that Nicky might not pull through—now on the final stretch of our journey to freedom. I knew how he must have felt when Julio died next to him. As hard as I tried to block my thoughts, I was aware of every move René was making behind me. Some part of me guided our small craft on through the dark waters, instinctively performing all the necessary motions. But tonight I wasn't living; I was just waiting.

The faintly glowing hands of my Rolex read 1215. The gas can't last much longer, I thought. The gauge needle was almost resting on E. If we don't see the Key West light very soon, we'll be in a lot of trouble, unless the sea condition improves. We lost Alonso and now if Nicky doesn't make it, I'd almost be glad if we all went down together. I got everyone into this ghastly mess with my infallible plan. Some plan!

My depressing thoughts were interrupted when René placed a hand on my shoulder. I reacted with an instantaneous burning sensation in my stomach, as if sharp claws were tearing at my insides.

"If you have a minute," René said, "there is someone here who wants to see you very badly."

"Is he all right?"

"Why don't you ask him yourself? It's time for me to relieve you at the helm."

"Keep the needle as close to 027° as you can," I said as I passed the steering to René and went with great apprehension to Nicky's side.

He looked at me in silence, his expression grave and unresponsive. When he spoke at last, it was in a low voice. With the faintest trace of a smile, he said something which I could not quite make out—his weak voice was drowned out by the whistling of the wind and the noise of the engines. I leaned down and asked, "What is it, Nicky?"

"I owe you my life," he answered.

"And I owe you mine," I replied.

Now in a stronger voice, he said, "I was out there alone in the middle of an angry, dark ocean—wounded and without much hope. If it hadn't been for you . . ."

"It was God's will. Besides, it was you who saved us all from that maniac, Garcia. Not that I give a damn, but what happened to our friend? We never caught sight of the son of a bitch."

"The minute we hit the water and I saw him swimming with jerky strokes and moving his head right and left, I realized that he was doomed. I tried to help him, in spite of it all, but he cursed me and told me to stay away from him—that I was attracting sharks with all the blood I was spilling."

He was right about that, I thought. But in the end, he turned out to be the victim of his own incredible hatred and resentment.

"Don't feel too sorry for him," I said. "He would have taken you down with him if he could have. In fact, I'm surprised that he didn't try to shoot you again in the water."

"He couldn't," Nicky replied. "Here—this is for you." With great effort, he pulled Garcia's Makarov pistol from underneath the blanket.

"I can't believe you! You held onto that thing when you were close to drowning."

"At first, I thought I'd give it to you as a souvenir. Later, I forgot I had it with me. What I can't believe is that it looks like we made it after all."

"It sure looks like it," I replied. To myself, I said, "If we don't run out of gas first." We took a heavy roll that reminded me of our helmsman's limited experience.

"René," I said, "you may be a great surgeon, but as a helmsman... Well, let's just say you could use a little more practice. If you don't mind, I'll take over."

"Mind? Not at all. I think I'll check on my other patient, and then hit my rack for awhile."

"My, God!" I said. "Do you mean Alonso is still alive?" I could not believe my ears.

"He has a chance," René answered, "but he needs surgery. I'm limited in what I can do for him here. The sooner we reach Key West, the better his odds."

My spirits fell. With so little gas left in the tank, I could not be sure when, or if, we would make Key West. "You go get some rest, René," I said as I got us back on course. "You've earned it."

As we continued cruising toward Key West and freedom, a whole new bundle of worries weighed me down—my cousin's condition, the rapidly dwindling gas supply, my own exhaustion which was sure to affect my performance. Still, we were all alive, and that alone was an almost incredible feat considering all that had happened in the last few hours.

After a short while, René came back and said with admiration in his voice, "Alonso's strong constitution is putting up a good fight for survival."

"I must see him," I replied. "Please take over for a couple of minutes."

It was dark below, and the whole compartment gave off a strong smell of blood. I turned on my flashlight. Alonso, lying asleep on his back, looked as white as paper, but he was breathing regularly. The placid expression on his face seemed to indicate that he wasn't in great pain, and this gave me hope. "Maybe," I said under my breath. "Just maybe . . ."

Back on deck, as I took the helm, René asked, "How are we doing?"

"Not so good," I replied. "If we don't pick up the light pretty soon, we are going to run out of gas."

"That bad, huh?"

"Just look at the gauge," I replied, pointing to the needle which now sat on the E. "We're running on the reserve. But forget the gas. Tell me about our patients," I said, ignoring my own wounded back, and its constant annoying pain.

"Like I told you, Alonso regained consciousness for a few minutes when I was last with him."

"Was he lucid?" I interrupted.

"He sure was. He knew exactly where he was and what was going on, and that's the best sign in a case like this. Garcia had pleaded with him to untie his feet so that he could go to the head. Feeling sorry for the guy, Alonso finally agreed, and when he bent down to untie the rope, Garcia stabbed him in the back."

"That—like most of our failures—was my fault. I didn't search him. Well . . . it would have been hard to foresee Garcia's actions. René," I said interrupting myself, "do you see how the condition of the sea has improved?"

He nodded. "I sure do."

"Well, that's excellent for more reason than one. It means we're going to be using less gas, but, more importantly, it shows that we're no longer in the Gulf Stream. I think that we are very close to our destination."

"I sure hope you're right."

"Me too. But let's get back to our friends. What about Nicky?"

"I'll tell you, he is some specimen of a human being. His

biggest problem is the huge amount of blood he has lost, but he is very young and even stronger than he gives the impression of being." Pointing with his finger to a spot on his chest, he continued, "The bullet entered at the level of the lower of the two floating ribs, bruising the bone and tearing some vessels, but not causing an irreparable damage. What caused most of the superficial injury with its large loss of tissue was the fact that the pistol was fired at such a close range."

"Will it leave a large scar?" I asked.

"I saved as much of the epidermis as possible when I cleaned the wound. If we can get him to a hospital within twenty-four hours, the apposition of the wound could be accomplished without too much scar tissue. But now we are talking about esthetics. The important thing is that he is in no danger at all."

"I agree, at least other than running out of gas and floating around out here for several days..." Suddenly, something caught my attention, and I concentrated on searching the dark horizon.

"Do you see anything?" René asked.

"I don't know yet." I pulled my binoculars from their case and once again scanned the horizon. Through them I saw a light, a beautiful, reassuring light, off our port bow. I observed it for awhile without saying anything—no point in getting René's hopes up for no reason.

I carefully read the sequence of flashes several times, until there was no longer any doubt in my mind—this was it! I had recognized the characteristics of the Key West approach navigational light!

"René," I said with great joy in my heart, "we are in Key West."

Lying half-asleep on his bunk behind the steering wheel, Nicky asked, "Carlos, did you say something about Key West, or was I dreaming?"

As I came to port a few degrees and headed straight for the light, I looked quickly over my right shoulder and said, "No, Nicky, you weren't dreaming. Key West light is dead ahead—about six miles from us. We are free men!"

"We are really in American waters! Thank you, dear God and Virgin Mary!" Nicky said. "Can you see anything? Are there any other vessels around?" he asked excitedly.

"Not so far, but the lights ashore are quite visible."

"Could you lift my back a little? I would love to take a look."

"Go ahead," René said. "I can easily keep us on this course. The rough seas are gone."

I let René take over and went to assist Nicky. "Here," I said as I propped him up. "And that's the land of the imperialists," I said, pointing to the shore.

"Yeah, the ones that vote for their leaders and are free to worship, travel, and educate their children."

"Yes, those are the ones," I replied.

"God bless them all," Nicky said.

The hesitation and coughing of the engines interrupted our conversation.

"What's happening?" René asked.

"Nothing much. We've just run out of gas," I replied.

"Are you kidding?" Nicky questioned.

"Not kidding at all. It's not a big problem. We'll just drop anchor, and in the morning someone is bound to come along and help us out."

"But how do you know that it's shallow enough to anchor here?" René asked.

"Because I did my homework and studied the chart. If we had run out of gas just a few miles farther out, we would have missed the continental shelf, and our anchor would have been useless."

"But we didn't," René said triumphantly.

"You're right about that," I replied on my way out of the cabin. On the bow, I pulled the anchor from its compartment and dropped it with a loud splash. In no time at all, my calculations were proven accurate; the anchor was holding.

I walked back into the cabin and told René, "Let's go down. I would like to give José the good news."

I sat on the edge of my cousin's bunk and said quietly, "Alonso, wake up. How are you feeling?"

He opened his eyes slowly and tried to pull himself up, but grimaced in pain as his injury reminded him of what had happened. "I forgot about my back," he said weakly. "But where . . . Where are we?"

"How about Key West?" I answered.

"We are in Key West? I can't believe it."

"Well, not exactly in Key West. More like three miles off the coast, at anchor, and out of gas," I said.

"Still... beautiful," Alonso said. "Now," he continued as he made a visual search of the compartment, "Where is that fine human being, Garcia?"

"Where he belongs," René replied for me. "Carlos, let me brief him. You look like you need your rest very badly. Why don't you go up and lie down?"

"I won't argue with that. But you two also try to rest. Both of you have more than earned it," I said as I got up and, holding both sides of the hatch, pulled myself out of the compartment.

Once in the cabin, I turned the anchor lights on and sat down on the bunk across from Nicky. He was awake, resting with his head propped on a cushion. He turned to me, his face illuminated by the bridge red light and said in a voice filled with relief and gratitude, "We have come a long way from Tarara, haven't we?"

I nodded. "Yes, we have, but we must try to forget what happened. I don't like even to talk about it. There are only three people in the world who know—you, me and Tony."

He paused for thought and then added, "And we don't have to worry about Tony."

"No, we don't. And speaking of Tony, he and Cathy should be on today's flight to Miami. Their exit visas were confirmed."

"Excellent," Nicky said, more to himself than to me. I took my shoes off and crawled under the blanket. For awhile, not a word was spoken, as if both Nicky and I wanted to absorb the peace that surrounded us after the nightmare we had lived during the last hours. The *Sirius* was riding anchor comfortably, the night was pleasantly cool, and the lights on the coastline were reassuring.

Breaking the momentary silence, Nicky said, "You know Carlos, I feel good. In spite of these ugly-looking ribs, I feel real good."

"I know what you mean," I said, glad that René's shot of pain killer had prevented Nicky from feeling any real discomfort. "I'll tell you what, let's celebrate by opening a couple of bottles of coke. You know, we've had practically nothing to eat or drink since we left Havana."

"You're right. Let's open those cokes. Do you know what's really funny? I don't know if I can get used to not always being afraid—always expecting someone to pop up out of some dark corner and gun us down."

The expression on my face must have changed drastically because Nicky suddenly looked startled. "What's the matter, Carlos?" he asked with distress in his voice. "Do you know something I don't?"

"Not really. It's just that I wish I could share your vision of normality."

"Carlos, don't play with words. Tell me what you're thinking."

"Very well. What I think is that G-2 and the fellow travelers have long arms—longer than ninety miles. It's true that we no longer have to be constantly afraid, but at least for awhile, we must still be cautious. But there's plenty of time to talk about that. I'm going to try to catch some sleep, and you should do the same."

"Fine, go to sleep. Now that you've got me worked up, you can relax. Sometimes I don't know about you."

"Sometimes I don't know about myself either," I said, already half asleep. "Buenas noches, Nicky. Don't worry about anything."

I couldn't tell what the dream was all about, just that I knew it was pleasant and that Judy was in it. Then Nick's voice pierced through the layers of sleep and ended it abruptly.

"Carlos, wake up. Come on, hurry."

"What's the matter?" I asked incoherently, my tired body refusing to be aroused.

"A boat! A motor boat is coming this way. Can't you hear it?"

I jumped to my feet and rushed out of the cabin, the cool morning air alerting my senses. A small fishing vessel about thirty feet long and loaded with fishing nets was cruising less than a mile off our port quarter. Sooner than I expected, it acknowledged my signals and was headed our way. I looked at my watch—0530.

Once alongside, the fisherman, a middle-aged, heavy set black man with a pleasant face and an easy smile asked, "How can I help you?" About five minutes later with three free gallons of gas in our tank and a warm feeling toward the first American we had come into contact with, we were heading for the Key West Coast Guard Station.

René was down in the berthing compartment getting things organized and helping Alonso clean up. Nicky was sitting on the bunk behind me with his legs under the blanket. He handed me a small piece of paper and said, "These are the phone numbers of my parents and Elena. Would you call them for me? I'm going to have to wait for the ambulance that René said he is going to call for Alonso and me. You'll probably be able to get to a phone right away."

"I'll call as soon as they let me."

"And who are you calling?" Nicky asked. "Thais or Judy?"

"Both."

He shook his head and said, "I believe you." After a pause, he added, "And after you make the calls, are you going to the hospital?"

"No, I'm going on vacation. I'll drop you a postcard from St. Moritz." Then I turned around and grinned at him. "You idiot! Of course I'll go to the hospital—the minute I'm finished with formalities."

"I thought so," he muttered confidently.

Returning my full attention to the steering, I reduced our speed and headed toward the Coast Guard pier.

A new day had begun in more ways than one. It was a sunny day with clear skies and a gentle breeze. I hoped it was an omen. Let it truly be a new beginning, I prayed.

Commander Mario J. Lamar was born in Havana, Cuba, and graduated from the School of Dentistry, University of Havana, and from the Cuban Naval Academy. While serving as executive officer of the Cuban Underwater Demolition Team, CDR Lamar defected from Castro's Navy in a 24-foot cabin cruiser in October 1960. He arrived in Key West, Florida, running out of gas three miles off the coast. He later joined the Cuban Brigade and in October 1961, participated in the Bay of Pigs invasion as executive officer of the ship *Seagull*. He was later commissioned in the U.S. Navy, graduated from the U.S Army Infantry School at Fort Benning and graduated with distinction from Officer Candidate School in Newport, Rhode Island. After serving in Vietnam, Lamar served as operations officer aboard USS *Spiegel Grove* (LSD-32), staff navigator with commander, Second Fleet, and Navy liaison officer with SOUTHCOM staff, Canal Zone. He was transferred to the Dental Corp in 1980. Commander Lamar holds the Bronze Star with Combat V for heroic achievement, Navy Commendation Medal with Combat V for meritorious service, and the Cross of Gallantry from the Vietnamese government. He currently lives in Florida with his wife, Karol, and the two youngest of their four children.

HISTORICAL FICTION & NONFICTION
AVAILABLE FROM BRANDYLANE PUBLISHERS, INC.

CODE NAME: KAIBIGAN
Dorothy Fleming

Based on real events, this powerful novel takes place in the closing months of World War II as the Allies advance on the Japanese-occupied Philippines.
6 x 9", paperback. ISBN 1-883911-18-4. **$14.95.**

SHORTCHANGED
John H. Harding Jr.

A young man finds himself in the army and in Korea, where he faces the realities of war. Struggling to stay alive, his memory takes him back to his childhood in Virginia.
6 x 9", paperback. ISBN 1-883911-22-2. **$13.95.**

TABOO AVENGED
Griffin Garnett

Follow the protagonist of *The Sandscrapers* as he unravels a strange and forbidding murder at the National Theater in Washington D.C.
5 1/2 x 8 1/2", paperback. ISBN 1-883911-16-8. **$14.95.**
The Sandscrapers, 5 1/2 x 8 1/2", paperback. ISBN 1-883911-10-9. **$15.95.**

WHEN CIVILIANS MANNED THE SHIPS
James A. Kehl

Join the unforgettable crew of the LSM 911 and other landing craft in this story that reveals the colorful side of this distinctive group of civilian sailors during World War II and their untested ships.
6 x 9", paperback. ISBN 1-883911-15-X. **$13.95.**

THE APPROACHING STORM:
U-Boats off the Virginia Coast During World War II
Alpheus Chewning

Stories of the men and U-Boats that came to America and the survivors who were brought to Virginia ports. Includes photographs, thorough documentation, and appendices.
8 1/2 x 11", paperback. ISBN 0-9627635-9-4. **$18.95.**

1600 MEN
A Personal Remembrance U.S. Naval Academy 1932–1936
Robert Sleight

A member of the Class of 1936 recounts life at the Naval Academy.
6 x 9", paperback. ISBN 1-883911-23-0. **$12.95**

To receive a complete catalogue, call:
1.800.533.6922 or 804.435.6900 • Fax: 804.435.9812
e-mail: brandy@crosslink.net • www.eaglesnest.net/brandy
Visa and MasterCard accepted

FICTION & NONFICTION
AVAILABLE FROM BRANDYLANE PUBLISHERS, INC.

SHOUTS AND WHISPERS:
Stories from the Chesapeake Bay
Jim Charbeneau

Fourteen tales that cover the period from the 1840s through the 1990s infused with history and folklore, bring to life a diverse collection of situations—stories about family, about the natural world, and about the power of love and personal honor.

6 x 9", paperback. ISBN 1-883911-11-7. $12.95.

INTERLUDE:
Letters from a Foreign Correspondent
Mary Archer St. Clair

After a chance meeting in 1924, Roger D. Greene and Mary Archer St. Clair corresponded until 1936. Roger Greene, a young writer, was soon to become a journalist with the London office of the Associated Press, and Mary Archer was a vibrant young woman in her twenties. Through his letters, we are allowed a personal glimpse into the evolution of Greene's infatuation with the lovely 'Mary Lou.' The story captures the improbability of a relationship separated by distance and personal circumstance. His letters also provide a first-hand account of the life of a foreign correspondent, as well as the history of our times from the Jazz Age to the Great Depression.

6 x 9", paperback. ISBN 1-883911-21-4. $14.95.

DOWN FOR DOUBLE
Gordon M. Graham, Lt. Gen. USAF (Ret.)

Gordon Graham's book is based on conversations recorded that document the experiences and historic context of his remarkable life and career as a fighter pilot during World War II, Vietnam and other conflicts.

6 x 9", paperback. ISBN 1-883911-06-0. $14.95.
AUDIO CASSETTE: **Down for Double: Biography, Interview, Readings.**
60 min. $10.95.

LEGENDS FROM THE FROSTY SONS OF THUNDER
William Trall Doncaster

This work focuses on the legends and stories of nineteenth century Somerset County, Pennsylvania. Since their occurrence in 1889, the controversial Nicely brothers murder trial and the Johnstown flood have become enduring legends. These stories and others along the Old Forbes Military Road are explored in this account of rural life punctuated by backwoods superstitions and romantic heroes and antiheroes.

6 x 9", paperback. ISBN 1-883911-25-7. $13.95.

To receive a complete catalogue, call:
1.800.533.6922 or 804.435.6900 • Fax: 804.435.9812
e-mail: brandy@crosslink.net • www.eaglesnest.net/brandy
Visa and MasterCard accepted